More Critical Praise for Laurie

for *Death of a Rainmaker: A Dust I*

"Set in Vermillion, Okla., in 1935, this superb series launch from Loewenstein . . . beautifully captures the devastation of the land and people in the dust bowl." *—Publishers Weekly*, starred review

"Loewenstein movingly describes the events and the people, from farm eviction auctions and hobo villages to Dish Nights at the movies. She vividly brings to life a town filled with believable characters, from a young woman learning her own worth to the deputy sheriff figuring out where his loyalties lie. This warm and evocative novel captures a time and place, with well-researched details shown through the lives and circumstances of one American town." *—Kirkus Reviews*

"The plot is compelling, the character development effective and the setting carefully and accurately designed . . . I have lived in the panhandles of Texas and Oklahoma; I know about wind and dust . . . Combining a well created plot with an accurate, albeit imagined, setting and characters that 'speak' clearly off of the page make *Death of a Rainmaker* a pleasant adventure in reading." *—The Oklahoman*

"Set in an Oklahoma small town during the Great Depression, this launch of a promising new series is as vivid as the stark photographs of Dorothea Lange."
—South Florida Sun Sentinel, A Best Mystery Novel of 2018

"After a visiting con artist is murdered during a dust storm, a small-town sheriff and his wife pursue justice in 1930s Oklahoma. A vivid evocation of life during the Dust Bowl; you might need a glass of water at hand while reading Loewenstein's novel."
—Milwaukee Journal Sentinel, Editor's Pick

"Laurie Loewenstein's new mystery novel . . . expertly evokes the Dust Bowl and the Great Depression . . . Loewenstein's novel sometimes reads like a combination of a Western and a mystery. But that genre mishmash works." *—Washington City Paper*

"The plot is solid in *Death of a Rainmaker*, but what makes Loewenstein's novel so outstanding is the cast of characters she has assembled . . . *Death of a Rainmaker* is a superb book, one that sets the reader right down amid some of the hardest times our country has faced, and lets us feel those hopeful farmers' despair as they witness their dreams turning to dust." —*Mystery Scene Magazine*

"*Death of a Rainmaker* is far more than a murder mystery set in the Dust Bowl of the 1930s. It is a poignant recollection of the desperation of farmers whose land, livestock, and household are in foreclosure, a stunning description of a dust storm that leaves imaginary specks of dirt on the reader's neck, a sensitive rendering of tough times and their toll on the psyche. Some books have such fine character detail— McCance's choice of a Common Sense Traveler's Notebook, suitable for a professional lawman, not a 'CCC pity case,' for example—and complex, nuanced storyline that the reader naturally slows down to savor the experience. This is one of them."
—*Historical Novel Society*, Editors' Choice

"Loewenstein is establishing herself as a master of nuanced historical fiction, especially when it comes to the political infighting and swirl of intrigue around small communities in the early half of the twentieth century. Loewenstein is a talented researcher with an eye for the historical detail, but also a gifted storyteller capable of breathing life into a wide cast of characters. For historical fiction readers, this is an author to watch." —*CrimeReads*

"Readers will be completely absorbed in the lives of Loewenstein's characters who epitomize the extraordinary resilience of small-town folks caught in the throes of the Great Depression . . . Loewenstein manages to connect an enticing murder mystery with riveting historical fiction that places the reader directly in the dusty shoes of her characters." —*Reviewing the Evidence*

"Reading *Death of a Rainmaker* is like slipping through time right into a 1930s black-and-white movie. It's odd for a story about a murder to be gentle and generous, but this one is. I fell in love with everyone in town . . . Laurie Loewenstein has a knack for writing the early twentieth century. I sure hope this is a series, because I'm smitten."
—Robin Oliveira, author of *Winter Sisters*

"As if the black blizzards of the Dust Bowl weren't worrisome enough for an Oklahoma sheriff and his spunky wife, in *Death of a Rainmaker* Laurie Loewenstein piles on even more troubles: a murder victim's corpse buried in a sandstorm, an array of possible perpetrators, a small community already fractured by secrets and swirls of distrust, and a contentious election in which the sheriff's honesty and competence are on the ballot. Like the storms themselves, the plot powers its way across the landscape and seeps into everything it encounters."

—Dayton Duncan, author of *The Dust Bowl*

"During one of America's most devastating periods, the Depression-era Dust Bowl, a huckster is murdered as a dust storm hurtles toward a small Oklahoma town. What follows is an authentic tale of the drought-stricken southern plains, and a lovingly and eloquently told murder mystery. It is not only the unfolding plot and the metaphorical obscuring of truth by dust, but Loewenstein's masterful prose—with its tender language and skillful resonance—that will captivate readers and keep them enthralled. *Death of a Rainmaker* is both a gripping tale of murder, and a glimpse into resilience and love in a time of savage loss, scarcity, and fear."

—Leslie Schwartz, author of *The Lost Chapters*

"When the wind comes sweeping down the plain in *Death of a Rainmaker*, Laurie Loewenstein takes your breath away. Her haunting and vivid prose deftly describes the opening chords of a dust storm that left families sick with dust pneumonia or dead broke. In this gripping tale of a sheriff searching for a killer in a dying town, Loewenstein rounds up characters with true grit, cunning, and kindness."

—Mary Kay Zuravleff, author of *Man Alive!*

"*Death of a Rainmaker* is a jewel of a novel. The scenes and characters are so vivid and alive that you forget that the Internet and interstate roads haven't been around forever. Loewenstein is a born storyteller who writes scholarly based page-turners. Overlaying it all is the rainmaker's story and death. It's a read you won't forget."

—John Bowers, author of *Love in Tennessee*

for *Unmentionables*

• A January 2014 Midwest Connections Pick, Midwest Independent
  Booksellers Association

"Exceptionally readable and highly recommended."
> —*Library Journal*, starred review

"Engaging first work from a writer of evident ability."
> —*Kirkus Reviews*

"Marian Elliot Adams's tale is contagiously enthusiastic."
> —*Publishers Weekly*

"*Unmentionables* is a sweeping and memorable story of struggle and
suffrage, love and redemption . . . Loewenstein has skillfully woven
a story and a cast of characters that will remain in the memory long
after the book's last page has been turned."
> —*New York Journal of Books*

"*Unmentionables* starts small and expands to touch Chicago and war-
torn France as Laurie Loewenstein weaves multiple points of view
together to create a narrative of social change and the stubbornness of
the human heart."
> —*Black Heart Magazine*

"A historical, feminist romance in the positive senses of all three terms:
a realistic evocation of small-town America circa 1917, including its
racial tensions; a tale about standing up for the equitable treatment
of women; and a story about two lonely people who overcome obstacles, including their own character defects, to find love together."
> —*Milwaukee Journal Sentinel*

"*Unmentionables* is a love story and a journey of self-discovery."
> —*Historical Novel Society*

"Like all good historical fiction, *Unmentionables* uses the past as a way
to illuminate large, pertinent questions—of race and gender, of love
and death, of action and consequence. Meticulously researched and
exquisitely written, *Unmentionables* is a memorable debut."
> —Ann Hood, author of *The Book That Matters Most*

FUNERAL TRAIN

A DUST BOWL MYSTERY

LAURIE LOEWENSTEIN

Published by Akashic Books
©2022 Laurie Loewenstein

Paperback ISBN: 978-1-63614-052-0
Hardcocver ISBN: 978-1-63614-051-3
Library of Congress Control Number: 2022933224

Kaylie Jones Books
www.kayliejonesbooks.com

Akashic Books
Brooklyn, New York
Instagram, Twitter, Facebook: AkashicBooks
E-mail: info@akashicbooks.com
Website: www.akashicbooks.com

Also Available from Kaylie Jones Books

Death of a Rainmaker by Laurie Loewenstein
Unmentionables by Laurie Loewenstein
Cornelius Sky by Timothy Brandoff
The Schrödinger Girl by Laurel Brett
Starve the Vulture by Jason Carney
Between the Devil and the Deep Blue Sea
by André Lewis Carter
Here Lies a Father by Mckenzie Cassidy
City Mouse by Stacey Lender
Like This Afternoon Forever by Jaime Manrique
Little Beasts by Matthew McGevna
Some Go Hungry by J. Patrick Redmond
Inconvenient Daughter by Lauren J. Sharkey
The Third Mrs. Galway by Deirdre Sinnott
The Year of Needy Girls by Patricia A. Smith
The Love Book by Nina Solomon
The Devil's Song by Lauren Stahl
All Waiting Is Long by Barbara J. Taylor
Sing in the Morning, Cry at Night by Barbara J. Taylor
Flying Jenny by Theasa Tuohy

From Oddities/Kaylie Jones Books

Angel of the Underground by David Andreas
Foamers by Justin Kassab
Strays by Justin Kassab
We Are All Crew by Bill Landauer
The Underdog Parade by Michael Mihaley
The Kaleidoscope Sisters by Ronnie K. Stephens

To my mentor and friend David Hollis

There's a little black train a coming
Set your business right
There's a little black train a coming
And it may be here tonight
Go tell that ballroom lady
All dressed in the worldly pride
That death's dark train is coming
Prepare to take a ride

—Traditional gospel song from the 1800s

C HAPTER ONE

THERE WAS A RAILROAD crossing out that way. The engineer cast out two long calls. Then a short blast. Then another. The thick chords vibrated across the plains. If there had been jalopies or farm wagons at the grade, they would have juddered to a stop. But this afternoon only dust devils skittered across the rails.

The train's desolate song suited the time and place— December 1935, smack in the crosshairs of the Great Depression and the Dust Bowl. Together, they had done their worst to this raggedy piece of the Oklahoma panhandle. Some farmers and merchants had packed up and deserted the meagerly populated High Plains. Some had stayed but shrank into themselves, ashamed of their collective poverty.

The four-part wail bloomed then faded as the train rattled west. A farm wife was rolling out biscuits when she heard the engine's cry. She considered the chain of crowded cars embroidering the horizon. Imagined them gently rocking as they traversed the crossing. The silhouetted passengers might be the only folks she saw for the remainder of the day.

And what of the passengers? As they leafed through newspapers or dozed, the train's cautionary chords paci-

fied them too. The engine's song implied safety—promising
that accidents could be prevented and collisions averted.
The passengers rearranged their legs.

In this way the folks inside the train and those standing at their kitchen windows took comfort in the train's
song. But in fact, the chord was a warning. A warning
that there might be danger ahead. A warning that all parties better take care.

Sheriff Temple Jennings was driving back to town. In
the distance he heard that same westbound train blowing
her horn at the crossing. Rubberized shadows of fence
posts stretched from one side of County Road 15 to the
other, flattening under the tires of the sedan in the late-
afternoon sun.

Grit spattered the windshield. Temple cranked up the
heater. He'd spent the afternoon crouched inside a ring
of sage staking out a brush-filled ravine. A local farm had
called in a tip that morning about a whiskey still operating there. Generally, Temple didn't get too worked up
about small-time moonshine operations. There was no
way he could stamp out all of them and get any other
work done. Most times he took care of the issue by casually approaching a bootlegger and saying, "I hear you're
farmin' in the brush," and the boilers, coils, mash barrels,
and other apparatuses would vanish by nightfall.

Whiskey and all other hard liquor were still illegal
in Oklahoma even though the federal government had
repealed the Eighteenth Amendment two years previous.
In Oklahoma, beer was legalized. But that was it. People
who wanted something stronger than suds had to buy
their booze under the table. And there were a number of
moonshiners happy to keep up with demand.

If an operation got too big, Temple felt obligated to go after it. But it was part of the job that stuck in his craw. He relished a drop of the hard stuff as much as the next man. And tracking down and closing the operation was a thankless task. Take today, for instance. After three hours of surveillance the only things moving in that gorge were tree sparrows and a couple of squirrels. Temple was left with nothing to show for his time but the numb fingers and stiff knees of a fifty-six-year-old man. He'd put Ed, his young deputy, on an overnight watch.

Neither middle-age aches nor the fickle heater could bring Temple low today. His wife Etha was due home at nightfall after six days in St. Louis. Seemed mighty like six years. When she had brought up the idea of visiting her friend Lottie, Temple initially fancied the notion of temporary bachelorhood. In his mind's eye this translated into shoving pie directly from the tin into his mouth. Leaving the bedclothes tangled from one day to the next. Shaving every other morning. But all that fun had quickly worn thin. He missed his wife. That evening she'd step off the train and he'd embrace her mightily. Now, he saluted the afternoon express as it whizzed past.

A sappy ballad trickled from the radio. Temple fingered the dial. He needed something snappy. In that moment the heifer materialized.

"Jeez!" he shouted, smashing his boot on the brake pedal. The car shuddered, considered skidding sideways but thought better of it; managed to stop not more than a foot from her long tawny face. So close Temple could have counted her eyelashes.

The Jersey cow swiveled her head toward the windshield. Her gaze was indifferent. A moving-picture star playing the role of a duchess. Apparently seeing nothing of interest, she continued processioning across the road with a rolling gait. Her heavy bag swayed. In her wake she left a busted section of fencing on the right side of the road.

Damn you, Gwendolyn. There was no question about who the heifer was. Most folks in this section of Jackson County knew her by name. She loped up their farm lanes and sauntered into their truck gardens.

The heifer belonged to Joe Melampy, who was a good enough farmer but couldn't string a wire fence to save his life. Temple considered letting Joe chase her down. But by the time Melampy got himself back here, Gwendolyn would likely have ambled out of sight. Temple pulled the car off to the side.

Ignoring his throbbing knees, the sheriff maneuvered out of the driver's seat. He suited up against the biting wind: heavy suede gloves, slouch-brimmed hat. He wrapped a wool muffler around his ruddy face— the once-pale skin now permanently weathered. There was rope in the trunk. A couple of hundred yards away, Gwendolyn was cropping at a clump of sage. Scrawny, as were all livestock these days, she likely still weighed six hundred pounds or more.

Temple approached carefully. "Easy girl," he murmured.

His fingers knotted the rope into a loop while his voice crooned reassurances. He was within three feet of his quarry when the sole of his boot ground loudly against a rock. She jerked. Temple froze.

"You're a ways from home, Gwendolyn," Temple said in low tones. "Mighty cold out here."

As if in answer, a length of glistening snot unfurled

from her nose. She stepped backward. Temple patted the air with his hands. Her blocky flanks retreated.

Temple considered the situation, weighing the rope between his hands. If he lunged forward, would he have time to toss the loop around her neck? Herding cattle was not his strong suit. He'd grown up in a small city in Pennsylvania, not on a farm crouched among the vast expanses of the plains.

Gwendolyn kept her eyes on him. Temple sprang forward. The heifer swung her haunches, trotted a couple of hundred feet, and twisted to see if he was following. *Shoot!*

Hands on hips, Temple studied the ground. How much time did he have to invest in this cat-and-mouse game? Etha's train was due in four hours—at 7:34 p.m. He'd planned on having at least an hour to straighten up the apartment. Etha'd be sore if she came home to dirty dishes and crumbs on the linoleum. And he needed time to buy her a Christmas present. The twenty-fifth was only six days away.

Temple and Gwendolyn continued their slow-motion race for another ten minutes, until they both abruptly called it off. His knees and the weight of her bag won out. Giving her hind legs wide berth because, no matter what, Temple understood Gwendolyn could still kick, he stiff-legged it along her flank and dropped the loop around her neck.

"You are one ornery critter. I'll give you that." The pair headed back the way they'd traveled. Gwendolyn likely regretted she'd gone to the bother of escaping for nothing better than a couple mouthfuls of withered sage. Temple was thinking on Etha. Was she thinking on him?

More likely she was reading a book with her shoulder pressed against the cold window of the passenger car, as the train swayed westward through the brown dusk.

When the road and his parked car finally came into view, deep fatigue was creeping up Temple's thighs. He led Gwendolyn back through the broken fence, untied the rope. She promptly trotted toward the barn. Temple crouched beside the bent wire, fumbling to bend it into some semblance of fencing. A barb pierced clear through the suede and bit his finger. He pulled off the glove and sucked the bright blood. Then he levered himself upright, climbed into the sedan, and drove up to the Melampy place to set Joe down for a talk about how to mend a fence as well as the cost of a citation for public nuisance. Mrs. Melampy would want to serve him a slice of pie and coffee and the whole visit would take at least an hour. But simply dialing up Joe from the office wasn't an option because, like most farm families in Jackson County, the Melampys didn't have a phone or electricity. Or running water, for that matter. Those luxuries were mostly reserved for the folks in town.

Back in Vermillion, the seat of Jackson County, Temple checked in at the sheriff's office on the first floor of the courthouse. Deputy Ed McCance, hunched over a typewriter, paused to ask, "Spot the bootlegger?"

"Nope." Temple poked at the papers filling a wire basket on his desk. "Anything stirring here?"

Ed tipped back in his chair, clasping his hands behind his head. "All quiet."

"Mind holding down the fort a bit longer?"

"Sure thing. Viviane left work early to visit her folks.

Her granny's poorly. Seems I'm on my own for supper."

Temple laughed. "Married only two months and already back to scrounging for yourself?"

Ed shrugged.

The third floor of the courthouse housed both the four-cell county jail and the official sheriff's residence. Walking into the apartment, Temple sniffed the sour odor of unwashed dishes and damp towels. He set to scrubbing pots and smoothing sheets. Newspapers heaped beside the easy chair and the john were bundled into the trash. After a quick shower and shave, Temple changed into his last clean shirt and hurried down the street to Model Clothing.

Vermillion's only ready-to-wear shop had opened thirty-six years ago as a small dry goods concern. Over the years the owner, Meyer Klein, had transformed it into a first-rate retail store.

This Christmas season, Meyer had taken extra care on the shop's window display. He'd invested in a three-foot cardboard Santa and a dozen papier-mâché bells. Usually it would be his daughter, Lottie, twisting garlands of red crepe paper across the shirts and dresses on display. But four months back Lottie had taken a job as a buyer in his cousin's St. Louis department store.

Meyer was refolding a stack of men's handkerchiefs when Temple rambled in.

"Sheriff, you are a sight for sore eyes. Foot traffic has been slow today." A grin extended across Meyer's round face.

"Wish I could say the same. I've been on these dogs since dawn."

"So sit. Sit!" The rotund merchant gestured to a

leather armchair reserved for waiting husbands. Temple dropped heavily into the seat. He removed his Stetson and finger-combed his hair.

Meyer said, "I am grateful that your Etha has been visiting Lottie. I worry about my daughter, even though she is a grown woman."

"For me, Etha can't get home soon enough. Another night of my own cooking and I'll be sick for sure." Temple slapped his thighs, indicating a change of subject. "I'm in need of a Christmas present."

Meyer's eyes lit up. "Give me a couple of minutes." He bustled over to the women's department. Temple stretched out his legs, folded his hands over his stomach, and closed his eyes. Maybe he'd take Etha to the Maid-Rite for a late dinner when she got off the train. No, to the Crystal Hotel. Treat her to a nice meal. Meyer trotted back with an armload of goods, which he deposited on counter.

Temple yawned, stretching his arms and tugging his wrists. "Whatcha got?"

Holding up a tweed dress, Meyer said, "Now this would be very becoming on your wife. She is slender and petite."

Temple cocked his head. "I'm not sure. She is sorta particular . . ."

The sheriff also shot down a bulky handbag.

"I saved the best for last." Meyer winked and made a show of arranging the item just so before turning dramatically back to Temple. "You cannot go wrong with this." He was cradling a narrow pelt between his palms. "What do you think?"

"What is it?"

"A fur coat collar. And I have cuffs to match. It's a

set." He handed the fur to Temple. "Very good quality. It will extend the life of her winter coat. Freshen it up. Hide any worn spots."

Beyond the display window, two nurses from the county hospital hurried past, clenching blue wool capes close to their necks.

"See those young ladies?" Meyer gestured. "Their cheeks are red and their noses are running."

Temple stroked the collar. The fur was both dense and silky. He imagined Etha burying her face in the pelt when she stepped out into the frigid gusts.

Meyer continued: "Lovely variegations of dark and light, don't you think? It's mink brown."

"Mink? I can't afford this!" Temple thrust the collar toward Meyer, who held up his hands.

"You misunderstand. The *color* is mink. But the fur is pieced squirrel. Only the belly portions, which are the softest."

Temple gazed toward the women's department. This fur collar might not be the most costly, but it sure looked it. He shook his head. As much as Etha deserved something nice, this would send the wrong message. The county sheriff was a public servant. After a bitter primary fight in August which, praise the Lord, resulted in a November victory, Temple understood that appearances mattered. Even if it wasn't mink, if folks thought it was, hackles would rise.

"I'm sorry, but I can't. People will talk."

Meyer folded his hands on his taut belly, which made a handy shelf. "Let me explain. Drought, foreclosures, tightened belts. Everyone is making do as best they can. But . . ." he raised a finger, "and this is important, we are all trying to keep up appearances. For the sake of pride. To keep one another's spirits high. So how does this work? We all play a little game. The housewives, they make meatloaf as always but add more bread than meat. They cut up and sew together feed sacks to dress the family. The farmer uses the labor of his wife and his children, even the youngest, where once a hand would be hired. Everyone knows that the meatloaf is not the same, the dresses are made from sacking, the scanty crop has been harvested by the children, but no one says it out loud. We all pretend that things are as they were before. We all pretend that our lives will eventually return to what they were."

"So you're saying folks will know this isn't mink?"

"That's what I'm saying."

Temple looked away. Dusk was coming on and soon he'd be at the depot, waiting for Etha. Fifteen years ago, well before the Depression, when they were still living in Illinois, they'd lost their only child, a boy of nine, in a drowning accident. After that, nothing had been the same. The sheriff turned to Meyer. "Do you think things will return to what they were?"

Meyer shook his head.

Across the street, a rusted sign screeched in the wind.

"Me neither," Temple said.

"So?"

Temple flung up a hand. "What the heck. I'll take it."

Humming softly, Meyer wrapped the fur pieces in tissue paper and laid them inside a gift box. The store's standard wrap, a print of holly leaves and berries, came next. Then all was tucked into a paper bag printed with *Model Clothing*. As if this were a department store in a big city and not a struggling shop in a shrinking town.

CHAPTER TWO

DADDY WARBUCKS WAITED expectantly at the back door.

"I'm coming, I'm coming. Keep your trousers on." Ruthie-Jo plucked her cloth coat from a peg in the kitchen and pulled on her husband Cy's hunting cap. The early evening sky was a chill purple.

Her routine on Thursdays, Cy's late night at the store, was unvaried. After finishing up the account books she kept for Mitchem's Hardware, the family business, she got supper underway and set the table. Then she'd take Daddy Warbucks, the little terrier, out to the backyard for his constitutional.

Daddy would piddle and sometimes she'd lift her dress and piddle alongside him. It was her yard after all and no one's business. But that did not apply to Ruthie-Jo herself. She made it her business to know everything possible about everyone else.

On this evening, however, it was too cold to lift her coat, and besides, she didn't need to go. Often on these jaunts, Ruthie-Jo left Daddy exploring the yard while she passed through the back gate and into the weedy wasteland that skirted the train tracks running behind the house. She didn't go far. A few dozen steps one way and then the other, never crossing over the rails. Ruthie-Jo maintained that this constituted an outing. When Cy asked if she'd left the house that day, she could answer that she had.

On this particular evening, soon after she set out tramping along the rails, she heard quick footfalls approaching from behind. Her eavesdropper's ears picked up a faint metallic jangle accompanying each of the interloper's treads. Ruthie-Jo swung around. The footfalls, the clanking, drew closer. She held her breath. A figure detached itself from the gloom, loping along the rails. He seemed unaware of her presence. *What's he up to?* she thought.

"Hey you!" Ruthie-Jo called in sharp tones.

The figure paused, his shadowy face only five feet away, close enough for her to hear an adenoidal wheeze before he darted past. There was a thud as something was pitched into the underbrush. The intruder sprinted into the darkness before she could call out again.

Living alongside the tracks, Ruthie-Jo was accustomed to the furtive movements of bums, thieves, and other flotsam drawn to the rails. Her curiosity was pricked. What had been tossed away?

She returned to her backyard. Busily excavating his months-long project, a shallow pit alongside the fence, Daddy had to be persuaded to go inside. Ruthie-Jo nudged him through the back door with her instep, grabbed a flashlight, and returned to the tracks. After pushing through the weeds, she uncovered a short length of chain fastened with a padlock. The key was still in the lock. Ruthie-Jo concentrated the flashlight on its brass surface. She couldn't make out the lettering without the magnifying glass she used for reading. She pocketed the key, leaving the lock and chain behind, returned to the kitchen, and briskly stirred the hash warming on the stove. Ruthie-Jo dumped a can of corn into a saucepan and set the table. She checked her watch. Fifteen minutes until Cy got home. Enough time, she figured, to examine the key. With her magnifying glass she could make out the letters *AT-SF RWS* engraved into the brass. It didn't take an egghead to figure out that this was a railroad key of some sort. Everyone called the Atchison, Topeka and Sante Fe Railway, the line that ran through Vermillion, the AT&SF. She wasn't sure what *RWS* stood for. Railroad something.

She was shoving the key back into the pocket of her housedress when a screech of steam brakes and the thunder of crashing steel rocketed up the tracks. Within seconds, a massive roar of light and sound erupted. It sent rolling tremors under the house. Ruthie-Jo's eardrums were close to bursting. For a moment she was frozen with terror like those stone people in Pompeii. Then her brain took over—telling her it was likely a train wreck. She snatched up Daddy, who was yapping his head off, and retreated to the basement. They crouched in the musty darkness. After a while the sounds of shouts and screams reached the cellar. Ruthie-Jo slinked upstairs. She moved from room to room. Nothing was damaged.

She and Daddy were safe. *Thank God!* Ruthie-Jo's hands shook. She patted the pocket of her housedress. The key was still there. She'd study on it more tomorrow. You never knew when something might be of use.

C HAPTER THREE

TWENTY MINUTES EARLIER, the westbound passenger train was passing the Mooreland Station, the last stop before Vermillion. Travelers and locals were crowded in its three coaches, dining car, and single sleeper.

Etha Jennings's knitting needles were clicking along like clockwork when, out of nowhere, a yawning hole appeared in the tidy rows of stitches she'd completed only five minutes before. *Damn it to hell.*

Etha collapsed the mess of needles and yarn, intended as a hat for her niece Vadie's younger son, into her lap. With Christmas coming up fast, and hats to knit for the two boys and her niece's husband, time was banging on the door. Vadie's family was motoring over from Arkansas for the holidays. Vadie's husband Everett had, again, lost his job. Vadie worked in a canning factory. Etha knew the family was barely scraping by, even though Vadie's pride kept her from saying so. During the visit, Etha was determined to talk Vadie into moving her family to Vermillion. They could share the apartment until housing was found. The boys could enroll in the local school. Surely Temple could find Everett some work.

Beyond the window of the swaying passenger train, farmhouse lamps sparked sporadically in the early darkness. The train sounded its horn. It was a four-hour ride from St. Louis to Vermillion. Etha had spent most of the trip knitting and flipping through a dated issue of *Ladies' Home Journal*. Her eyes burned with fatigue.

"Sure you don't want some?" The man sitting across from her, by the name of Vince Doll, extended a wrinkled bag of peanuts.

"I am sure." Etha's closed lips dipped down at the ends. Her mouth fell naturally into this position, as did her mother's. And like her mother, Etha was milk-bottle pale except for the high color in her cheeks.

"Suit yourself." He cracked open a peanut, tossed the kernel into his mouth, and dropped the shell onto the floor among the others. The scab of August's contentious primary, when Doll had attempted to unseat her husband as sheriff, still smarted. Even before the campaign, she'd never understood why the grain elevator owner thought so much of himself.

Etha toed the pile of hulls away from her shoes. At age fifty-four she had largely shrugged off the habit of knee-jerk agreeability. Not that she was rude—simply firm.

"Heading home?" Doll asked.

"Hmmm." Etha busily unraveled the yarn to start the hat anew.

Doll smoothed the chain of his pocket watch, which lay across his high-waisted trousers. He continued the conversation as if Etha was participating: "Me? I was at an auction. Foreclosure of a grain elevator back Alva way. One man's disaster is another's fortune. 'Specially in these times." Doll raised one leg to pull his thick ankle on top of his thigh. "Yep. Can't say the thirties have been kind to our state. But once the drought breaks everything will come to rights."

Etha mouthed the number of stitches as she cast on.

"Heard you were visiting your friend, that Jewish gal, in St. Louis."

Down came the knitting. "Do you mean Lottie?"

Doll plowed on: "So, who's been feeding the prisoners and washing their didies while you were gone? Temple, I expect. I don't know what I was thinking, wanting that job. And my Carrie, I can't tell you how relieved she was when the election was over. She was afraid we'd have to move into that apartment. My Carrie is accustomed to a real home."

Etha stood and picked up her coat.

"Hey! What's eating you?" Doll's face, permanently flushed, grew a deeper crimson.

"I'm going for fresh air."

Etha stomped up the aisle of the swaying coach, planting her palms on alternating seat backs for balance. The lavatories at the car's end smelled of urine and powered soap. She held her breath. At the exit door, Etha stepped into the noisy swaying space between coaches.

Doll's words stung. The sheriff's apartment was comfortable by any standard. Yes, there was the jail on the same floor, but it was secure. Who wouldn't be happy to have a living room, dining room, bedroom, and tiled bath? The kitchen was generous and airy. There was a single cell for lady prisoners in one corner but it was rarely used—and made a handy spot for storing root vegetables.

The cold air of the vestibule swelled with the clattering vibrations of the train's wheels. Etha clutched the grab bar and regarded the dark landscape. The only drawback to the apartment, which was usually not a problem, was the single bedroom. But with the family arriving on Christmas Eve, it would be cramped. No getting around it.

As the floor lurched beneath her feet, Etha counted up her spare blankets, sheets, and chair cushions that might combine into a serviceable pallet for Vadie and Everett in the dining room. The boys, ages eight and ten, would share the bunk in the kitchen jail cell. Besides the sleeping arrangements, the other and more serious concern was that Everett was a drinker. Vadie denied it up and down and every which way, but Etha knew the signs. For didn't the county jail fill up regularly with men and, sometimes, women in the same sour condition? Booze on the breath, slurred words, quick temper. What if he got soused during the visit? She and Temple weren't teetotalers by any means but hard liquor was still illegal in Oklahoma and, as the sheriff, Temple had to be careful.

Etha was constantly worrying about Vadie. She fretted that Everett wouldn't find a job, that he would make a spectacle of himself, that he would pour his sporadic earnings down his throat. And then where would Vadie and the kids be?

And now, in five days, the cause of all her niece's misery would be sleeping in Etha's dining room. A man she didn't like much even when he was sober. With all of them squished into the apartment like sardines, how long would it be before Everett acted out?

Moments earlier, as Etha was making her way up the aisle and leaving Doll to his pile of peanut shells, Cleo Bluett was wheezing down the corridor of the colored car. Beneath her Sunday best, Cleo's chest was as rigid as an oil drum. She badly needed a dose of air. Sidestepping satchels and suitcases, she struggled toward the rear door. She'd always had weak lungs. Was prone to shortness of breath. But she hadn't had a single spell during the three days of the Women's Missionary Society's statewide convention. And likely she'd have made it all the way home if it wasn't for that white man and his cigars. He'd moseyed in after the train had passed through Alva, settled in behind Cleo, behind the panel that separated the colored section from the smokers, and lit up one stogie after another. Her throat tickled, and then scratched. Politely asking the man to put away his smokes was risking outrage and insults. Instead, she had pressed a hankie against her lips, but it was no more effective against a full-blown coughing fit than the wet rags she had to shove around windows when a dust storm barreled in.

Reaching the rear door, Cleo shoved on the push bar. It didn't budge. She tried again, leaning into it. Nothing. The exertion ignited more coughing. It was then Cleo saw, through the door's porthole, a white woman in the passageway. Likely wanting some fresh air too. Cleo adjusted her crimson beret and rapped on the window but the lady didn't turn around.

The train's horn blew four times. Long. Long. Short. Long. Crossing coming up. The train whipped by a truck idling at the grade. The driver was a young farmer, who was taking the opportunity to spit a wad of tobacco onto the road.

Standing in the doorway, Etha checked her watch—a pretty little thing Temple had given her one Christmas. Only ten minutes out from Vermillion, she noted.

Behind her, from the colored car, Etha became aware of a rapid knocking. The face of a sturdy woman, her brows creased in worry, was on the other side of the door. She waved Etha over. Etha guessed the door was stuck. The doors between the cars were notoriously in disrepair, as was almost every other aspect of the train—the cone-shaped paper drinking cups leaked, the upholstered seats sagged.

Between Etha and the forward car was a flimsy gangway, a rickety space hanging above the huge couplers linking the coaches. Like a skater testing the ice, Etha toed the slippery steel floor plates and took a step. The hinged plates jostled against one another, transmitting the pounding wheels up through her pumps. On either side of her, rudimentary canvas walls, pleated like bellows to accommodate the motion of the cars, heaved in and out. She noticed that the bottom of one wall did not meet the steel flooring. The blur of fast-moving rails was only inches from her feet. Nothing much rattled Etha, but now fear funneled into her chest. She saw that the woman's face under the crimson beret mirrored her own tense expression.

Etha shakily trod across the plates. When her shoes found purchase on the sturdy platform of the next car, she exhaled. Relief flooded the other woman's eyes. They exchanged tight smiles. Etha pulled the door's grip. Nothing. She yanked. The other woman pushed. The door was stuck tight. In that instant the metallic shriek of brakes exploded in Etha's ears. The vestibule lurched. Lights flickered and Etha felt the door let loose. The woman stumbled out, wheezing with each intake of breath. Etha was opening her mouth to speak when the passageway went dark, and the car tipped to the side. The screech of splitting wood burst through the blackness.

Etha was slammed against the doorframe. There was the burning reek of a kettle boiled dry. As she fell she glimpsed a dust storm, strangely white, rolling through the colored car. Screams mingled with the hiss of steam. The train listed and pitched as if a ship plunging into the depths. The pounding and screams ascended. Etha tried to stand but everything was in motion and a heavy wetness inside her coat pulled her down. Was she drowning? Beneath the surface something pierced her thigh. Her head swam in a dark current.

At some point, she thrashed back to consciousness. Cries and shouts, which must have been going on all along, reached her ears. Abruptly all motion stopped. Etha understood. The train had crashed. And toppled. Sideways? Upside down? Impossible to know.

"Over here!" Amid the creaking of steel and the screaming of passengers, voices from the outside world penetrated.

A light swept into her eyes. She jerked.

"Ma'am, stay still. I'm going to get you out." The voice was agitated.

The light snapped off. Calloused hands gripped hers. The man tugged. Etha's thigh blazed as if a hot knife was twisting into her flesh. Her rescuer carried her from the wreckage and laid her among the brown winter grasses. He leaned over her. She saw a long face with oversized ears. "Oh God, oh God, oh God," he was mumbling.

Etha said, "Go for the others."

He pulled a bandanna out and blew his nose. "I seen

some town folks coming out to help. I'll send them your way."

"There was another woman beside me," Etha whispered hoarsely.

But he was gone. Off toward the screaming wounded and the crack and snap of white-hot steel.

The rustle of dried bluestems murmured in Etha's ear. She squinted into the night sky. The pain was almost unbearable when her eyes were open. She squeezed them shut.

The stony ground was bitterly cold. Her fingers and feet stiffened. Time passed and no one came for her. Not far away, voices muttered but did not approach. The stench of burning flesh hung everywhere. Twisting her head, a rusted tin can and petrified wad of chewing tobacco came into view. *I've been forgotten,* she thought. Despair washed over her. *Is this the end of me?*

She gingerly touched her cheeks and nose. Only scratches. Her hat was missing. She unbuttoned her coat, ran her hand across her bosom and stomach. The flesh was dry and whole. But her right thigh was wet and sticky. The smell of iron was strong. She pressed on it. Pain spattered like hot grease across her body. She rebuttoned the coat.

Grunting, she rolled onto her stomach. She tried to stand but her leg throbbed painfully. The ground and sky spun like a record on a phonograph. She crawled. Lights and voices buzzed in the distance. She passed out twice. The second time, the loud blast of a siren galvanized her. She crept forward with her eyes half-shut. The quivering lights coalesced into a single glowing space—an open train shed. She pulled herself up on a support pole.

"Grab her!" someone shouted.

Etha buckled. She was again laid out—this time on a blanket. This time with a blanket to cover her as well. This time with battered passengers on either side and anxious tenders bending over her. She had pushed through. Gutted it out, as her brothers used to say.

C HAPTER FOUR

WHILE ETHA HAD BEEN PUTTING DOWN her knitting and heading to the vestibule, Temple had been leaning across the station counter jawing with Herschel, the station agent. Etha's train was coming in early, according to Herschel, but the two still had a couple of minutes to discuss baseball.

"You're crazy if you think Dizzy Dean will get traded," Herschel proclaimed. "The Cardinals know he's got what it takes."

"'Spect they do. But there are rumors the Reds want to sign him."

Temple turned and addressed the gloomy travelers huddled around the station's coal stove. The AT&SF was known to skimp on coal in its stations and heat in its passenger cars. "Care to take a side?"

No one took the bait.

"Look-it here . . ." Herschel was saying when his voice, the ticking of the station clock, and the shush of coal rearranging itself in the stove were obliterated by the shriek of shredding metal. And then an ear-piercing explosion. Plaster flew from the station's ceiling. Temple hunkered down. His first thought was a fast-moving dust storm. But the shadowy scrub beyond the shattered windows was motionless. Then Temple's churning brain sorted out what his ears were telling him. *Train crash. Oh God. Etha.*

He stumbled to his feet. Herschel was already flicking the phone's rotary dial.

On the platform, a couple of track hands tore past.

Temple bolted outside and up the weedy ditch along the tracks. "Which train?" he yelled to the workers, but got no reply.

With heaving lungs, he closed in on the carnage. The stink of steam and burning flesh was strong. He'd been a kid when an infamous flood roared through his home-town of Johnstown, Pennsylvania—destroying homes and, ironically, igniting fires. He'd never forgotten the stench. Nor the sounds. Same as now. Shrieks and moans. The pitiful pleas of women and children told him this was the inbound passenger train from St. Louis and not a freight. *Please God that Etha is safe.* He reached the en-gine. It was thrown on its side between the rails running west and the siding. The eastbound track was clear. Final gouts of steam were issuing from its smashed boiler.

Beyond the locomotive, dissipating clouds exposed a nightmarish hash of broken hardware, bits of clothing, smashed seats, and severed limbs. Survivors stumbled blindly among the stew. The track crew was struggling to free those trapped in the two forward coaches, which had also derailed. Temple hastened along the edge of the wreckage, ignoring the cries of the wounded. His only thoughts were of finding Etha in the rank fog.

He called her name as he advanced. At the rear of the train one of the coaches remained upright. Passen-gers tentatively emerged as the conductor urged them to quickly move away. None were Etha. Temple pivoted and tramped back toward the locomotive. His glance slid across jumbled heaps of seat backs and grips. Here was a baby's cap. There an empty boot. Chunks of metal. Bits of flesh.

Finally, after what might have been ten minutes or ten hours, the track foreman, a man by the name of Milt Redfield, grabbed Temple by the elbow.

"Sheriff, what are you doing? We need your help."

Temple stared numbly beyond Milt's shoulder. "My wife . . ." His words dribbled away.

"Etha on this train?"

Temple nodded.

"We'll find her. You leave that to the crew and the rest. A bunch of folks from town just got here. Doc Hinchie and nurses from the hospital. Orderlies too."

Temple's eyes were unfocused.

"Listen to me!" Milt shook the sheriff's arm. "The AT&SF will send a detective out. Standard procedure for a derailment like this. I need to fill you in on everything before the company brass arrives. One of my men took note of something that seems out of place."

Roughly pulling away, Temple said, "My deputy can handle whatever that is. I'm not doing anything until I find Etha." He spun around and waded back into the wreckage. Every bit of light from the setting sun was now extinguished. In the darkness of night the twisted remains of the train loomed. The flashlights of rescuers only briefly illuminated stricken faces, mangled bodies, before moving on.

Temple stumbled randomly among the debris. His mouth hung open. It was only when he heard the voice of his deputy shouting his name that he remembered to close it. Temple watched as Ed approached.

"Did you find her?" Ed asked.

Temple shook his head.

"Look. You're not going to want to hear this, but you've got to start acting like the sheriff. Folks injured, rescuers running around like chickens with their heads cut off. Lookie-loos clogging up the works." Ed flapped a hand toward the silhouettes massed beyond the rails. "Whatever evidence that will tell us how this happened—if this was an accident, mechanical failure, or whatever—will get trampled. Not to mention the crowd is getting in the way of the folks trying to tend to the wounded. You got to take charge. You know you do. I will find Etha. I—"

"Don't try to tell me how to do my job," Temple snapped.

The deputy bowed his head.

I'm not thinking straight, Temple realized. *I've wasted precious time wandering around.* He could barely make out Ed's face, but he knew it was earnest. Part of his responsibility, as Temple saw it, was to set an example for his young deputy. "Sorry. You're right. You promise to find her?"

Ed nodded, then switched the heavy flashlight back on and loped off.

The sheriff hurried toward the front of the wreck where a canvas-roofed truck was slowly jolting toward the rails and scattering bystanders with horn blasts. Behind the wheel, Temple spotted Commander Leroy Baker from the CCC camp. As soon as the brakes squealed and the truck halted, young men piled out from the back.

Cavalry's just in time. Temple's mood inched up a notch. President Roosevelt's CCC boys, young men whose families were on relief, toiled in every state. They planted trees, dug irrigation lines, cleared brush. Most were solid. Now these once lost youths twitched like horses at the starting gate—primed to pitch in on the rescue efforts. After motioning them to wait by the truck, Baker marched over to Temple.

"What can we do, sheriff?" Baker's West Virginia burr was long and slow but the man himself was all spit and polish. Matching brass collar pins. Regulation tie tucked between the second and third buttons.

Temple motioned toward the ghoulish throng. "It would be mighty helpful if your boys could keep the gapers up there at bay and if a couple could guard the train cars."

"Sure thing."

"And thanks for getting here so quick."

The sheriff plodded up the tracks. The sooty air echoed with shouts. A CCC fellow with a flop of dark hair sprinted toward him.

"Sheriff Jennings!"

Temple didn't break stride. The CCCer caught up. Tapped the sleeve of the sheriff's overcoat.

"Hey," Carmine panted. And when at last Temple turned, Carmine said, "Heard Mrs. Jennings was on the train. Is she all right?" The youth's face was drawn.

Four months back Carmine had been Temple's prime suspect in the murder of a traveling rainmaker. During the time the kid had been in the county lockup, Etha had seen something in the street tough that Temple couldn't. While the sheriff had believed in the kid's guilt, Etha felt differently. Eventually she was proved right. But Temple still didn't trust the kid. Even though Carmine was innocent of the murder, he'd sprinted away from the sheriff when Temple was trying to interview him. In Temple's experience, those who ran from the law were usually guilty of something. Despite warning Etha to keep the kid at arm's length, he'd often come home to find Carmine seated at the kitchen table inhaling a slice of Etha's pie—the two of them gabbing away.

"We haven't found her yet. But we will."

Carmine dropped his head, cupping his palms over his eyes.

Temple sighed, both irritated and touched. "Etha's tough. You know that. Now get on back to the corps. We need every pair of hands we've got."

Carmine wiped a sleeve across his nose and made his way back to the crew.

Temple hastened ahead, scouring the crowd for the track foreman.

Milt, a burly man with muscled shoulders that strained his overalls, spotted Temple first. Surprisingly agile, Milt nimbly maneuvered the debris field. "Etha all right?" he asked.

The sheriff rubbed his forehead. "Don't know yet, but Ed's got it covered. Help me reconnoiter the scene so I get the big picture."

With Milt in the lead, the two men headed toward the final car. Along the way, Milt described the likely time line of the derailment. It had started with the engine jumping the rails and plowing between the main track and the siding. When it tipped over on its right side, the boiler exploded, spraying scalding steam. An instant later, the combination mail and baggage car was thrust up and over the engine. Next in line was the colored car. It had smashed to bits directly in line with the ruptured pipes. Live steam had gushed into the car. The temperature, likely two hundred degrees or more, would have instantly scalded those exposed. The next coach car also fell sideways but escaped the steam. The third coach, dining car, and Pullman sleeper at the rear remained upright.

A surge of nausea flooded Temple's throat and mouth. He bent over, hands on his knees. *Scalded to death.* "What about the engineer?"

"Not found but likely crushed under the cab."

"Family notified?"

"The company takes care of it. The driver wasn't from here. The crewman who fires up the boiler made it out alive. Badly burned but might help put the picture together at some point."

Temple examined the ground, gathered himself. "Something else you wanted to show me?"

"One of my men spotted something out of line. Maybe intentional." Milt pointed east up the track.

Temple frowned. "What? Vandalism?"

"It happens," Milt said.

But as the two men began walking eastward, a track hand shouted for them to hold up. "Herschel says the division superintendent is on the line."

The section foreman tightened his lips and turned to Temple. "Sorry. I got to take this call."

The track hand had a mess of greasy hair jammed under his pinstriped work cap. He said, "And sheriff, I'm supposed to tell you that the AT&SF detective is coming in tomorrow morning. He wants to meet with you first thing."

Milt lingered to ask, "Did Herschel say which detective?"

"Claude Steele."

"I know him," Milt said to Temple. "Good enough investigator but sort of an odd duck."

Temple sighed. Another load to carry.

Milt trudged toward the station. Temple figured they'd connect up in a bit. Then Milt could show him what the track hand had noticed earlier. It was difficult for Temple, even with all his experiences as a lawman, to believe that somebody would purposefully wreck a train—maiming and killing with cold-blooded intent.

As the night wore on, the ongoing chaos around the wreckage kept both Temple and Milt hustling. It would not be until the next day that Temple would learn what the track hand had observed.

C HAPTER FIVE

AFTER SWEARING TO TEMPLE that he'd find Etha, Ed calmly strode into the wreckage. *In an emergency, a leader is the steady anchor*, he thought. The deputy was anxious to present himself as a man going places—like those fellows he read about in Dale Carnegie's *How to Win Friends and Influence People*.

He passed a gang of CCC boys joining arms to keep back the spectators. He'd been a member of the CCC himself before becoming deputy. And before the CCC, well, it had been a life of riding the rails, working the carnie circuit, loading coal—whatever came his way.

Ed's flashlight illuminated the unwholesome terrain beneath his boots. Bodies, springs, bearings, metal struts, disemboweled seat cushions, and shredded clothing. He thought of Viviane, his bride, and was grateful she was not here to witness this. Grateful that she was safely out in the country doing nothing more dire than spooning gruel into her granny's mouth.

From this pandemonium, someone shouted in Ed's direction: "Need help here!"

The deputy focused his flashlight in the caller's direction. The fellow, who had one of those hangdog faces, was attempting to scale a passenger car that had smashed into

the locomotive. The car's wooden walls were squeezed
together like an accordion. Ed realized it was the colored
car. He'd spent enough time hanging out in train yards
trying to catch a ride on a boxcar to know the setup of
both freight and passenger trains. Always coupled behind
the baggage and mail cars near the front of the train, the
colored cars were notoriously sooty, noisy—and vulnerable. They were inevitably constructed of wood and were
decades old. Behind the colored cars, shiny steel passenger cars carried the white folks. In case of a wreck, the
flimsy colored car was liable to be rammed from behind
and smashed into the cars ahead. Sweat sprang across
Ed's forehead.

"Boost me up!" the fellow yelled.

Ed maneuvered to the man's side, entwining the fingers of both hands and bracing himself.

The fellow planted his boot and swung up. He teetered across the car's torqued coupling and peered into
the coach. "Can't see." He extended his hand to the deputy.

Ed clambered up beside the rescuer and directed his
flashlight into the maw of the wreckage. What it revealed
was truly horrific. The entire front end of the coach had
been torn away—likely by the force of live steam from
the exploding boiler, which then rolled through what
looked to be a crowded car. Ed glimpsed bodies with
hands clenched in death agony—coated with soot but otherwise whole. Others were missing arms, legs, skullcaps—
doubtless sheared off by rods, bolts, and all manner of
shrapnel spewed by the blast. Blood, pulpy masses of tissue; the stench of burning flesh was everywhere.

"Oh my God," the man sobbed.

Ed clapped his hand over his mouth and squeezed

his eyes shut before gathering himself. There might be survivors. Ed called down to several able-bodied men stumbling numbly among the debris: "We're going in for a rescue. Set up a relay to pass along any injured until they're clear of the wreck. And someone go find the doctor."

"There's a field hospital set up in the train shed!" someone yelled from the rear.

"Good. Let's make this fast."

Ed's mate was already on his stomach, with head and arms dangling into the coach's gaping wound. "I think I see someone," the man said, wriggling farther inside. "Give me your hands!" he shouted into the car.

Two palms reached upward. A woman. Deep burns covered her arms and hands. She screamed in agony as the man pulled her out. Ed bent to grab her waist. Together the two men hauled her through the mangled gash of twisted metal that had been the front of the coach.

Death was not new to Ed. Once, while riding the rails, he'd slid open the doors of a boxcar during a blizzard. A hobo was curled in the corner, his face sunken, his limbs waxy and stiff. And in recent months, as a deputy, he had been called to several fatal farm accidents, suicides, and the murder of an itinerant rainmaker.

He sensed death might be coming for this woman too, but her wheezing breaths gave him hope. He lowered her into the open arms of a track crewman below.

"I don't see nobody else moving. I'm going in," Ed's partner said.

Ed followed. He dropped into the cockeyed space, scrambling to find purchase on what were the remnants of the car's windows. Debris splintered beneath his boots.

The man with the hangdog expression was a few feet inside, his hand resting heavily on a luggage rack, his face a crumpled wad of sorrow. The reek of burned flesh was overwhelming.

"Rest are dead."

The two men bent their heads, then climbed out.

The deputy knew he was needed elsewhere. "Gotta go. Name's Ed, by the way."

The fellow stretched out his hand. "Lonnie."

At this hour, the only lights remaining were those illuminating the station platform and the lanterns of the rescuers. Ed wondered how he was going to keep his promise to Temple in this shadowy bedlam. But as he prepared to jump from the tipped coach, he spied the field hospital about a quarter mile away. He hustled over.

There were no neat rows. No separations between the living and the dead among the sixty or so on the ground. Wending through the makeshift ward, Ed winced at the passengers covered in singed clothing, bloody bandages, and thin blankets. Low moans and shouted orders swept through the open space and out across the grasslands. Ed sought out the injured who were of Etha's small build. Twice he thought he spotted her but, moving closer, the dazed eyes and bloodied scalps belonged to others.

A kneeling matron was holding a tin cup to the lips of a sufferer when Ed bumped into her. Rocked back on her heels and onto her bottom, she hissed, "Goddamnit!" It was Minnie Hinchie, wife of the county's general practitioner.

"I am so sorry," Ed said quickly, reaching down to help her to her feet.

After brushing off her coat, Mrs. Hinchie turned to

the deputy. "It's about time you lawmen showed up. My husband's about to drop from exhaustion and still the wounded stream in. Why hasn't the hospital sent the ambulance? Where is Musgrove with the hearse?"

Ed took the verbal pounding without any lip. Dale Carnegie advised listening rather than arguing—even when the criticism was meritless. "Yes ma'am. Both on their way as we speak."

"And where is Temple? I've seen neither hide nor hair." The corners of her mouth sagged with fatigue.

"He's here. You know, Etha was on the train."

Mrs. Hinchie pulled back, and her eyes welled. "Oh my Lord. I had no idea."

"He searched for quite a while until we convinced him to take charge of the smashup. I promised to find Etha."

Shouts and the gunning of an engine echoed across the wreck's dark hulk. The rise and fall of a siren announced the approach of the ambulance; its headlights careened side to side over the rough ground.

The deputy squeezed Mrs. Hinchie's hand. "I'm going to keep looking. If you find out anything here, send someone to find me."

"Of course."

Ed moved off into the darkness toward the second tipped passenger car. He searched the smoldering wreckage for an hour. Two hours. He was hurtling toward despair when a high voice rose behind him. "Mr. McCance. Sir," the kid said, panting. "Mrs. Hinchie—"

But Ed was already dashing toward the shed where he found two orderlies sliding Etha into the ambulance. Above a worn sheet, her face was a pale nub. Her breath came in short gasps. But she was breathing. Ed's eyes grew glassy. He blew his nose. Then he galloped off to find Temple.

C HAPTER SIX

THE SHARP TWANG OF RUBBING ALCOHOL plucked at the drowsy recesses of Etha's consciousness. The clatter of pumps crossing linoleum washed into her ears. *Shush shush*, whispered a blood pressure bulb in the palm of the nurse. The nurse moved away.

Etha drifted, but quickly resurfaced. Remembered the rubbing alcohol, the linoleum. Understood she was in the hospital. Understood that the warm weight covering her hand was Temple's. She opened her eyes to the early morning light.

"There's my old sweetie," Temple said, his voice gummed with fatigue.

Etha rubbed the gray whiskers speckling his jaw. "Need a shave," she rasped.

"Yep. And a bath and at least twelve hours of sleep and something stronger than the swill this establishment calls coffee."

"Help me sit up."

"You got to stay flat for now."

Etha frowned. "On whose say-so?"

"Hinchie's."

"Oh, him. What does that old codger know?" Etha

pushed herself up on one elbow. A sharp pain zipped across her leg, drawing tears. She buckled.

Temple bent over her, his voice tight with worry. "Please."

"No, I . . ." she began. It rushed back. The train. The crash. Coarse hands pulling her from the debris. Her long crawl through the weeds. Etha regarded the ward. Every bed was filled. Nurses hurried from patient to patient. The murmurs of the staff, the groans of their charges, and the clatter of instruments in metal trays swelled in the vast space. Etha gripped Temple's hand. "Did everyone come through all right?"

Temple shook his head.

"Sweet Jesus." Etha paled.

"Thirteen dead, as far as we know so far."

"Thirteen!"

Temple studied his hands. "Hinchie says you've got some serious injuries. Lacerations and such. He'll be coming by to give you a good going-over." He brushed the salt-and-pepper wisps off her forehead. "But until he gets 'round, you need to lie quiet. If you get too wiggly I'll have to distract you by singing or something. And we both know that's no good."

A weak smile creased Etha's face. All this talk was exhausting. She closed her eyes.

When she opened them again, midmorning sun lit the ward's tall windows. The hills and valleys of her sheets glowed. Etha wiggled her toes, which seemed to be in working order.

When I was sick and lay a-bed,
I had two pillows at my head,

And all my toys beside me lay,
To keep me happy all the day.

When their son Jack was laid up with the mumps, Etha had kept him occupied by playing checkers and reading aloud from *A Child's Garden of Verses,* which included that poem. Etha was about to ask Temple if he remembered the lines but heard him gently snoring in the chair at her bedside.

The ward was even more crowded now. Clumps of dazed family members camped beside thickly bandaged patients. Nurses, orderlies, and tray girls wove in and out between the beds like shuttlecocks. The slightest twist sent Etha's right thigh throbbing. She felt neglected and irritable. On her immediate left, a screen blocked her view of her neighbor. On her right, she glimpsed Hinchie patting the hand of a young woman with two blackened eyes and a headdress of gauze. Vermillion's GP tossed the stethoscope over his shoulder, the signal he was moving on, and stepped toward Etha.

"You didn't think I forgot you, did you?" he asked. His round face was drawn and damp with sweat.

"It did occur," Etha said wryly.

At the sound of the doctor's voice, Temple roused. "She's wanting to sit up and you know Etha when she gets it in her mind to do something."

"Um-huh," Dr. Wilburn Hinchie commented neutrally. He was the county's only doctor. On the side, he acted as Jackson County's medical examiner when a suspicious death arose. His wife Minnie was Etha's friend and the two couples played pinochle the third Saturday of every month. In addition, twice a week the sheriff and the doctor occupied adjoining stools at the Idle Hour. Over beers, they commiserated on county politics, money troubles, and rheumatism.

Hinchie tugged his stethoscope back in place and pressed it against Etha's chest. "Lie still now," he said, folding back the sheets and unbuttoning a man's work shirt that, due to the overflow of patients, served in place of a hospital gown. He palpated the ribs. She didn't yelp. "Nothing broken." Hinchie buttoned up the shirt then pulled the covers down to examine the cut on her thigh that he'd hurriedly dressed the previous night.

The dressing was stained dark red and completely saturated.

"Nurse!" Hinchie called.

"What's wrong?" Etha asked, her face drawn with worry. Temple gripped her hand.

A nurse in a wrinkled overapron and crooked cap appeared at the side of the bed.

"Basin, tweezers, and a fresh dressing," Hinchie said. She hurried off. To Temple and Etha he said, "I'm going to take a closer look than I got last night. Temple, step away for a couple of minutes."

The sheriff hesitated. Etha shooed him away. "Hinchie knows what he's doing."

The nurse returned. She handed Hinchie the implements and rolled a second screen to the foot of the bed. Hinchie pulled off the soggy dressing and dropped it in the basin. The wound, jagged and angry, smelled of rotten eggs. Bending closer with a magnifying glass, Hinchie encountered a foul garden of wood and glass splinters embedded in the raw flesh.

"Damnit," he muttered.

"I heard that," Etha said.

Hinchie straightened. He knew Etha was a fellow pragmatist. "Right now, the laceration is teetering on infection. I need to pluck out all the slivers I can and clean up the edges with a scalpel. I can't tell how deep this wound goes. If it has penetrated the thigh muscle and gets infected, we'll have a real mess on our hands. But I'm thinking positive."

Etha listened with her lips tightly rolled under her front teeth. "Then I'm looking on the sunny side too. You can poke around my leg all you want but I draw the line on being your pinochle partner. You don't know trump from a hole in the ground."

"You may be right on that," Hinchie replied.

Temple's nervous pacing had taken him halfway down the aisle when Hinchie called him back to the bedside. "Come in and squeeze Etha's hand while I'm working. This is going to hurt. I'll be quick as I can."

Temple rounded the screen, pale as marble.

"Give me that paw," Etha said.

Hinchie and the nurse bent to their task. Temple liked to wring Etha's hand right off. A couple of squeaks burst from Etha. Tears drizzled into her ears.

"All done," Hinchie announced after littering the nurse's outstretched basin with metal filings, glass shards, and bloody gauze. "Just going to dress it lightly for now."

Etha lifted her head. "No stitches?"

"The gash is too wide. I want you to stay here for three or four days so we can keep an eye on it. Then you'll be packed off home for complete bed rest."

"With my niece and family coming for Christmas? And the tree to trim?"

Hinchie turned to Temple. "It is clear that I am not succeeding with your wife. So I am telling you. It's a dirty wound. Tried to clean it out best I could but it needs to be kept open for a time until I'm sure I tweezed out all the contaminants. Running the sweeper, cooking, doing wash—all that moving around will aggravate both that laceration, and me. The risk of infection, including blood poisoning, is high. I'm telling you straight—she could lose the leg or, worst case, her life. It will be your job to keep her still. This is not something to mess around with. Got it?"

The sheriff's face sagged.

Etha patted his hand. "I'm a fast healer."

Hinchie snorted. "Don't let her bamboozle you. Time and bed rest." He rolled the instruments up in surgical toweling, handed them to the nurse, and whisked past the screens to greet the next patient.

Flicking a hypodermic of morphine to remove air bubbles, the nurse swabbed Etha's arm, inserted the needle, then marched off.

Etha smiled drowsily. "Alone at last. Guess you'll have your hands full in a couple of days."

Temple kissed her forehead. "You're going to have to play by the rules for once. Do what Hinchie says."

"I know," Etha mumbled, her eyelids slowly lowering.

The village of Mooreland, little more than a crossroads, was one stop east of Vermillion. Generally, the engineer simply slowed while passing through the village so that a canvas mailbag could be hooked on the fly as the train rolled on to the county seat.

On this day, things were different. Claude Steele had

requested that the driver pause at Mooreland's depot for a full five minutes. The engineer had grumbled about his timetable, but Claude had responded that this was official AT&SF business and the man would just have to make up the lost time. As the train screeched to a stop, Claude swung outside of the coach and hit the platform at a trot. The depot was marginally larger than a garden shed. Claude peered into the ticket window that opened onto the platform. The office beyond was empty.

"How do? Needing some help!" Claude shouted. A door shut toward the back.

"Hold your horses." Moments later the station agent trotted in. He thumbed both suspenders into place. "Sometimes a fella has to use the facilities."

"Agreed. But as you can see," Claude said, cocking his thumb behind him, "I'm holding up this passenger train to conduct some AT&SF business, so time is of the essence. I'm a company detective." He flipped open the cover on his badge.

The agent, a man in his thirties with the upward-rising brows of the perpetually worried, snapped to attention. "You here about the derailment down the way?"

Claude nodded. "I'm wondering if you were on duty when the 7:18 came through last night by way of Ponca City."

"Yes sir."

"Awake?"

"Unequivocally."

Claude turned, casting his eyes across the street to the grain elevators and single saloon crouched in their shadows. "I wouldn't hold it against anyone if they admitted to having a catnap after dinner. These backwater stations get awful quiet. This one was built in 1887, if memory serves."

"Not me. I was wide awake."

"Glad to hear it. So about last night." Claude pulled off his spectacles and rubbed them with a wadded handkerchief.

"That particular train doesn't stop here regular, unless I let them know a passenger is boarding. The train came through on time."

"And the weather?"

"Clear."

Claude abruptly looked up from his eyeglasses and stared pointedly at the agent's face. This was a technique he believed guaranteed a truthful response. "What about speed?"

"On the money."

Claude thrust out his hand. "You've been a big help. Thanks, young fella. By the way, that looks like a dog spike."

"What?"

"That there old rail spike you're using for a paper weight. Shaped like a dog head. Pretty scarce. Now don't say I never told you nothing useful."

"That?" the clerk frowned. He pointed to the rusty iron spike resting atop a pile of papers.

"Yep. I collect them. Don't have that one, though." Claude raised his eyebrows.

The clerk spread his palms, his voice incredulous. "You want it?"

"If you're not needing it."

"No. Take it!"

Grinning, Claude pocketed his treasure and trotted

off to the waiting cars. He clutched the grab bar, cocked two fingers at the engineer, and the train rolled out. The conductor checked his watch. Three minutes behind schedule now.

Dropping heavily into his seat, Claude examined the spike. It still bore the individual nicks where the blacksmith's hammer had struck. *A jim-dandy*.

Claude had grown up in a house along the tracks. His father had been a sergeant with the Kansas City police and expected his son to follow in his footsteps. But patrolling a beat in uniform with a nightstick tucked into his belt held no allure for Claude. His entire world was the railroad. He could identify any train by the distinctive harmony of its horn. Memorized locomotive numbers. Subscribed to *Railroad Stories* magazine, rereading each issue until its pulpy pages disintegrated.

In the spring of his senior year, Claude told his father he'd set his sights on a job with the railroad. Specifically as a locomotive engineer. His father was first stunned and then angry. For months, family dinners were misery as the father alternately berated and pleaded with his son. But Claude held firm. The day after graduation, he filed an application with the AT&SF for training as an engineer. Three days later he was called in to take written and physical examinations. Claude passed the aptitude test easily. However, when presented with an eye chart, even those letters not halfway down were fuzzy. The bigger blow came when the company doctor pressed a stethoscope to his chest, heard the telltale wheeze of an asthmatic, and declared Claude unfit for the position of engineer. It was a tough summer. Claude got an interim position as a ticket seller at the city's station while he ruminated on his next step. During his lunch breaks, he roamed the loading platforms of the freight and passenger trains, interrogating conductors, brakemen, postal workers in the mail car, track workers—anyone who would talk to him about their work lives. By August, he had settled on the position of railroad detective. There were a number of advantages, as he saw it. Working out of a regional hub, railroad detectives often investigated cases within a radius of one hundred miles or more. The idea of working at different stations, and with a variety of train and work crews, had a lot of appeal. He was confident that his wide and deep knowledge of every aspect of railroading would be a major asset.

Claude applied and was immediately hired. That had been thirty-two years ago. He took to the whole shebang enthusiastically. His deep dedication to railroading now extended to include an abiding allegiance to one road in particular—the AT&SF. The railroad detective was a company man through and through. A seminarian couldn't have been more devoted to his calling than Claude was when he'd sworn to protect AT&SF assets and its good name. He dedicated his heart and brains to the company—and if those didn't do the job, the holstered pistol strapped to his shoulder and cast-iron knuckledusters in his back pocket would.

Now Claude fished a notebook out of his shapeless topcoat, lit a cigar, and logged what he'd gleaned from the station agent.

Seventeen minutes later the train steamed into Vermillion, after switching to the eastbound rails. These were the only operational tracks until the wreckage was cleared. Claude peered out the window. He spotted a lanky middle-aged fellow on the platform wearing a Stetson and topcoat. The man was eyeballing the passengers as they debarked. His sallow, unshaven face drooped. *Like as not the sheriff. Up all night.* Claude had buddied up plenty with local lawmen on cases. Most were good eggs but some could be tetchy. Territorial. From this distance, Claude couldn't tell which camp Temple was in. He shrugged. *Don't matter. I'm easygoing as they come.* This was one of many convictions Claude had about himself that didn't hold water.

CHAPTER SEVEN

THE TRAIN JERKED TO A STOP. Oily, day-old stink from the derailment hung heavy in the wintry air. Most travelers pressed handkerchiefs or mufflers across their noses.

Temple, waiting on the platform, didn't take any notice of the reek. All he could think about was Etha flat out in the hospital. What had Hinchie said? *A dirty wound.* That sounded bad. Going from task to task was the only way to keep from becoming crazed with worry.

A dozen passengers stepped out of the cars. *Won't be hard to figure which is the railroad detective,* he thought. Most of the AT&SF policemen that Temple ran into over the years were ex-cops who continued to dress the part: spit-and-shine uniforms, brass buttons, epaulets, and visored caps bearing shields. None of the travelers matched that look. A stranger who did approach him, hand out, was outfitted in a bulky topcoat, woolen suit jacket, and greasy vest. Sagging gray trousers overflowed a pair of unbuckled rubber boots—their clasps flapping with each step. Temple swallowed his surprise.

"Claude Steele, railroad detective. I'm thinking you're the sheriff."

"I am." Temple gripped the beefy hand.

Claude rubbed his palms together. "Let's get started, then."

Temple picked up the leather satchel slumped at Claude's feet. "I'll put your bag in my car for now. Give me a second."

When Temple returned, the platform was empty. *What the hell?*

A trackman, shovel over his shoulder, slouched past.

"Have you seen an older fella in big rubber boots?"

"Up at the engine." The worker discharged a spout of tobacco juice and lumbered on.

The destroyed locomotive and forward cars remained on the weedy ground between the siding and main rails. The rest of the train's coaches had been shunted to a sidetrack. The scene was still crawling with track workers and volunteers, including the CCC boys, who were doing a final search of the wreckage.

"Getting the lay of the land," the detective explained when Temple approached. A thick cigar jerked up and down between his lips, scattering ashes.

With its undercarriage exposed, the engine resembled a dead roach: a jumble of blackened and bent appendages. Claude picked his way across the rocky ballast and marched right up to the underbelly.

"This here," he said, distributing more ash as he tapped at a cable with a stout finger, "is part of the braking system. Intact. So we might have to look elsewhere for the reason this train derailed. I need to see the cab."

A ladder was fetched and, as the burly detective mounted the rungs with topcoat flapping, the sheriff took note that the man packed a stubby Colt Police Positive revolver. Temple himself didn't routinely carry a weapon.

Once Claude maneuvered himself to the open window of the cab, he motioned Temple to join him.

Claude cautiously lowered himself into a squat. "Might be a clue here."

"Such as?"

"Won't know until I see it. My super told me the stoker made it through. Anyone talked to him?"

"Not as yet. He's in the hospital. Thought between you, me, and my deputy, we'd split up the questionings. But before that, Milt, the section foreman, told me there might be a reason to think this wasn't an accident."

"I heard the same." Claude descended, his big belly brushing against the ladder's rungs. "Let's find this Milt."

They located the foreman relieving himself beside the track. *Poor guy. Can't even take an uninterrupted piss,* Temple thought sympathetically.

Introductions were made as Milt buttoned up.

"We'd appreciate it if you'd show us what caught your section hand's eye," Temple said, aware of Claude off to one side, jiggling on his toes in agitation.

Milt said, "Let's go."

"Man after my own heart," Claude said. "Lead on."

Milt tramped eastward, past the wreck, and continued for almost a mile. Claude and Temple followed. The air was cleaner out this way. No stink of soot and boiled bodies. They came to a stop at a signaling device on a cast-iron stand.

Claude whistled. "Appears to be tampered with."

The base was a block of iron, with a lever sticking out one side. A two-foot pole rose from the center. And on the top of that was a metal disk.

"How so?" Temple asked.

"See here, this lever . . ." Milt began.

"The lever here is the crucial piece," Claude cut in, as didactic as a high school physics teacher. "It moves a section of the track ahead—guiding a train to either stay on the main track or shunt off to a siding. It should either be fully up or fully down. This is cocked halfway. Which means that the main and side tracks are not smoothly connected. It'd be like you were driving a car and there was a junction up ahead. You need to bear right or left but there is nothing but a big old gap."

Temple almost expected the detective to finish with, *Questions?*

Instead Milt added, "The train's wheels didn't know whether to take the main track or siding, so they cut the difference and derailed."

Studying the rudimentary mechanism and thinking that it might be responsible for so much death and injury, including to his own Etha, roused Temple's anger. "This is ripe for vandalism. Anybody could tamper with the switch!"

Milt shook his head. "Nothing can happen—either with the signage or with the switch—without accessing the lever. And the lever is secured with a padlocked chain."

Temple propped a boot on the rail and rocked back and forth. He scrutinized the landscape, down toward the station. "Then it must be missing from this signal because I'm not seeing anything."

"Agreed. Could have been snipped off by a miscreant, but you need a mighty strong pair of bolt cutters." Claude appeared to be enjoying his role as instructor and investigator.

"So let's say, for argument's sake, that we find the lock and a chain that hasn't been snipped."

Milt said, "That means the culprit used a—"

Claude's voice overrode the supervisor's: "Used a railroad key to open it."

Temple grunted. "So if someone purposefully unlocked the stand and cocked the switch, they'd either need a bolt cutter or key. Who has keys?"

"Every man on the track and train crew," Claude said.

Milt tugged on a small chain attached to the riveted button on his bib overall's strap. At the other end, a key popped out of his pocket. "Universal key. Opens all the locks on this stretch of track. Most of us keep them attached to our uniforms—if we lose them, it is instant dismissal."

"How many men have a key?" Temple asked.

"Track gang currently stands at six. Plus Herschel and the train crew." Milt removed his cap and shoved back an oily hank of hair.

"Could it have been misaligned by accident? A worker was changing the switch and got sloppy?" Temple asked.

Milt said, "Happens sometimes. But the bigger issue is that this switch stand shouldn't have been touched at all. I checked the schedule—no need for the train to be directed to a siding. Straight shot to the station and beyond."

Claude rose, brushing off the glowing tip of his cigar on the signal stand and dropping the soggy remnants in his pocket. "Sheriff, how about we head to your office? Draw up a list of who needs to be interviewed and divide it up between you, me, and that deputy of yours. I could use a cup of coffee too."

Etha woke abruptly. Across the aisle, a woman was sliding a meal tray onto a bedside table. She wore a tightly clamped net over sandy strands of hair. White uniform cuffs squeezed her thickset arms. The woman, a stranger to Etha, looked to be in her late twenties.

The aide tapped the sleeping granny's shoulder. The old woman, who had the collapsed lips of the toothless, pushed the hands away. But the young woman persisted, shoving an extra pillow under the patient's head and pulling her into a seated position. A spoonful of soup was ladled toward the sunken mouth, which abruptly clamped shut. Liquid ran down the old woman's chin.

Pity—that most Midwestern of traits—bubbled up in Etha's throat. But then her mind took a leap into unconsidered territory. She imagined herself as the toothless crone—ending her days as a nursling. She was not all that far from it now—lying feebly in a hospital bed and already nearing sixty.

The meal cart's squeaky wheels turned her way. The aide, whose name tag read *Thelma*, was at her bedside announcing, "Regular diet. Roast turkey with brown gravy, carrots, peas, and mashed potatoes."

Etha nodded her thanks and added, "I'll get to it in a bit."

Thelma frowned. "Doctor says you are to eat. Let's sit you up." The aide began reaching behind Etha for the pillow, as she'd done for the old woman.

"Stop it!" The command exploded unexpectedly from Etha's lips.

Both women stiffened in surprise. There was a pause.

Etha's brows rose in regret. *What is wrong with me?* "Sorry for snapping. I don't feel myself and . . ." She sensed some inner battle behind the other woman's tight face.

Finally, in a controlled voice, Thelma said, "Ma'am, I need to check off on your chart that you et two bites. If I don't, I'll get the reprimand."

A clipboard hung off the end of Etha's bed. Thelma held it up and pointed to a black box on the paper chart near the bottom. "I need this job. I don't want nobody saying I'm not doing what I'm supposed to."

Etha sighed. "All right. But I can feed myself. Go ahead and make your check mark."

Thelma folded her arms over her bosom.

Etha scooted herself upright and took up the fork and knife. "One," she said, swallowing. "Two."

Thelma drew a thick pencil from her pocket, marked the chart, gripped the cart handle, and pushed it to the far end of the ward. All the while her back remained rigid, her eyes darting from one side to the other.

Etha shoved the plate away. A small metal pitcher held hot water and alongside was a cup, saucer, and tea bag. The fabric screen around her bed was gone. To her left, a patient lay on her side, brown legs curled inward, her pale soles facing Etha.

It must be because of the train wreck, Etha thought. Having colored and white folks mingled in the same ward was unusual. Etha's experience with colored people was limited. Her general association was of privation. And as the Great Depression deepened and spread, she had come to see more clearly that privation was often the result of injustice or greed.

On the far side of the patient, a man occupied the visitor's chair. His folded hands hung between open knees. His broad brown face was grim.

The tea was only temporarily distracting Etha from

the pain. She needed something more to take the edge off. The earlier bustle of nurses had melted away. Maybe the man sitting in the visitor's chair would be willing to track down a nurse for her.

"Sir," Etha whispered.

The man's jaw contracted but he didn't respond. Etha decided her leg could wait. Fifteen minutes later, with still not a nurse in sight, the pounding pain in Etha's thigh was unbearable.

"Sorry to bother," Etha tentatively said, "but would you mind finding a nurse for me?"

The man glanced up, then pushed on his thighs and rose from the chair. He wore a three-piece suit with a watch chain and fancy stickpin in a striped tie. "I'll try, ma'am." His voice was polite but reserved.

The ward was long and narrow. At the far end were several small rooms, almost closets. One where patient meals were assembled. Another in which pills were counted out. Nurses clutching cloth-covered trays of hypodermics were, at last, issuing from the third. The afternoon light was chill. Feeble. It was spitting snow.

Against the beige linoleum, the man's shoes creaked. The nurse, who accompanied him back to Etha, took her pulse, checked the dressing on her leg, and administered a hypodermic.

"That's your wife in the next bed? Hurt in the crash?" Etha asked the man, who was standing nearby.

He nodded. "Cleo. And I'm Henry Bluett."

Etha introduced herself. "Is Cleo all right?"

"No. She is not all right. She hasn't opened her eyes or said a word since the accident. She's in a bad way."

Etha's throat constricted. The policeman who had

come to the door all those years ago had used those same words about her boy Jack. But "in a bad way" had only been easing the way for the officer to inform Etha and Temple in his next breath that, in fact, their son had accidently drowned while swimming in the river.

Her voice caught. "What does the doctor say?"

"Fractured skull. Burns. Luckily she wasn't scalded to death like all the other colored people on that train. Every single one—including a baby—all dead except Cleo."

"Oh my God," Etha pressed her palm to her mouth. "But your wife survived."

"No idea why. She was traveling in the same rickety wooden coach as the other colored folk. Up front, right behind the locomotive and mail car. Rammed directly into the steam from the smashed boiler."

Something tugged in the back of Etha's mind. Her thoughts lurched to the moment when the slippery floor of the train vestibule pitched and rolled beneath her feet. When she'd glimpsed a woman's face—her mouth open, her lips stretched tightly across her upper and lower teeth, her eyes glistening in terror—on the other side of the jammed door.

"Was your wife wearing a red beret?"

"She was coming back from the Women's Missionary Society's convention in St. Louis."

"I think I saw her right before the crash. She was trying to open the door into the vestibule. I pulled and she pushed, and it finally opened."

Peering over his shoulder at the still figure of his wife, Henry blotted his eyes with a handkerchief.

"I am so very sorry."

Henry nodded in silence.

After a moment, Etha asked, "Are you and Cleo from Cozine?" Cozine was a small all-Negro town one county over.

"I'm the postmaster. Cleo teaches Sunday school."

When she'd first heard of Cozine, Etha thought it might be a good idea. A town founded by colored people who governed their own affairs. Held leadership positions. It would be a way for them to garner respect from the outer world. She had no idea if this was so. In her fifteen years in Vermillion, the doings of Negro folks in a remote town had rarely crossed her mind.

"You take care," said Henry, returning to his wife's side.

Sometime later, urgent murmurs woke Etha. Opposite her bed, two nurses huddled. "Get Hinchie," one said. The toothless woman was grunting rhythmically, emitting small exhalations of pain. Hinchie soon bent over the small figure. The groans faded. Then stopped altogether. He pulled a sheet over the woman's face. Etha stared at the roughly tented form. The woman's feet were small. Two small bumps jutting from a rumpled landscape. For a time, no one attended to the woman. She was beyond help, left on her own in the busy ward. Then Thelma approached, pushing her food cart. Etha watched the aide step to the patient's bedside. She smoothed the sheets so they lay neatly along the planes of the body. After a long moment, Thelma moved off.

C HAPTER EIGHT

EARLIER THAT DAY, four blocks from the hospital, in the house beside the tracks, Ruthie-Jo thumped shut the hardware store's account book. She always did her bookwork first thing in the morning and stopped at noon.

Meals were simple in the Mitchem household. Ruthie-Jo didn't fuss over what was, when you got right down to it, an annoyance. Cooking and eating—both a waste of time, in her thinking. A necessary but unwelcome distraction from the real business of life—which was work and getting your due.

She hooked an apron, stained with gravy and grease, over her head, rolled up the sleeves of her housedress, and plopped a loaf on the cutting board. Daddy Warbucks pawed her legs, yipping and begging, knowing what was coming: a slice of bologna for Cy, a slice dropped on the floor for him. For Cy, she smeared mustard on the bread then slapped the meat between slices. She herself would have a couple of molasses cookies after Cy went back to the store.

During his lunch break, Cy would fill Ruthie-Jo in on the local doings. She herself never mingled. It had been four months since she'd stepped foot in town. That had been to attend the Jewel Movie House's inaugural Dish

Night. She'd endured the wait in line, the bodies pressed against her, for the china cup and saucer given free to all patrons. She hadn't stayed for the movie, of course. In the following weeks, as more cups and plates and even serving pieces found their way into the eager hands of the movie patrons, she wasn't among them. She'd told Cy the china pattern was not to her liking.

Daddy's abrupt yipping and vertical springs announced Cy's arrival. Her husband came in the back, as directed by Ruthie-Jo. *I don't want you tramping through the dining room and messing up my paperwork.*

"Cold one," Cy declared, stepping into the kitchen, his naturally pleasant face crimson from the biting winds.

"Any sales this morning?" she asked.

"Seems to be more folks in town helping out with the wreck and all. Sold a couple of sody-pops from the case. And Joe Shrubb bought a box of upholstery tacks."

"That all?" Ruthie-Jo slid the bologna sandwich in front of Cy's place at the table and thumped onto her seat. "I thought with the accident—"

Cy broke in: "It's a sorrowful thing. Musgrove called. Needing a load of pine boards for coffins. Those are sales I'd rather not have, I tell you true." Taking his chair, he surveyed the sandwich.

"Don't even ask," Ruthie-Jo snapped.

"What?"

"Umph." For years, Cy had been hinting, every now and then, that he'd like a hot lunch. She had better things to do and him asking only stiffened her stubborn streak. "I had no idea." Ruthie-Jo pressed her fingers to her mouth. "How many?"

"How many what?"

"Dead. I never dreamed."

"I heard thirteen. The hospital orderly who bought the pop said the number might rise. Couple of passengers in the hospital are hanging on by a thread."

Ruthie-Jo contemplated the yard beyond the kitchen window. *To think Daddy and I were safe in the cellar when only yards away people were dying.* She'd never given any thought to her own mortality. Her people were long-lived. Scots-Irish and tough as nails.

Cy pressed the last corner of crust across the plate, gathering the remaining crumbs. "Might not have been an accident. Some supposing it was done on purpose."

Ruthie-Jo frowned. "Who is saying that?"

"Couple of track hands."

Snorting, Ruthie-Jo rose from the table. "Nothing but rumors. Calamities attract them like flies. And those men can't be trusted. Roughnecks stinking of creosote."

Cy shrugged. "Might be something to it. Heard AT&SF sent one of its detectives to investigate. Find out if someone vandalized the switch."

Ruthie-Jo opened her mouth to rebut Cy but paused. The figure that flew by her last night right before the explosion. The man who tossed the lock and chain into the weeds. "All this pointing to anyone in particular?" she asked casually, picking up his plate and carrying it to the sink.

"Don't know." Cy bent to scratch between Daddy's ears.

After he left, Ruthie-Jo sat down with a cookie and cup of coffee. The AT&SF's roadmaster was due to stop by that afternoon. The man wasn't the brightest—minus some buttons, as they said—and couldn't handle keeping the payroll and inventory records straight. He paid Ruthie-Jo on the side to do it for him.

Maybe he'll have a suspicion about who'd sabotaged the train, she thought. That might be a worthwhile piece of information. She shoved her hand in the pocket of her housedress, fingering the railroad key she'd found in the lock.

Ruthie-Jo returned to the dining room where the bookwork was laid out, patting the stacks of paper organized in rows across the table. Everything connected to Mitchem's Hardware—unpaid customer invoices (with the majority being owed by the failing chicken hatchery), stock orders, daily ledgers—marched across the top row. This was the legit part of her work.

The second row was made up of three current under-the-table jobs. These consisted of the drugstore's account books, her multiple correspondences pressuring Jess Fuller, the owner of the hatchery, to sell her his business in lieu of his debt, and the roadmaster's books. None of these side projects were known to Cy, especially the deal she was pressing on the hatchery. Her husband was too naive to cut off any customer, deadbeat or not.

The dining room was the heart of her operation, but strands stretched into several other rooms. The sterile parlor was untouched, though the kitchen was crammed with niches that held potentially ripening fruit. Things she'd heard—mostly from Cy or over the telephone party line—and made note of were tucked in the tiny drawers of a wooden spice cabinet, along with dusty nutmeg seeds and crumbs of thyme. The drawers had the advantage of being alphabetized in stenciled letters. *C* for cinnamon . . . or a cheating husband. *S* for sage . . . or a spendthrift.

G for ginger . . . or a gambler. Under-the-table ledgers of years past were archived in the attic.

Before getting started on her afternoon bookwork, Ruthie-Jo mounted the stairs. In her bureau, under her hosiery and underpants, was a dented cookie tin where other secrets nested. She didn't actually need to go to the trouble of secrecy. Cy, who slept across the hall, never ventured into her domain. Ruthie-Jo was not always certain what use these secrets might have, but she had an instinct for putting her hands on something that might prove unsettling to someone. Something that he or she might want to buy back in some fashion. Such as the compass from the hardware store that the banker's son had lifted from the counter, according to Cy, and that had surprisingly found its way to the Mitchems' doorstep in the middle of the night. Likely, Ruthie-Jo reasoned, the miraculous appearance had been pressed on the son by his father, as a way to "make things right." Rather than handing the compass over to Cy, who would only put it back on the shelf without a word to sonny boy, she'd kept it. You never knew. There was more like that in the tin. The Methodist minister's hardware order, on the back of which, in his own handwriting, the telephone exchange of the local bootlegger was carelessly scribbled.

Into this hidden cache she dropped the key, which she'd wrapped in tissue paper. The rumors about possible vandalism made it potentially valuable. She'd go outside later for the lock and chain.

Back downstairs, she pulled out the AT&SF account book. On her typewriter, she began composing a report of the weekly labor expenses for the hundred-mile section of track the roadmaster supervised. This included the salary for Vermillion's section foreman as well as the members of the track crew. She noted the materials purchased. One hundred pounds of ballast. Fifty gallons of tar. Two crates of spikes. All this from the scrawled notes that the roadmaster, Tom Fetner, had provided. Ruthie-Jo looked more closely at one of the notes. There was a mistake in Fetner's arithmetic. The payroll didn't add up right. Was it sloppy addition or something else? Ruthie-Jo's antennae twitched. Fetner would be knocking at the back door in an hour. She wanted to have the paperwork ready. And now she had another question for him besides the speculations about the cause of the wreck.

C HAPTER NINE

SEVERAL LESSER WOODEN BUILDINGS had served as Jackson County's courthouse in its early years. By 1901, however, the white settlers had entrenched themselves firmly on land that had formerly been granted to the Cherokee, Cheyenne, Arapaho, and other tribes, and the current three-story brick building with sandstone steps and arched windows was erected.

Temple led Claude through its tall wooden doors and into the marble-walled foyer. The sheriff's and county clerks' offices were on the right, and a staircase, open to all the upper floors, on the left.

In the sheriff's office, Ed was at typing at his desk. After introductions, Temple said, "Grab yourself a seat, Claude."

Temple filled Ed in on the switch with the missing lock and chain. "Right now, that's the focus of the investigation, I'm thinking. Was the switch purposefully cocked by a railroad worker with a key? Or by vandals who clipped off the chain? That your take on things, Claude?"

"Yep. First thing is to interrogate both the track and train crews."

The young deputy scribbled in his pocket-sized notebook, designed for traveling salesmen, with a smartly dressed businessman on the cover. Ed believed it lent him an air of professional polish.

Temple said, "How about Ed and I talk to the local track crew? You take the trainmen. As far as I'm concerned, this is a joint venture."

Claude clicked his tongue approvingly. "You'd be surprised, or maybe not, how territorial some local lawmen are."

Ed passed a list to Temple. "I went ahead and got the names of the track gang from Milt."

Temple skimmed the names. "All live in town. We've had run-ins with two or three. Mostly drunk and disorderly." He passed the paper to Claude. "Anyone familiar?"

Claude rang a finger down the list. "Nope."

"Fair enough. So besides interviewing all these fellas, what else?" Temple asked.

"Need a statement from the stoker," Claude said. "He'll be able to confirm whether it was the switch that caused the derailment or something else we haven't yet uncovered. With the engineer and brakemen dead, he's our only witness from the front of the train."

The clip of high heels sounded outside the office door. Ed's wife Viviane entered with a tray of sandwiches from the Maid-Rite and a tin pot of coffee. "Sorry to interrupt, but thought you might need a bite." Viviane was the secretary in the county clerks' office one door down.

"You are a keeper," Temple declared, taking the tray from her hands.

She hesitated in the doorway, then asked softly, "How's Etha?"

A tight smile crossed Temple's face. "Fair to middling. She's got a nasty open cut on her leg. But Hinchie says it will heal. She'll have to take it easy, though. Hearing that riled her pretty good."

Ed chuckled.

Viviane's brow pleated in concern. "Why don't you join us for supper tonight?"

"Thanks, but I'll be at the hospital."

Viviane squeezed Temple's arm. "I'll bring over some pie later. Leave it upstairs for when you get home."

"Mighty kind, but—"

"Won't take no for an answer. And gentlemen, let me know if you need any phone calls made regarding the wreck." With that, Viviane clipped back down the hallway.

Temple passed the greasy bundles around and gestured to the coffeepot. "Help yourselves."

Claude pushed himself up from the chair and poured a cup. "Didn't have a chance to show you fellas before, but I think you'll find this mighty intriguing." He pulled the rusty spike from the baggy pocket of his topcoat.

Ed, with half a sandwich in his mouth, said, "That caused the wreck?"

"What? No! This is a rarity. Called a dog spike. Scarce as hen's teeth. Got it earlier today in Mooreland."

"Why?" Ed asked.

"I collect spikes. Fascinating stuff. By the by, there are about ten thousand spikes in each mile of track. Would you believe it?"

Ed pulled his head back with a vague smile. "Never gave it a lot of thought. You collect them?"

Temple was staring abstractly across the room. Now he turned. "Interview the stoker. What else?"

The railroad detective stuffed the spike back into his pocket. "I hopped off in Mooreland on my way here.

Talked to the station agent. He's the one that gave me the spike."

"And?"

"Said the train was traveling the correct speed. Jibes with the conductor's observation, so that can be ruled out as a cause."

"Okay."

Claude's gaze traced the ceiling. "Someone needs to inspect the area near the switch. Might be the lock and chain are nearby."

"We've got plenty on our plate, so let's get moving." Temple balled up the sandwich wrapping and tossed it into the waste can. "Ed, you give the ground near the signal and beyond a good going-over while there's still daylight. See if you can find that lock setup. Then you and I can start interviewing the track crew. Claude, let's go talk to the stoker."

Claude stood, absentmindedly stroking his belly. "Before we head to the hospital, Sheriff, mind if I line up some lodging first?"

"Sorry. Forgot all about that. I'll drive you over to Mayo's and get you set up."

Once crisply whitewashed, Mayo's Rooming House had fallen on hard times. Now its clapboards had absorbed the grit of the swirling dust storms and taken on the color of a turbid creek. The front porch offered a view of tangled prairie grass and discarded tires. Temple braked. The two men stepped out.

"Lean pickings for lodging. It's Mayo's or the Crystal Hotel. This place will save the railroad some coin on your upkeep."

Claude grinned. "I'm not particularly particular, if you know what I mean—being an old bachelor and all. Clean sheets, soft mattress. Enough said."

The ears of Myra Mayo had apparently taken in the crunch of tires on gravel. Or maybe the word *bachelor* caught her ear. The widow met them at the door with flushed cheeks. "Hello, Temple," she said perfunctorily before turning to Claude. "This must be the railroad detective. And I'm guessing you're in need of a room."

"Oh-ho!" Claude laughed. "The proprietress is a medium as well as businesswoman. Claude Steele." He made a little bow.

Myra grinned, exposing an irregular assortment of teeth.

The three moved into the hallway, making a racket with Claude's floppy galoshes, Temple's leather boots, and Myra's heavy pumps. There was a small alcove halfway down where Myra checked in roomers.

As Claude bent over the registry, Myra said, "Where do you hail from, Mr. Steele? I hope it's warmer than this. The winds out here are playing havoc with my chilblains. My doctor says—"

Temple cleared his throat. "Mr. Steele and I need to be back on the job right quick, so if he could leave his bag here?"

Myra jerked. "I'm just trying to make small talk."

"Don't get your back up," Temple said.

A door banged down the hall.

"Beatrice, did you finish upstairs?" Myra called out.

A woman of about forty carrying a stack of towels appeared in the doorway. "All done."

"This is my daughter," Myra said.

After introductions were exchanged, Myra continued, "I'm going to show Mr. Steele up to 208 before he has to be on his way. He and the sheriff have a busy schedule." The pair disappeared upstairs.

Temple turned to Beatrice. "We're investigating the wreck. Guess you figured that out. I believe some fellows from the track gang live here?"

"Jim Miller, Mack Otis, Toady Davis." Beatrice's expression was neutral. Her hair hung in wet wisps around her face—like that of a lathered horse run too hard.

Temple pulled out a pad, writing down the names. "When might we catch them, do you think?"

"Normally they come in to clean themselves up around dinnertime. They go to the Maid-Rite for a meal before heading to the Idle Hour. But I haven't seen any of them since the accident. Working overtime."

"We'll track them down. Longtime roomers?"

Beatrice pulled on her lower lip. She was not an unattractive woman, with her finger-permed hair and large brown eyes, though a receding chin took away from the effect. "Jim and Toady going on three years, I'd guess. Mack is new. A couple of weeks."

Temple made a note.

"Miss Beatrice, you sure do know how to keep a room spick-and-span," Claude said as he emerged from the staircase with Myra trailing behind.

Beatrice studied her hands.

Grabbing Claude's elbow, Myra said, "Now, when you get back I'll have that pick-me-up ready I was telling you about. Don't forget. I'll be waiting!"

Minutes later, the sheriff steered the county sedan into

the gravel lot of Vermillion General Hospital. Claude was rattling on about call boxes, switch signals, duty rosters, and other railroad minutiae.

Late afternoon and already the edges of the sky had a violet tinge. Inside, anxious kin occupied every chair in the waiting room. A number of men leaned against the walls. Temple and Claude pushed through the crowd to the reception desk. When the sheriff asked about the train's injured stoker, a beleaguered woman in a collared dress directed them to the men's ward on the second floor.

As they mounted the steps, Temple turned to Claude. "I'd appreciate it if you'd interview the man on your own. I'd like to look in on my wife."

"Sure! Don't give it a thought. This particular crewman and I go way back. He'll give me the lowdown. You go check on the little woman."

Up another flight of stairs, in the women's ward, the sharp smells of rubbing alcohol and disinfectant did battle. Patients dozed open-mouthed. Nurses scurried, water pitchers in hand. One shook out a thermometer with such vigor it seemed the mercury might shoot out the other end. Etha's bed was in the middle, on the right. She was sitting against a bank of pillows and talking to a visitor. As Temple drew closer he saw it was Carmine. *What is that kid doing here?*

"Look who found me," Etha sang out as her husband approached. "And he brought me a magazine!"

"See that," Temple replied.

Carmine smiled uncertainly at the sheriff. "I got permission from Commander Baker to stop by."

Temple didn't answer.

Carmine stood. "I'll be heading out then."

Etha frowned. "Already?"

"He knows you got to take it easy," Temple said.

After Carmine's boots receded out of the ward, Etha asked, "What was that all about?"

"What?"

"Why can't you be civil to the young man? You, not Carmine, made the mistake of arresting him last August. You should be going out of your way to be kind."

Temple snorted. "The first time I went out to the CCC camp to talk to him, he took off running. Why run if you're innocent?"

"He was!" Etha shouted into the ward's quiet murmur. A number of heads turned.

Temple stood, alarmed. He patted the air with his hands. "Don't get upset. You'll pull out your stitches."

"I don't have stitches," Etha muttered.

Flushed, Temple sat back down. "I know now he isn't a killer, but . . . I'm just not sure he's trustworthy. You have gotten attached to him and I don't want you to get hurt. In my work, I come in contact with a fair share of sweet talkers and con men."

Etha flopped back onto the pillows. "He's just a boy. And I am a grown woman. I know when someone can be trusted." She closed her eyes.

Temple deliberated on his hands. *Maybe so. But I need proof.*

Meanwhile, one floor down, Hinchie had fallen with a thud across the rumpled blankets of a cot in the hospital solarium. His legs and back pulsed. The night before he'd been dozing contentedly in front of the radio cabinet, the tubes behind its fabric grille radiating heat, when the telephone rang with news of the wreck. He hadn't had a wink of sleep in the twenty hours since. *Too old for this*. He'd muttered this phrase for decades. The weight of responsibility—caring for the sick and dying—dug into his shoulders like straps on a harness. And now, at age seventy-two, he *was* too old. Hinchie's gaze drifted across the ceiling, shortly followed by an old man's moist snores. Not ten minutes later a nurse cleared her throat beside the cot. Hinchie jerked upright.

"What?" he asked, startled and confused.

"A detective from the railroad is asking if the stoker can be interviewed."

"Is the fellow even conscious?"

The nurse nodded. Hinchie swung his legs to the floor, ruffling his hair. The sour smell of an unbathed pensioner rose up.

Outside the men's ward, Claude was knocking ashes off a cigar. Introductions were exchanged.

"Doc, I'm hoping to talk to Luther. Find out what was going on in the cab right before the derailment."

Hinchie jerked his neck to one side, attempting to loosen the kinks. "You realize he has third-degree burns on both legs, most of his torso, and his right arm? The fellow may very well not make it. And he's heavily sedated. I don't know how much you'll get out of him."

"Understood."

Hinchie led Claude through the ward and into a private room at the far end. A nurse was adjusting a pillow behind the patient's neck. The fellow's jaw was slack, his eyes unfocused. Heavy bandages covered three of his four limbs.

"Thanks, Annie," Hinchie said. "We won't be long." He gently touched the patient's shoulder. Heat rose from the skin. "Someone here to talk with you. Can you manage?"

The man's face remained tightly sealed. Far away.

The railroad detective approached the bed, leaning in close. "Hey, Luther. Remember me? We met when I was working that theft case on your line a couple of years back."

Luther's eyes opened.

"Can you hear me?"

Nothing.

"Can you tell me what you remember about the approach to Vermillion?"

An exercise in futility, Hinchie thought. *This Luther is too far gone*—his breath carried the distinctive smell of acetone. The doctor knew it well. The fruity odor which often heralded the breakdown of the body as death approached.

Claude repeated his question, to which Luther weakly pawed at blankets with his unbandaged arm. The detective bent close to the stoker's face. "Did the engineer call out?"

The man jerked his head, staring wildly into Claude's eyes. "Dick?" he said.

"Yes. In the cab. Dick Perkins, the engineer. Did he call out?"

Luther rushed to the surface of lucidity. "We derailed."

"Yes." Claude pushed his nose only inches from the stoker's. His voice was quiet. "Right before. What happened?"

"Dick . . . um . . . cried out."

"What did he say?"

Luther's eyelids sank.

Claude abruptly grabbed the man's good arm. "What did he say?" he demanded loudly.

But the stoker slipped under. Hinchie observed Claude's jaw lock in anger.

"You're going to have to leave this man be. He's on his way to the other side."

The railroad detective grimaced.

Hinchie slumped into the visitor's chair. It seemed as good a place to catch a nap as the solarium.

CHAPTER TEN

IN THE WASTELAND on either side of the tracks, shadows thickened among the desiccated bluestems and spiny burr grass. Hands on hips, Ed tilted his face to the fading afternoon sky, cricking his back and neck this way and that. For the past two hours, he'd been tramping from the switch stand westward down the rails—eyes alert for the dull gleam of a lock and chain. Breathing in oily creosote from the ties, stumbling over the ballast, and kicking up the powdery soil with nothing to show.

It was coming on dinnertime. When Ed had passed the train station, he'd seen Temple jawing with Herschel at the ticket counter. Ed knew the sheriff was not a layabout. He was undoubtedly questioning the agent about the crash.

Shoot, Ed thought. *All this searching around for a lock and chain could very well be a fool's errand.* It seemed like that railroad dick had been flinging out theories here and there with no basis in fact. Could be, Ed cogitated, that the lock had been stolen by vandals days before the derailment. That the missing equipment had nothing to do with the wreck. And, more likely, it was sloppiness on the part of the engineer that caused the derailment. Temple gave Claude too much credence.

Now Ed was eight hundred yards down the line, coming up on the clump of houses that clung to the tracks like the burrs on his socks. He and Viviane were saving to buy their own house and they'd already decided it had to be in town and not out in the county, like her parents' soddie. Not even on the edge of Vermillion, like these here. Right in town, they'd agreed, in one of those houses with a sidewalk and a grassy yard and a tree strong enough to hold a tire swing. That last requirement had only been added to their fantasy five weeks ago when Viviane discovered she was pregnant. It was their secret for now. She hadn't even told her ma. Privacy was important to Viviane. She'd grown up in a one-room house, sharing a bed with her younger brothers. "I want this to be hush-hush until after Christmas," she'd said to him.

Knowing a child was on the way was yet another reason for Ed to press ahead on his after-hours project. Most evenings, while Viviane washed the dinner dishes, Ed labored on writing what he was calling *A Manual for County Sheriffs and Deputies*. He had hopes it would be used by offices all over Oklahoma. Maybe even boost his chances of a law enforcement job with the state.

He'd never have dreamed, when he left his family's apartment in Chicago's notorious First Ward at age sixteen, that he'd accomplish so much. Like many young men in the Depression, he'd bummed around—riding boxcars and picking up odd jobs. Then he'd applied to and gotten accepted into the CCC. That's when things turned around. And now he had a profession, a wife, and a baby on the way.

He pondered the three houses ahead. Milt, the section foreman, his pale wife, and their kids occupied the farthest. The operator of Vermillion's service station, Lou Harriman, lived in the middle.

The first house in the row, with unpainted wooden siding, belonged to Cy and Ruthie-Jo Mitchem. Cy, with his ready grin and corny jokes, rated high in Ed's book. He was not the brightest fellow but a good egg.

Head down, Ed trod slowly toward the Mitchem place, sweeping his boot from side to side, pushing away the weedy clumps. Ed was thinking he'd halt the search at the foreman's house, when he spotted a metallic glimmer near Cy's back fence.

"I'll be jiggered," he mumbled.

A steel lock and chain were curled, snakelike, among a clump of weeds. Yanking his handkerchief from his trouser pocket, Ed squatted to gather the evidence. This was very likely the missing setup from the switch stand. The deputy examined the greasy apparatus. No signs of tampering. No nicks from a bolt cutter or a fumbled attempt to open the chain link with pliers. *AT&SF* was engraved on the lock. No key, though. When he plucked the setup from the ground, he noticed that the bent weeds underneath sprung back. Likely the rig had been dropped there only a few days back—at most.

If this was from the switch stand, then the chances that this was a deliberate act increased, Ed reckoned. Someone had used a key to remove the chain and lock, pushed down the stand's lever, and partially opened, or cocked, the switch. If the setup had been legitimately removed by someone on the track crew, it wouldn't have been tossed more than a mile from the stand.

Ed would need to send his find to the state lab. As with many rural sheriff and police departments, Jackson County did not have the equipment or personnel to analyze fingerprints, handwriting, bloodstains, or tread marks. These advanced methods were only available at state forensic labs and, of course, the Federal Bureau of Investigation. Temple had filled Ed in on a tour he'd taken of the state crime laboratory in Oklahoma City two years before.

"You would not believe the number of microscopes and test tubes," Temple had said. "And there was this helixometer."

Temple had gotten the chance to peer into that last item—a specially constructed telescope inserted into the barrel of a pistol. Trained detectives could analyze the markings and tell if the gun had been recently fired. A puffed-up bureaucrat gave the tour, Temple had said, all the while bragging, "We're one of best-equipped crime labs in the country."

As he juggled the lock and chain in his handkerchief, Ed decided that he'd try to finagle one of those tours for himself in the future.

"Before the derailment, did you notice anything out of the ordinary?" Temple asked, leaning across the ticket counter at the station; the muscles of his lower back screamed with fatigue.

Herschel thought on this, absently folding a shipping invoice into a tight square. Then unfolding it. Then folding it again.

Temple peered into the agent's office beyond the counter. Bills of laden, train schedules, and memoranda with the official AF&SF seal were neatly tucked into wall racks. Herschel's stiff-brimmed uniform cap hung on a hook. An Underwood and the telegraph setup, now largely supplanted by the telephone, occupied a chipped desk. Everything had its place. Temple envied Herschel his small bead-board kingdom. So much of a sheriff's work was done on the fly—when a theft was called in, a smashup at an intersection reported, a domestic dispute boiled over. There was nothing close to the regularity of a train schedule. Temple thought he might favor more routine at this time of his life.

It had taken Herschel so long to contemplate the question that the sheriff jerked when the agent finally answered. "Can't say I did. You were standing right where you are now when it happened. We were jawing. The freight train was running late, so . . ."

"Wait. Another train was due in *before* the passenger?"

The invoice was in its third iteration as a square.

"Got a call from regional twelve minutes before the freight's scheduled arrival."

Temple frowned. "Was this freight also heading west?"

"Yep. The passenger was given the go-ahead. That's why it rolled into Vermillion a tad early."

Temple scribbled in his notebook. "Who else knew about the change in schedule?"

"Train crew. The update order would have been passed from the Mooreland station master to someone in the cab. We use a fishing-rod type setup so the engineer can grab a message without stopping or even slowing down."

"Would a change like that make an accident more likely?"

"Not at all. If it weren't for the derailment, the passenger train would have pulled in early, unloaded, took on passengers, and then waited to move out at its appointed time."

"Okay, so then—"

The waiting room door banged open and a farm couple swayed in, gripping cardboard suitcases. The woman slumped onto a bench.

Settling his cap on his head, Herschel said, "Could you give me a minute to get Mr. Dunn squared away?"

Temple retreated to a bench to review his notes as the farmer, Sunday trousers sagging over his boot tops, approached the ticket window.

Crossing his legs and balancing a notebook on one thigh, Temple reflected on his jottings. The maze of operations, the organization of the railroad workers, the intricacies of the equipment was, he was beginning to understand, a world unto itself. Temple had never worked for an operation larger than the Jackson County Sheriff's Office, which consisted of himself and Ed.

The stale air in the waiting room was chill. Temple was opening the door to the coal stove when Ed strutted in, a big old grin papered across his mug.

"Looking peppy."

"You betcha. Got something."

The sheriff shook the grate free of ash and tossed in a shovelful of coal, then resettled himself on the bench. "Shoot."

"I've spent the last hours hunting down that lock and chain. Tell you, if I never see another clump of spiny burr grass, I'll die a happy man." He picked a couple of stickers off his socks. "Viviane's going to have a fit when she sees my hose and trouser cuffs."

Ed drew the handkerchief from his pocket, cupping the bundle in one hand and pulling the corners open, revealing the chain and padlock.

Temple's eyes lit up. "Hey!"

"Way past the station. Right near the Mitchems' backyard."

The sheriff reared back. "Quite a ways from the stand. No key?"

"Nope. And the chain wasn't cut or fiddled with. See?"

Temple stared above the coal stove, his eyes unfocused. "That could mean that whoever removed it had a key. But why not cock the switch and then replace the lock and chain setup then and there?"

Ed shrugged. "Maybe the fellow ran out of time."

Temple's eyes lit up. "Hershel just told me the train was coming in early."

"So he did the deed and ran away, throwing it after he was clear of the station."

Temple tapped on Ed's notebook. "When Milt was showing me that switch stand yesterday, he said all the railroad men have universal keys that would open locks on switches, signals—anything needing to be secured."

"Like this padlock?"

"Yep."

Ed drooped. "So everyone on the track, station, and train crews has a key. That's a lot of suspects."

"And an acquaintance or family member of these folks might also have access. That makes it even more complicated."

"Shoot." Ed twisted his mouth to the side. "Could also be some stranger pilfering one."

"Milt said the crew generally clips the keys to their overalls. Lose a key and you're immediately fired."

The air grew chill again. Temple rattled the clinkers and shoveled another load through the stove's door.

"So that probably means there are extra backup keys. Viv has one hidden under a flower pot on the back step just in case we lock ourselves out."

"Good point. And maybe the person to ask about that is right over there."

Simultaneously both men turned toward Herschel who, finishing up with the farmer, sensed four eyes on him.

"What?"

Two chords of a train horn sounded up the tracks.

"Another question for you." Temple stood, shaking his legs to resettle the trouser cuffs over his boots.

The station agent shrugged on his uniform coat. "Gonna have to wait. That there's the 5:03 freight. I've got incoming goods to inventory, mail to load." He jogged from behind the counter and out onto the platform.

Temple pressed his tongue against his molars and made a clicking sound. "Guess we know who's in charge here and it sure ain't us. It's the company."

After his unsuccessful interrogation with the stoker, Claude had tracked down the conductor who was bunking temporarily in the train's sidetracked caboose while waiting for reassignment. The detective questioned the man and walked away with the same story he'd been hearing all along. From St. Louis to Vermillion, smooth sailing. No mechanical issues until it jumped the tracks pulling into the Vermillion depot and then all hell broke loose.

Milt was shouting into the phone when Claude strolled into the foreman's office—a cramped space enclosed by flimsy partitions and wedged into the corner of the toolhouse. "I mean pronto! Can't get the track cleared without it."

Claude settled into a stiff-backed chair and lit a cigar as Milt slammed down the receiver. "I don't see how the company expects me to take care of this without a wrecking derrick." The foreman stared glumly at the telephone.

Claude said, "I'm sure the road is doing the best it can. They want these tracks cleared as much as you do."

Milt bit his upper lip as if fighting the urge to rebut the detective. That didn't trouble Claude one iota. He wasn't ashamed of being a company man. For standing up for who buttered his bread. And a finer railroad organization he'd never encountered, and he studied all of them. Had subscriptions to *Railroad Association Magazine* and the *Railroad Trademen's Journal* since he was nineteen. Kept all the back issues neatly catalogued on a bookcase devoted solely to railroading manuals, periodicals, and pamphlets.

It could be that Milt sensed all this since he kept his mouth buttoned.

Claude continued: "I won't take up much of your time, but I'm trying to get to the bottom of what caused the derailment. Talking possible manslaughter charges if it was deliberate."

Milt sighed. "What do you need from me?"

"Particulars about the signal and switch setup before and after the wreck. My understanding is that the train was coming in a little early due to the change in schedule by the freight. According to the conductor, the passenger train was slowing to the posted speed in anticipation of stopping at the station. Sound right so far?"

From the other side of the partition, the shed's wide doors banged open. Two men slowly pushed a handcar inside the toolhouse.

"Give me a minute," Milt said, rising from his desk and squeezing his bulky frame past Claude.

"Take your time."

Milt approached a colored trackman who was sitting on the edge of the handcar pulling off thick leather gloves. Claude listened to the exchange.

"Any progress on getting that bent rail out?" Milt asked.

"Can't go much further until the derrick shows," the man responded. "The ballast is a mess. We can start on that."

"Okay," Milt said. "I'm almost done here and then I'll call regional again."

Back in his office, Milt said, "Sorry for the interruption. My crew is mostly reliable but I got to stay on top of them. That fella Daniel I was talking with is my most dependable track hand."

Claude nodded. "Price of doing business. So, specifics on the switch stand?" His pen hovered above the notepad.

"It was used two days before the wreck to switch a train to the siding. No problem."

"Checked after that?"

Milt plucked a file from a pile on his desk. Opening it and running his finger down a set of numbers, he said, "After that train was switched, I checked the stand myself. The day of the wreck, Daniel did a routine check at 3:44 p.m. Everything was in order."

A plume of cigar smoke eddied upward from Claude's lips. "And after the derailment?"

"You saw for yourself. Chain, lock, and key gone and the switch only partially set."

"Any thoughts on who might have done it?"

Milt slapped the file back on top of the pile. "Seems to be a purposeful tampering occurring shortly before the train pulled in."

"I wouldn't argue." Claude flicked the ruined mass of wet tobacco into the waste can and wiped his lips on his sleeve. "In that case, what first comes to my mind are bums. The whole range—tramps, derelicts, teenage hooligans riding the rails. The company's cases of vandalism have gone up tenfold. Bad times, idle hands. Work sheds tore up for kindling, kegs of spikes overturned just for the fun of making a loud noise, signal lights stoned. And, of course, the thieving. My God, you would not believe the thefts I've investigated."

"Don't doubt it. I hate to hurry you along, but . . ." Milt drummed his fingers impatiently.

"What I'm saying is there are a lot of bad elements out there looking to cause trouble for the AT&SF. Have you noticed any no-gooders sticking around? Rock-throwers? Loiterers?"

Milt shook his head. "Can't say I have. My hands and me, we keep an eye out for that kind of thing."

"What about thefts? Did you see or hear reports of looting after the wreck?"

"I think that might have been a problem if the CCC boys hadn't come out to lend a hand. A big crowd of spectators had accumulated but the corps kept them away from the cars."

Claude paused. "You know I got to ask this. Any chance one of your men did this on purpose? Bad apple?"

Milt shook his head. "Got a good crew on board now."

"But in the past?"

"Sure—there are always one or two a year. If I get wind of lollygagging, I fire them."

"When was the most recent?"

Milt glanced at his desk calendar. "Couple of weeks ago."

"Any blowback from him? Resentment?"

Milt shook his head. "Nope. I heard he left town right after. Off to California."

"Tough to fire a man in these times."

"That's so. Nowadays, most that don't work out . . . and even those that do . . . end up hopping a freight west."

"And this particular fella's in California?"

"So I was told."

Claude cogitated on the ceiling. "So right now my gut is telling me this is probably a case of vandalism by an outsider who intended to wreck a train. Don't know why as yet. Could be simple as mindless maliciousness against God-fearing, hardworking folks."

Milt stood. "If you don't have any more questions, we're losing daylight."

Claude stood too, shaking out crumbs, shreds of tobacco, and other leavings. He extended his hand. "Thanks for your time. Could you point me to a local hangout where the riffraff loiter? I want to see if I can't sniff out someone willing to rat on who might have done this."

"The Idle Hour in town. But you might have better luck at the Oke Doke, a roadhouse two miles down

Route 15. Near the tracks. Besides the locals, it tends to attract drifters."

Claude passed out of the toolhouse. It was getting on dinnertime. He wondered if that Crystal Hotel Temple had mentioned had a restaurant. A good beef steak would do the trick.

As it set, the sun cast an orange glow across the sheets in the ward and the nurses' uniforms, which flickered like flames as the women moved between the beds. Etha crammed a pillow behind her neck so she could study her surroundings. A kitchen maid named Alice, who had a sweet smile and a name badge pinned crookedly to her collar, brought Etha a sugar cookie and hot tea.

The screen beside Cleo's was pushed back. Henry was gone. Cleo was on her side, facing Etha. Her eyes glittered in the dusky light.

"You awake?" Etha said.

"Believe so." Cleo's voice was hoarse, her face ashen.

"Your husband was here not long ago."

Cleo's lips drew slowly upward. "He'll be back. Probably having a cigar. You on the train?"

Etha nodded. "I'm just lying here thinking about all the things that need doing back home."

"Nothing like home." Cleo's every word seemed to be an effort.

Their conversation was interrupted by a rumble of words from the bed on the other side of Cleo. It had been vacated earlier in the afternoon. Now an orderly was transferring a woman of middle age from a gurney.

The patient was venting her dissatisfaction in a righteous tone. At first Etha couldn't make out the words, but as the woman gained steam she gained volume as well.

"I refuse to be tended to in the same ward as a colored woman. As if the indignity of being parked on a stretcher, waiting for a bed, wasn't enough. My left wrist has a hairline fracture, I'm told." She held her lightly bandaged limb aloft: Exhibit A in a criminal investigation. "And now that I have finally reached the Promised Land, I find myself sharing it with a Negress."

Etha felt a dark flush creep up her neck. Cleo's face did not register the insult. Perhaps the thick padding of morphine cushioned her senses.

Living in Illinois and later Ohio, Etha had absorbed the generally accepted notion among many white citizens that the North was more receptive to Negroes. That the harsh Jim Crow laws of the Deep South were not practiced above the Ohio River. Oklahoma, where she had lived for fifteen years, seemed neither Southern nor Northern, nor even Midwestern. Oklahoma, from Etha's perspective, was mostly a sparsely populated expanse sprinkled with small towns and farms and plains that somehow produced a mutually agreed upon separation among the races. The Indian tribes clustered on their allotments. There had been a number of all-colored towns, like Cozine, established by Negro boosters. And then there were the white folks everywhere else.

The patient's words, her tone, set Etha's gut wriggling uncomfortably.

At the far end of the ward, Thelma was adjusting a tray table. She paused to stare in the direction of the tirade. Even from a distance, Etha caught the shift in Thelma's bearing. The aide strode to the bed of the outraged woman, paused for a fraction of a second, and

then pushed her face inches from the other's florid coun-
tenance. Etha was close enough to hear Thelma's whisper.
"Shush up."

The woman's eyelids widened, her mouth opened, but
whatever words were there dried up and blew away.

Thelma continued, "That colored woman is fighting
for her life. She's not bothering nobody. Stop carrying
on."

At first the patient did not move. Then she brought
her lips together and glanced around the ward as if trying
to assess whether the exchange had been overheard. Etha
wasn't sure if the woman was seeking a show of support for her position, or was hoping the altercation had
gone unnoticed. Finally, the woman collapsed against the
pillows—perhaps too fatigued right then to pursue the
aide's impertinence.

As Thelma tramped rigidly back to her task at the
end of the ward, a prick of admiration pierced Etha's
consciousness. Etha respected women who were straight
shooters. She herself was not always able to say what was
truly on her mind. More often than she'd like to admit,
the strong desire to remain polite at all costs bound her
tongue.

Around her, the low moans, the squeak of bedsprings,
the splash of water from a cloth wrung out over a basin—
all the usual sounds of the ward—continued. The angry
patient's words and Thelma's response had barely stirred
the hushed surface of the room's communal pond.

Cleo's knees were drawn to her chest. To Etha's gaze,
Cleo seemed to be sleeping even though her eyes were
open. Her brown irises distant. Removed.

C HAPTER ELEVEN

CLOAKED BY SHIFTING HUMMOCKS of clouds, the moon shone dimly. Ruthie-Jo, with Daddy Warbucks in tow, clomped across the frosted grass of the backyard. The silence was as thick as wool. Ruthie-Jo had purposely delayed their nightly ablutions. It was later than the night before, the night the train had derailed.

Daddy snuffled at the wash pole, peed, and continued his itinerary that looped past the cracked base of the concrete birdbath, continued on to the pile of rotting lumber no one wanted to buy, and ended at a tuft of weeds whose significance was a mystery to all but him.

The events of the previous evening unfurled in Ruthie-Jo's mind. She heard again the godawful explosion of iron and steam slamming up the rails and the screams of the injured. The shouts of rescuers rang in her ears. But before all that, she'd seen the shadowy figure running past—so close that she had inhaled the metallic stink of his sweat. Heard the jangle of lock and chain. She'd kept the key, but had tossed the rest. Now she understood their value.

Thinking on this, her lips stretched into a slight smile. Her eyes narrowed. *I have a pretty good idea who you are and what you did.* Five hours earlier, shortly before dinner, the roadmaster had stopped by, just as Ruthie-Jo was finishing up his accounts. Fetner's breath was whiskey sharp. It had not been difficult to wrangle out of him that indeed there were rumors of vandalism causing the derailment. And when Ruthie-Jo pointed out the error, mistaken or purposeful, in his payroll figures, his explanation, slurred and meandering, had been like a fleck of gold in an old-timey miner's sieve. It had not been an error after all. She'd carefully plucked out the shiny stuff, tucking it away in her spongelike mind.

"Come on," she called to Daddy now, tugging on the wire gate leading to the tracks and stepping through. She'd forgotten her gloves. The cold wire bit into her fingers. The terrier, intent on malodorous markers, ignored her.

As Ruthie-Jo turned to scold, warm air tickled the back of her neck, between her hat and coat collar. Puzzled, she lifted her arm to brush it away. In an instant, a heavy body pressed against her back. Ruthie-Jo's hat toppled sideways. Something encircled her throat and was pulled tight. Heart racing, her legs like water, Ruthie-Jo dug her fingers between the ligature and her neck. Her heels scrabbled frantically. She thrashed. The noose tightened. Suddenly every sinew, every vessel in her body burned for air. She fought back with everything she had. Tremendous pressure rocketed through the top of her skull, exploded down the barrel of her throat, and ignited her lungs. For a moment, she thought a train was approaching, but realized the roar was coming from her throat as she heaved and gasped for air. Eyes rolling frantically, she clawed backward at the attacker's face and hair. But quickly her vision tunneled, her brain swam, and she buckled—knees, torso, head—into the weeds. Now there was nothing but blackness. She did not feel the continuing pull, the knee in her back. Did not feel the weight of her body dragged across the tracks and into the brush. Eventually even the blackness dissolved. She lay alone. Her eyes half-open. Unfocused. Emptied of secrets.

CHAPTER TWELVE

HENRY BLUETT WOKE WITH A JOLT in the middle of the night. Had Cleo cried out? No. Her chest rose and fell steadily beneath the flannel hospital bedding. Still he felt anxious. *Bad case of the jimjams,* he thought, pushing against the arms of the visitor's chair and standing stiffly. Disinfectant mingled with sweat in the stuffy ward.

The moment he'd gotten word about the derailment, about Cleo's condition, he'd had a fire in his gut. He'd tamped it down so as not to convey to her, even in her unconscious state, his rage. But now it bubbled up and he had to lay eyes on the wreckage. See for himself, when no trackmen would likely be crawling around. This was his chance. Downstairs, he slipped out a side door, buttoned his topcoat, and strode toward the tracks.

Smudged shadows of the toppled coaches undulated as clouds scudded across the dim moon. His watch read 1:22. Alone among the debris, warily picking his way toward the train, glass and metal shards cracked beneath his soles. The locomotive remained where it had fallen. He passed it and the ruins of the mail car. Next was the colored car.

The front of the coach was tipped up against the loco-motive, tilted toward the sky. Henry paused, thinking on the pressurized clouds of steam bursting from the boiler, rolling in a wave toward Cleo and the other colored passengers. He pressed his palm against what was left of the coach's wooden siding. The windows were too high and it was too dark to see inside. But Henry could imagine the carnage that had unfolded there. In the past thirty-odd years there had been a number of protests by Negroes about the unsanitary conditions and dubious safety of the colored cars. Petitions were distributed across the South and West, including to Oklahoma's Corporation Commission charged with oversight of the state's public services. The petition, which Henry himself had signed, railed against "the pine hearses" in which Negroes were forced to ride. The phrase stuck: *pine hearses*.

Fresh rage pushed into his gut. His Cleo could easily have perished here, along with the others—all paying full price yet relegated to filthy, rickety coaches. He slammed his fists into the slats, which broke into kindling beneath his knuckles. *Bam. Bam. Bam.* Blood trickled from his clenched hands. It was five minutes before his arms fell to his sides. He needed to see the rest of it. Panting, his fists throbbing, Henry marched to the next coach in line. Despite the enormous dents in its steel frame, despite the derailment of its front wheels, despite the windows blown out by the explosion, it remained whole. The coach carrying the white passengers was a testament to the protective armor of steel plating. Where seconds ago Henry had been enraged, now despair rolled in. His knees shook. He crouched, sobbing.

Slowly he stood, swabbing his face with a handkerchief. He should get back to the hospital. *What if Cleo is awake and I'm not there?* The fast-moving clouds were gone, the sky clear. Bare cottonwoods clattered in the wind as he moved down the tracks. Dim lights from the hospital, about a half mile away, glimmered unevenly. Ahead a couple of darkened houses hunkered in the cold.

He narrowed his eyes. One, no two, murky figures emerged near the closest house. The forms moved jerkily, twisting and merging. Likely tramps tussling over a bottle. Henry moved on quickly. The last thing he desired was an encounter with two liquored-up hobos. He left the tracks and turned toward Center Street.

In the shaded light marking the hospital's rear entrance he examined his knuckles. The cuts were sticky. Already starting to scab over. But Henry knew they could reopen at any moment. Some wounds never healed.

CHAPTER THIRTEEN

THE RAZOR SKITTERED ACROSS Temple's jaw, his concentration broken by pounding on the apartment door. There was a bright nick of blood on his chin. *Damnit.* He swabbed the remaining skim of shaving cream off with a towel. It was just coming on seven in the morning, two days after the smashup. He planned to visit Etha in the hospital and then get to the office at 8:15 sharp, as usual.

Cy Mitchem stood in the hallway, kneading his hat brim with quivering fingers. Like Temple, he was only partially dressed. Cy's overcoat was unbuttoned, revealing trousers, suspenders, and a tight sleeveless undershirt that cupped his flabby breasts.

"What?" Temple asked.

"Ruthie-Jo's missing." Cy's words emerged in a desperate bark. "I don't know where she is. I can't think where she'd be. It's not like her to just up and . . ." He whimpered to a stop.

Groaning, Temple ushered Cy inside and pulled out a chair at the kitchen table. Cy plopped down with a thump. Striking a match, Temple lit the gas range and slid the coffeepot on top.

"Argument between you two?"

Cy shook his head. His moans liquefied into thick tears. Temple fetched a clean hankie from the bedroom.

"Speak up."

Squeezing his eyes shut, Cy's blubbering trickled away. "Alarm went off at six o'clock. Brushed my teeth, started getting into my duds. Then I heard barking. Daddy Warbucks was running back and forth in the street, yipping his head off. Ruthie-Jo never lets him loose outside our yard. I thought maybe the front gate had blown open and he'd taken advantage. I knocked on her door. She usually doesn't get up until after I leave. She didn't answer so I poked my head in . . ." Cy broke down again.

Temple said softly, "Wasn't there?"

"No. And her bed was all made up. I figured she'd gotten up early for some reason. But downstairs was empty too. Daddy was still barking. When I stepped outside he ran off. I walked around back but no Ruthie-Jo. I called her name. Nothing."

From the cupboard, Temple removed two cups, poured coffee from the pot, and handed one to Cy.

"So you came here?"

"Straightaway. My God, where could she be? You know she hardly steps more than a yard or two from the house."

Temple took a gulp, swishing the coffee from one side of his mouth to the other, swallowed. "When did you see her last?"

Cy sipped tentatively at the cup in front of him. "Last night. She made rabbit stew. After washing up we listened to the radio. I went to bed around ten. Ruthie-Jo is a night owl. Stays up until maybe midnight. Takes Daddy out one last time."

Temple absently tapped a finger on the table. "Did you hear her come to bed?"

"No. But most of the time I don't. Once my head hits the pillow I'm a goner."

"So anytime between when you went to bed at ten and when you got up this morning, she might have left the house?"

Cy nodded.

"Let me get dressed and then you, Ed, and I'll head over to your place. Find out what's what."

Cy glumly examined his hands.

Ten minutes later the three men pulled up at the Mitchem house. The front gate sagged. A skim of frost glazed the front steps.

They stepped inside. "Ruthie-Jo?" Cy shouted. Silence. "Daddy?" he added hopefully.

"Cy, I want you to get on the phone and call . . . No, never mind." Normally Temple would question the missing person's friends, but he realized Ruthie-Jo didn't have any. "How about family? Where are her people from?"

Cy waved him off. "Ruthie-Jo has kin in Tennessee, but they haven't communicated with her in years. Not even a Christmas card. For a while there, we'd get something from a cousin out that way, but the woman must have given up."

Temple nodded. "I'm going need another cup of coffee. How about making us some while Ed and I give the house a good going-over?"

Cy got busy measuring out grounds.

"Where did Ruthie-Jo keep her suitcase?" Temple asked.

"Do you think she's taken off? That can't be!"

Temple sighed. "I don't think so but we need to check."

Cy mumbled, "My closet."

Temple turned to Ed. "Check there and the entire second floor. I'll go over the cellar and the backyard."

In the basement, Mason jars, many clouded with mold, lined three rows of shelving. Otherwise the space was empty. The rear yard was scrapped and dusty. Poking around behind a stack of rotting lumber, Temple felt the squish of a dog turd beneath his boot. He backed up, wiping the sole on the ground and cursing. The back door bumped open.

"Nothing upstairs," Ed said.

"Suitcase?"

"In Cy's closet."

"This doesn't look good. Watch your step. Daddy has done his business all over the place." Temple rested his hands on his hips, eyeing the tracks beyond the fence. "If she was any other woman, I'd say we need to be thinking about her running off with another man. Or just running. But with Ruthie-Jo . . ." He shook his head. "You know how she is."

"Viviane calls her The Recluse. So now what?"

Temple stuffed his hands under his armpits. Even with his gloves on, his fingers were icing up.

"You got an attic?" Temple called as Cy cautiously negotiated the back steps with two mugs in hand.

The cups were handed off. "She wouldn't go up there for love or money," Cy said. "Especially now. Freezing cold up there this time of year."

"Just the same, we need to check it out. Give it a look-see, Ed, then we'll scour the track area beyond the yard."

"Opening is in the ceiling of her closet. There's a ladder against the wall," Cy said.

"Got it." Ed took a gulp of coffee and trotted inside.

While Ed headed to the attic, Temple and Cy sat on the back steps.

"I just can't think where she'd be at," Cy said

Temple sampled the coffee, weaker than punch at a church social. "Always been a homebody?"

"Mostly. When we first got acquainted, she was quiet. I met her at the train station in St. Louis. I was heading home from a sales trip—this was before Father died. We got to talking. She waitressed down the street from the station. Made it a habit, she said, to watch the trains on her day off. Once she got to talking, it was clear she was as smart as a whip. After that, I ran into her at the station a couple of times on my sales trips. Then my father passed away. I took Ruthie-Jo to a nice meal. Told her I was running the store. Felt it was time to settle down and asked would she marry me."

Temple raised his brows. "Closed the deal fast. Good marriage?"

Cy seemed to take mild offense. "We get along fine. More than fine! I run the store, she does the books and inventory. She's not much of a cook, but no one can touch my Ruthie-Jo when it comes to brains."

"And after you married, you two moved in here?"

"Yep."

Temple gazed absently through the window, across the yard, at the frost dripping from stiff weeds in the weak midmorning sun. His stomach rumbled. If she'd been home, Etha would have made sure he and Cy had

something in their stomachs before they bolted out the
door. He checked his watch. She would be propped up
against the pillows about now, the sun from the ward's
tall windows warming her face. Temple itched to wrap
this up and get to the hospital but tamped down that
impulse. It was a lawman's obligation to put duty first.

"Did Ruthie-Jo ever mix in with folks here in town?"

Cy shook his head. "You know how she was. After
we moved in she hardly ever stepped out. Every once in
a while, of course. To the dentist to have a tooth pulled.
That kind of thing. But she's been a homebody since I
married her."

Temple grunted noncommittally and drained the
mug. "I'm going to check around the tracks. Maybe she
was out with the dog and twisted her ankle."

"Think so? But why didn't she answer when I hollered?" The merchant's brown eyes muddied up.

"Let's not worry until we have to. Send Ed out back
when he's done in the attic."

The wire gate leading to the tracks was open. Temple
waded into the brush skirting the rails. About a mile to
his left was the train station. He turned right and ambled along the rocky skirt of ballast. The aroma of creosote was warm and resinous. Temple had fished the Little
Conemaugh off a railroad bridge in Johnstown, Pennsylvania, as kid. The scent was bound up in that memory.

The sheriff bellowed, "Ruthie-Jo? You here?" He didn't
expect an answer. He agreed with Cy: if she was nearby
and conscious, she'd have made that known earlier.

He stepped across the tracks and trod up the far side,
back toward the station. The scrub was dense among the
gnarled cottonwoods. He almost passed Ruthie-Jo by, but

the treads of her rubber boots glinting in the sun drew his eye. *Lordy.* He waded through the stalks. Burrs clung to her thick stockings. Temple knelt. Between cracked lips, her swollen tongue protruded. The bloodshot eyes registered outrage. *How could this have happened?* she seemed to demand. Putting his ear to her mouth, Temple listened. Nothing. The same wadded silence emanated from her heart when he pulled her coat open and laid his ear on her chest.

A two-inch band of mottled flesh encircled her throat. A ligature of some sort had probably been used. A cluster of shallow abrasions fanned across her collarbone. Temple knew from experience these were likely made by Ruthie-Jo's fingernails as she fought for air.

He sat back on his heels. "I'm sorry," he whispered.

He thought of Cy. The man would be shattered. After a bit, he headed to the tracks behind the house and shouted for Ed. Within moments, the deputy trotted through the back door with Cy following.

"Cy, could you hold up for a minute? I need to talk to Ed," Temple called.

"Is this about my Ruthie-Jo? Did you find something?"

"Let me be certain before we go trampling all around."

Cy appeared unconvinced, but stayed put. A couple of dry snowflakes drifted down and were quickly lost in the brush. Ed jogged over to Temple, who stood with one boot planted on a rail.

"We gotta keep him back." Temple pulled on his jaw. His voice was low.

"Ruthie-Jo?"

"Dead."

Ed pushed his hat back. "Christ."

Behind the two men, Cy called out, "Everything all right?"

Temple continued softly, "I'm pretty sure she was strangled. Is the camera in the car?"

Ed nodded.

"Try to get Cy to go inside with—"

But Cy was already upon them. Neither Temple nor Ed thought he had the gumption to ignore Temple's request. But apparently he did when it came to Ruthie-Jo.

"What's going on? I have a right—"

Temple pushed his palm into Cy's chest. "Stop."

Cy spotted the soles of his wife's boots at the edge of the brush. He tried to wrestle past Temple, who gripped his arm hard.

"You don't want to remember her like this."

Cy drew back, his face drained of color. "What? No! This is a mistake. She's as healthy as an ox."

Temple dipped his head. "She's gone. I'm sorry."

"I don't understand. She never had so much as a headache."

Exhaling heavily, Temple said, "There is no good way to say this. Someone took her life."

Cy stiffened. His mouth moved but no words came out.

Temple patted him on the back. "Ed and I will find out what happened."

"Who would want to hurt Ruthie-Jo?" Cy began blubbering. "Oh God. It can't be true."

Temple said, "I'm going to ask you to go inside and wait in the house. Is there anyone to come sit with you?"

Cy shook his head.

"How about Reverend Jacobs? You're Methodist, right? Ed will make the call for you."

Watching Cy, shaking with sobs, make his way back to the empty house, Temple thought he'd rarely seen a man so shattered. He turned to Ed. "I need you to telephone Jacobs and the undertaker. There is no way Hinchie can break away from the hospital right now. I'll have to serve as acting medical examiner. Ask Musgrove to send a couple of those farmhands he's got on the payroll to drive her body to the hospital morgue after we're finished. Hinchie can do the autopsy when he catches a break from the train wreck. Then get back here with the camera."

After Ed dashed off, Temple crouched down beside Ruthie-Jo. He could not shake the belief that her unblinking gaze was one of outrage. "I'll do my best by you," he murmured.

Etha had awakened before dawn. Dozed. Then woke again, at regular forty-minute intervals. It was now 7:35 a.m. and her thigh pulsed. She slipped her hand under the sheet. The wound was tender. Around her other patients stirred. Some called out for a bedpan. Others for water. Three nurses and several Red Cross ladies wove sluggishly among the beds, the starch seemingly kicked out of them. The train pileup was straining everyone.

The screen had returned to Cleo's bedside.

"Cleo?" Etha called in a low tone. "You there?" No answer.

A nurse, the one with freckles spattered like cinnamon on tapioca pudding, arrived and slipped a thermometer under Etha's tongue. As she noted the temperature in a chart hung at the end of the bed, Etha asked, "Normal?"

"Close."

"How's my neighbor doing?" Etha nodded toward Cleo's bed.

The nurse shook her head. "Slipping under, is what Hinchie says." She moved on. Etha noticed the young woman skipped Cleo's bed, as if the hourly charting was no longer of consequence. Tears glazed Etha's eyes. *Where's Henry?* When a Red Cross lady whisked past, Etha asked her to collapse the screen between her bed and Cleo's. Cleo's back was to her.

When Thelma appeared with the meal cart, more than thirty minutes past the usual breakfast hour, Etha was too distraught to eat.

"Just coffee, please," she said, noticing that Thelma's face was haggard. One cuff on her sturdy forearm was askew. Strands of frizzled hair fell heavily across her face. "You're looking peaked."

"What?" Ignoring Etha's request, Thelma wrestled the tray table into place and roughly arranged the plates.

Etha let it go. Maybe Thelma wasn't cut out for her job, though these days folks took whatever work they could find . . . even if they weren't suited. The cart moved down the aisle.

After a bit, Etha recognized the murmur of Henry Bluett's low voice. She pushed herself up to a sitting position. Sliding her injured leg over the edge of the mattress was another test. It took five minutes to beat back the pain and get her feet on the floor, but she managed and shuffled forward.

Henry was clutching Cleo's hand. Etha hobbled closer. "How is she?"

Henry rose. "Here." He pulled a chair around. Etha lowered herself gingerly. "Same."

"Are you by yourself?"

"Our grown children are coming later, after they get off work. A bunch of Cleo's lady friends in Cozine keep asking to visit but I want this time alone with her."

Etha pressed her palm against her lips and studied Cleo's face.

Henry sat down and continued, "We've been together since I stepped into her elevator at the T.J. Elliott department store. Prettiest thing I'd ever laid eyes on. Sitting on her stool, pushing the buttons." With a hankie, he dabbed at the saliva that had collected at the corner of Cleo's mouth. "She's not at her best right now but she has always been a fine-looking woman. You saw her."

"Oh my yes. Well, that hat!"

Henry smiled thinly. "You ladies and your hats." Then something shifted in his gaze. Frowning, he clenched the brim of the fedora in his lap.

Etha's throat thickened. "What does the doctor say?"

He shook his head and his voice rose in harsh tones. "Nothing. Nothing to do. Just dosing to keep the pain down."

"You didn't have a chance to talk with her?"

Henry's voice softened. "Oh, I've been talking but she hasn't talked back. Sleeping like a baby. But I tell her she's my honey bee. That's what I always call her. My honey bee."

"She was awake last evening. We talked. I told her you'd been here, holding her hand." Etha wanted to offer more words of comfort but her tongue stiffened. There was nothing to say. The usual phrases offered at such times seemed flimsy and false.

Etha pushed herself up. Her thigh throbbed. Collapsing into bed, she immediately fell asleep. Twenty minutes later she was awakened by Hinchie and the young nurse.

"Here to change that dressing, young lady," he said. His voice was chipper but the flesh around his eyes was purple with fatigue.

"How are you holding up?"

He shrugged. "Getting too old for these hours." The doctor pulled the bedclothes aside and tugged the adhesive at the edges of the bloody gauze. Etha scrutinized the gash, a nasty stew of glistening red flesh.

"Well?" she asked after Hinchie did his own examination.

"Holding its own. Not infected and we need to keep it that way." The nurse handed him a bottle of clear liquid that he poured over the wound. Woozy, Etha flopped back on the pillow.

"Yes, ma'am, I'm feeling my age," he murmured as he laid fresh gauze on the site. "Both wards are full up, of course, and we've got patients stowed in the solarium and hallways. Even in the staff dining room."

"Really?" Etha said, abruptly alert. "That many?"

The nurse broke in. "I can tell you, Mrs. Jennings, that every single member of the staff is about to drop. The hospital in Grove City is sending over doctors and nurses but they won't get here until day after tomorrow. We shipped the less serious patients over there right after the wreck and they are still busy with those folks."

The meal cart, now empty, squeaked past.

Etha grabbed Hinchie's arm as he pressed the tape into place. "When was the last time you slept?"

He laughed. "In my bed? The night before the accident, whenever that was. I'm losing track of time. But now it's time for you to rest up. No fretting."

Hinchie and the nurse moved on. Etha contemplated the landscape as a flurry of snow batted against the windows, then thickened. *I shouldn't be here. Not really. Others need this bed more than I do. I've got to get out.* Temple would have a fit, but she'd talk him down. She couldn't lie in a soft hospital bed while others slept on the floor.

"Knock-knock." Carmine stood at her footboard. "Care for a visitor?"

Relief washed over her. "Boy am I happy to see you. Slide that screen over so we can have some privacy. I need your help."

Carmine smelled of sweat and cigarettes and his thick ruff of dark waves needed a trim. Teetering on manhood, Etha thought. Which made her think of her son Jack, who had died a schoolboy and so remained that age forever. Like the kid in a class photograph who moved away after third grade. Jack, she fancied, might have looked something like Carmine at age eighteen.

"What's cooking?"

Etha clasped her hands to her chest. "A favor."

"Anything! You know that."

"You've got to get me out of here."

The young man examined her face. "What? Did you clear this with the doc? You're not looking too pert."

Etha straightened her spine against the pillows, ignoring the pain, and smiled gamely. "You've just caught me before I've had my coffee."

Carmine crooked his lips to one side. "Not convinced."

"Look, this is my idea and mine alone. But Hinchie would be fine with it." Etha leaned forward, which was a mistake. She grimaced and pulled back. "There are plenty of people here who are desperately wounded. Who need the care much more than I do."

Carmine quietly asked, "What does Mr. Jennings think about this?"

"Haven't told him yet."

Carmine backed away with his palms up. "Whoa, Nelly! You nuts? I can't get snarled up in this. If I—"

Thelma broke into the conversation, clumping over without so much as a "pardon me," water pitcher in hand. Bedraggled as she had been at breakfast with hair unreined and socks full of burrs, she was no tidier now. She filled Etha's glass and trudged away.

"Well?" Etha said.

Carmine shook his head. "You got to convince me."

"One, as I said, this bed is needed by others. Two, I will heal much faster in my own home. Everyone knows home is the best place for convalescing. Three, Christmas is almost here and my niece and her family are coming soon. And four, because I'm asking you."

Temple was only sort of warming up to Carmine and what she was asking of him now wasn't going to improve the relationship. He sighed deeply. "But if the sheriff comes at me with a shotgun, you best speak up fast."

Etha threw up her hands. "Of course! So?"

"So, I think I'm making a big mistake."

They found her soot-covered dress, coat, and boots crammed in a box under the bed.

"Turn your back," Etha instructed as she slowly stepped out of the work shirt serving as a hospital gown and into her own clothes. She shoved her underwear, stockings, bra, and girdle into her pocketbook. All that twisting and hooking would make her ribs holler. The bandage on her leg had been changed not that long ago, thank God. *How much gauze is in the medicine cabinet at home?* Carmine might have to run over to Bell's Drugs.

As she pulled on her overcoat and hat, Etha directed him to scout out the ward for Hinchie or Temple.

"All clear," he said, and extended the crook of his arm. She tugged her hat down low and flipped the coat collar up.

"That don't look suspicious," Carmine said, his voice thick with sarcasm.

Etha gimped down the aisle with Carmine at her side. As they passed Cleo's bed, she noticed Henry was tucking the blanket around his wife's shoulders. Etha wanted to stop and offer words of comfort, but this escape was taking every ounce of strength she could muster. If she paused, even for a minute, she might collapse.

In the hallway outside the ward, a young woman with her leg in a cast dozed in a wheelchair. Another patient with sorrowful eyes and greasy hair watched the pair from a narrow stretcher.

"I hope one of them gets my bed," Etha whispered.

A wheelchair with a saggy seat was stationed in one corner. Carmine maneuvered it behind Etha's knees. She dropped into it gracelessly. When the elevator doors opened on the first floor, Etha gasped. Gurneys lined both sides of the hallway, jammed head to toe, each holding a patient. Nurses, orderlies, and family members jostled in the narrow cattle chute between.

"I had no idea. This is awful," Etha said.

Carmine cautiously pushed the chair through the traffic. "Should we let someone know you're leaving?"

Etha waved him forward frantically. "Just get me out of here. I'll call from home."

They emerged into a chill wind.

"Like driving the Indy 500 back there," Carmine said.

Etha, aching all over, slumped in the wheelchair.

"You okay?" Carmine asked.

She slowly raised her head, took in the snow-dusted lawn, the vista of blue sky, the clanking flagpole chain, and smiled.

They congratulated themselves on the jail break. But then, Etha noticed the steps leading down to the sidewalk. The courthouse was a mile away. And there were three flights of stairs from the lobby to the apartment.

"How are we going to manage this? What a fool I am!"

Pulling on his lower lip, Carmine considered the situation. "I'm going to make a call. You wait here."

"And just exactly where would I be—" she began, but Carmine was already trotting back through the hospital doors.

Three minutes later he was back. "All set."

"Taxi?"

"I ain't saying."

The exhilaration of escape drained away. Etha ached all over and wanted only to collapse into her own bed, however she got there. From the far end of the street, a puff of dust grew into a large cloud from which emerged a CCC truck. It careened to the curb and two sturdy young men leaped from under the flatbed's canvas roof.

"To the rescue," Carmine said as he and the others picked up Etha, chair and all.

"Well, I never," she laughed as she was borne down the steps and hoisted into the truck. The driver made a tight U-turn, raising another load of grit, and gunned it down Center Street toward the courthouse.

In the back of the truck, one of the young men, a cigarette dangling from the corner of his mouth, patted Etha's knee. "We'll have you home in two shakes, Mrs. J. When Carmine called camp we were standing in the chow line, bored as—" he paused, adjusted his language, "as all get out."

"So you missed lunch?" Etha frowned, remembering that many of the CCC boys arrived at camp scrawny and hungry.

"The cook said he'd hold something back for us." The kid flicked the butt onto the street.

As the wheelchair rocked, Etha's injured leg protested. When the truck screeched to a halt in front of the courthouse she felt like one of those molded desserts—quaking and shivering as the hostess cut into it.

"Slow it up," Carmine told his buddies as they lifted her down. "She's on the mend."

One grabbed the footrest, another the push handles. Carmine and a third fellow grasped the armrests.

"On three," Carmine said.

They wrangled her inside the courthouse. The laceration on her thigh screamed bloody murder as they mounted the stairs to her apartment. Etha, tipped slightly back by her bearers, glued her eyes to the ceiling with clenched teeth. There was a book, a biography, she had read about Queen Elizabeth. A plate depicted the queen carried on a litter past a crowd of villagers. The skinny legs of the queen's bearers were encased in tights and garters, as she recalled. When she thought of the CCC boys lugging her up to the third floor in tights rather than ill-fitting uniform trousers, she laughed out loud. Thank goodness there were no peasants to witness this humiliation—only a farmer passing through to the county clerks' office to plead for more time on his tax bill. With head bent low in disgrace, the man failed to notice Etha's mortification.

By the time they rounded the landing on the second floor, sweat slicked the boys' faces. Carmine urged them on. Feeling light-headed, Etha wondered if she might pass out. But when the door to the apartment came into view, she recovered. The rescuers hustled her inside, then down the hall to the bedroom, and then—*thank you, Jesus*— lifted her onto the bed. Etha thought she'd never experienced anything as soft and warm as that simple cotton mattress. The bedclothes were fragrant with Temple's scent—a mix of sage and pencil lead.

Carmine covered her with a blanket. "I'm going to get you a cool washcloth and glass of water and then tell Viviane you're here."

"Thank you."

"Boys, meet me at the truck. I'll be out in five."

Alone in her bed, Etha investigated her bandages. They were soaked through. She withdrew her fingers, stained with bloody fluids. Hinchie had warned her that the risk of infection was high. *Maybe I should have stayed put.*

C HAPTER FOURTEEN

EARLIER THAT DAY, after Cy had first spotted him out-side in the street, Daddy Warbucks had zigzagged in confusion up and down Vermillion's sidewalks and alley-ways, crossed the makeshift baseball field, and nosed be-hind a jalopy jerking into a parking space at the Crystal Hotel—until finally coming to rest in a vacant doorway, panting heavily.

The routine of his day had been smashed to bits the night before when a stranger attacked the Female. Un-able to stop the assault, Daddy had run, circled, and run again. Now, thirsty, breathless, and lost, he shivered in the sharp scent of urine that was not his own—or hers.

After some time, a warm draft eddied into his cubby-hole. Daddy peered down the street. A door was propped open, emitting warmth and food smells. He approached cautiously and, when no strangers appeared, hurried inside. The ground was soft beneath his sore paws. He discovered some scattered pieces of popcorn. After this meager meal, an exhausted Daddy curled up against a wall and slept.

Meanwhile, Chester Benton, the owner of the Jewel Movie House, was struggling to replace a torn belt on the theater's projector. As he swore at the obstinate machinery, Chester realized he'd forgotten to close the lobby doors after the wholesale merchant dropped off the concession stand candies and cigarettes. He thought of the precious heat spilling out into the cold air. He counted off the steps from the projection room to the top of the steps, placed two fingers on the wall, and made his way to the first floor. Chester had been blind since the age of eight, after a bout of brain fever. He operated the projector, took tickets, easily maneuvered his apartment on the second floor of the theater, was a third-degree Mason, and, in all, moved through life as well as any sighted man—and more smartly attired than most. But it was not all roses, as they said in the movies. Lottie, Chester's longtime girlfriend, had broken off their relationship and moved to St. Louis several months before. He missed her. In retrospect, he acknowledged that he had not treated her as attentively as a man should his lover. But he'd never misled her into expecting marriage. That was all her fantasy and, well, he told himself, you can't dictate somebody else's dreams.

Downstairs, he closed the lobby doors. Rounding the corner of the concession counter, his toe pressed into something soft and squirmy. Chester yelped, thinking it a large rat. Daddy yelped, anticipating a heavy boot to the ribs.

When no blow fell, Daddy slowed the pace of his vocalizations. And when Daddy's yelp turned into a bark, Chester felt a modicum of relief. *Not a rat!* But a dog wasn't much better. Dogs equaled chaos, in his mind. Above all things, Chester valued order and tidiness— which enabled him to smoothly navigate the sighted world. He folded dollar bills the long way and fives the short. His socks were all the same color to eliminate mismatches. Once planted, the furnishings of his office and living areas were never moved. His apartment was stiff and staid—as was the man himself.

Certainly a dog had no place in Chester's orderly surroundings. Animals, he had been taught at the Oklahoma School for the Blind, were moving, darting obstacles that would trip up the unsighted at a moment's notice. Chester's first thought was to herd the animal outside. Grabbing a broom, he tentatively extended it toward the closed end of the L-shaped candy counter where, he assumed, the dog had retreated. In his mind, Chester envisioned the broom steering the dog toward the outside door. In reality, a growling Daddy lunged at the brush end, grabbed it in his teeth, and administered a healthy shake.

"Ack!" Chester dropped the handle and stumbled backward. How big was this dog? Larger than Chester had imagined. The growling and barking stopped. The theater owner considered the situation. Maybe some tidbits, scattered as in a fairy tale, out the lobby doors? The idea of dropping food across the carpeting was distasteful, but seemed necessary.

Chester retrieved a handful of diced ham from his icebox and dropped a piece of meat on the floor at the open end of the counter. A minute later a moist chorus of teeth, lips, and tongue sang out.

All right, then. Chester repeated the process. After five more steps, the dog was approaching the entrance. Chester cautiously pushed against the door with his backside, stepped through, and dropped the last piece of ham. As the dog's furry flanks brushed past Chester's shins, he stepped back inside, firmly closing the door and leaning against it in relief.

Daddy, however, was not so easily hoodwinked. Or gotten rid of. The scent of ham lingered on the other side of the door, daring him to breech the walls. This was best accomplished, he'd learned over the years, by yelping and relentlessly scratching his sharp little nails on the doorframe.

On the other side of the entry, Chester cringed. The high-pitched yapping pinged off his eardrums like hail. Worse yet, the scratching pierced his heart as he conjured up deep ruts marring the Jewel's walnut doors. Hands pressed against his ears, Chester moved toward the stairs to replace the projector's belt and set up the reels for that evening's screening. But he stopped abruptly, knowing himself too well—how the commotion at the lobby door would stretch his nerves to an unendurable tightness. Even if the soundproof projection booth blocked it all, he would know it was happening.

He turned and opened the door. The movie owner felt the animal brush against his cuffs.

"Don't get too cocky," Chester said. "We'll settle this later."

When Maxine, the thirteen-year-old ticket taker, appeared for her six thirty p.m. shift, Chester intended to coax her into sheltering the dog at her house until the owner was found. But for the time being, peace had been restored and Chester wearily climbed back to the projection room to do battle with the belt.

C HAPTER FIFTEEN

WHILE ED HUSTLED OFF to settle Cy and call the undertaker, Temple knelt to examine the body. Ruthie-Jo's lids were half-closed over the hazy eyes of the dead.

Temple stood, blowing his nose, stamping to get the blood flowing in his legs. The sputter of snow thickened in the pewter skies. *Where's Ed with the camera?* Temple's watch read 11:43 a.m.

He made a couple of notes on his pad about the state of the body, then resumed his examination. Everything below her neck appeared to be in order. Underneath her coat was a flannel nightgown, thick stockings, and rubber boots. No gloves. Sort of surprising given the cold. She'd probably not intended to be outdoors for long. Only a few moments for the dog to do its business. The left hand lay open on the frozen ground. Temple used his magnifying glass to observe the nails. A couple were broken—probably in the struggle.

The right arm was flung to one side. Beside it lay a flashlight. Temple couldn't figure why she'd brought that. Surely the dog could find its own way around the yard.

The Mitchems' back gate creaked and Ed approached with the camera bouncing against his chest.

"Cy settled?" Temple asked, rising from his haunches.

"The reverend is visiting at the far end of the county, but his missus is on her way to sit with Cy. Any clues?"

Temple filled him in on what he'd found—which wasn't much. "Snap your photos and then we can flip her over. Undertaker's boys on their way?"

"Within the hour." Ed pulled the camera from its case, removed the lens cap, and blew delicately across the glass. The deputy slowly circled the body, depressing the shutter release as it sounded its two-syllable *flit-to, flit-to, flit-to*. Temple pondered the weedy ground beyond Ruthie-Jo's feet. A trail of broken bluestems and cockleburs led to the tracks. Parallel grooves marked the bare earth. *Lugged here from where she was strangled. Put money on it.* He strolled to the wire gate. Temple imagined Ruthie-Jo and Daddy on their nightly errand. Daddy inhaling the scents of the night. Ruthie-Jo stepping through the gate, idly glancing up the tracks. Someone coming up from behind. A wide circle of trampled grass and dirt lay outside the gate. *That doesn't mean much. Regular use would do that.* If the killer was waiting nearby, where would he hide?

"Got what I need, Sheriff!" Ed called out.

"Be there in a sec."

A chicken coop belonging to the family next door squatted at the rear of that yard. Temple hiked to the rickety henhouse, where a couple of chickens, feathers fluffed, pecked aimlessly. Would a killer squatting on the far side of the coop at night be visible? He and Ed would need to interview the neighbors. See if they'd noticed anything suspicious.

He trotted back to the deputy, who was scribbling a few notes in his journal.

The lawmen crouched at Ruthie-Jo's feet. Temple lifted her right leg. The heels and back of the boots, as well as her calves, bore fresh dirt marks.

"She was dragged," Temple said.

"Why move her?"

Temple shrugged. "To buy time in case Cy came out looking for her right away?"

Above, a northern harrier soared, his orange breast illuminated against the milky-gray sky as he scouted for prey. The clouds continued to spit snow.

"Let's turn her. I want to see the back of the neck," Temple said.

As they rolled the body, Temple spotted something under the right arm. "Hold up." It was a hairnet. "Get a snap of this and then I'll bag it and the flashlight."

The bulb fleetingly illuminated the dreary scene. Temple bagged the evidence, then pulled the victim's hair to one side. The ligature marks he'd observed on the front continued all the way around. Here, though, the furrow was thick in the middle then thinned slightly at the sides.

"I've seen this once before," Temple said. "A strangling case from my first year on the job. The wider track is made as the killer pulls simultaneously on both ends to cut off the air supply. The two ends overlap." He checked his watch. "Maybe you should give Musgrove a—" he began, when the Mitchems' back door opened and the reverend's wife, Sarah, called out that the mortuary boys had arrived.

"Send them back," Temple instructed.

When the bodies started piling up after the derailment, Vermillion's mortician had hired two farmhands to hammer together pine coffins. Green around the gills

FUNERAL TRAIN 133

above their Sunday shirts and ties, these two came loping toward Temple and Ed. One carried a stretcher, the other a rough wool blanket.

"Watch where you're stepping, fellows," Temple said, leading them up to the body. Upon spying Ruthie-Jo, the one with the blanket broke out in a sweat, stumbled away, and puked in the weeds. The other, whose name was Pete, asked, "Mrs. Mitchem?"

"That's not for public consumption," Temple replied. "Musgrove must have cautioned you that this is all confidential for now. Put the stretcher right alongside her."

"Just asking," Pete muttered.

The stretcher in place, Ed said, "Go get the blanket from your pal. He's not done heaving. I'll help you with this."

Ed lifted Ruthie-Jo's upper half, Pete her legs, and on the count of three they swung her onto the litter. Temple shook out the blanket, gently laid it over the dead woman, and tucked her in. The three removed their hats and stood solemnly beside the body for a moment. A frosty gust rattled the dried bluestems.

"Amen," said Temple. "Now corral your buddy. Hearse out front?"

The farmhands grabbed the ends of the stretcher and shuffled around the side of the house. Temple and Ed followed. Mrs. Jacobs must have spotted them—she and Cy stepped out the front door. The widower's plump face had deflated in the last hour. The stretcher bearers shoved Ruthie-Jo's body inside without much grace. The Packard pulled away.

"That's it, then," Cy said. "I can't believe it. I'll never see her again."

"Come on inside and I'll make us a couple of sand-wiches," Mrs. Jacobs said. She turned to Temple and Ed with a bit of desperation in her eyes. "Want to join us?" Even a minister's wife struggled to make small talk with a grieving spouse.

"Thanks, but we want to get right on this," Temple said. "Couple of things left to check out back."

Beside the tracks, skims of snow were already filling in the depression where Ruthie-Jo's body had lain.

"I'm thinking that Ruthie-Jo's death is linked to the derailment."

"Because I found the lock and chain here?" Ed said.

Temple nodded. "I'm thinking maybe—and this is only a guess at this point—but maybe she saw something the night of the wreck. Saw someone tossing the setup right by her house. And maybe that someone spotted her. The next night the fellow comes back to make sure she doesn't talk. Let's both think on that. Right now I need to swing by the hospital. Meet you at the office in ten?"

"Sure thing," Ed said.

As Temple motored to the hospital he mentally or-ganized the murder investigation. First thing was to in-terview Ruthie-Jo's neighbors to find out if they heard or saw anything unusual the night before. Also to get Hinchie on the autopsy as soon as possible.

Inside the hospital, the heavy smell of stewed cab-bage greeted Temple. He passed down the center aisle of the Women's Ward, past nurses spooning soup into the mouths of unsteady patients. Past healthy-looking inva-lids shoveling roast beef into their chops. Past a colored man gripping the stiff hand of a woman in the bed next to Etha's. A kitchen maid with a sullen expression and wrinkled uniform shoved a meal trolley past him.

A phalanx of screens had been set up around Etha's bed. Temple said, "Anyone there?" When there was no answer, he peeped inside. The bed had been stripped. Stained sheets were puddled on the floor. *Oh my God.* Images of Ruthie-Jo's cold body rose in his mind. *Oh no. Not my Etha.*

Temple rushed to the first nurse he spotted. "Where's my wife?" he demanded.

The middle-aged woman, nursing cap askew, asked, "Who?"

Temple pointed to the bed. "Etha Jennings."

The woman peered around him. "I'm not sure. She's not my patient."

"I don't care whose patient she is. She's my wife. She's badly injured."

The nurse said, "Please keep your voice down. Her nurse, Miss Janey, is right over—"

But Temple was already striding toward Miss Janey, who was shaking out a thermometer at a patient's bedside. When she had inserted it under the patient's tongue, Temple, struggling to keep his voice level, said, "I'm looking for my wife. She'd not in her bed." He pointed again to the empty spot.

"I was told she checked herself out."

"What?"

"One of the orderlies told me awhile ago."

"But her injuries are serious."

Irritation swept across the nurse's face. "You'll need to talk to—"

Temple was already halfway down the ward. Back

on the first floor, the receptionist at the front desk knew nothing about it. She had no idea that the patient had left or where she had gone. *I know where she is,* thought Temple. *And I can take a guess who helped her get there.*

He jumped into the sedan, floored it to the courthouse. Steam gathered in his chest and pushed against his ribs.

After the CCC boys had gotten Etha into bed, Carmine had stopped by the county clerks' office. He filled Viviane in on Etha's condition, and she promised to go straight upstairs.

Etha was dozing when Viviane appeared at her bedside with a basin of warm water, washcloth, towel, and a tablet of Etha's geranium soap.

Waking, Etha said, "I forgot where I was for a second."

Viviane slid the basin onto the nightstand. "I'm raiding your bathroom cupboard. Be right back." She returned with rolls of gauze, adhesive tape, and a jar of antiseptic unguent pressed to her chest.

Pale and pinched, Etha's face told Viviane all she needed to know about the older woman's discomfort.

"I didn't think this through," Etha said. "And I'm sorry you got commandeered for nursing duty. My niece will be here in a couple of days. Until then, I'm sure Minnie Hinchie can swing by."

Viviane sat on the edge of the bed, pulled back the blanket, and unbuttoned Etha's dress. She raised her brows at the missing undergarments but made no comment. Soaping up the washcloth, she gently swabbed the patient.

"So why *did* you leave the hospital?" Viviane asked.

Etha knew she'd be asked this many times. The worst inquisitor would be Temple. He would not understand that there were those, much more seriously wounded than she, who were waiting for beds. "You would not believe the masses of sick and injured at the hospital. It is how I imagine it was in those field hospitals at the Somme."

The washcloth massaged her underarms. Her breasts. Etha turned her head, embarrassed by her naked flesh. But the sponge bath was soothing and her shame melted away.

Viviane pursed her lips. "*You* are one of the sick and injured, for goodness sake!" Although young enough to be Etha's daughter, Viviane was one of those women who didn't hesitate to speak her mind—which she continued to do after removing Etha's sodden bandages. "What on earth? This is nasty."

Etha peered down at her thigh. "A lot of that mess is from Hinchie poking around, plucking out bits of this and that."

With several pads of gauze, Viviane cleaned away the bloody fluids, dabbed on the unguent, and then dressed the leg.

"I'm going to make you a cup of tea and then I need to get back downstairs."

"Thank you, dear."

When Etha opened her eyes, Temple was standing above her, his face a cloud of worry and anger. His big hands, limp at his sides, shook.

"What exactly were you thinking?" he asked. "Do you have any idea of how worried I've been? At the hospital, your bed was empty. You know what my first thought was?"

Feeling she was in the right, Etha raised her head. "I do not."

"I thought you were dead. That's what I thought."

"Don't be silly," she said stiffly. "I'm not going to die. And of course that's not what I intended. I felt that others needed the—"

Temple waved her off. "Yeah, yeah. I heard this from you before. Others worse off. Others bunking on the floor of the solarium and needing your bed."

Etha sniffed. "That's the truth."

He slumped on the edge of the bed, dropped his head in his hands. "When I saw that empty bed, I was scared to death."

Seeing him broken took the starch right out of Etha. She tugged on his sleeve and when he leaned in to kiss her forehead, his face was wet.

Temple sighed, sat up slowly. "So, let me guess how you got yourself from the third floor of the hospital to the third floor of the courthouse."

"I talked him into it. He was as much against it as you are."

"But?"

She shrugged. "I was persuasive. He got some other CCC boys to help. It worked out just fine. And Viviane got me settled. She promised to check on me every hour or so during the workday. I'm sure Minnie will visit too. And in three days I'll—"

Temple put up a flat palm. "Whoa there. In three days your niece and the rest get in. Is that what this is all about? Leaving the hospital against medical advice so you can string popcorn and fill the boys' stockings?"

"Certainly not!" Etha snapped. Then, after a moment

of contemplation, she said, "Could be. I hadn't thought about it, but now that you mention it, making a Christmas for Vadie and the kids was probably in the back of my mind."

"Probably?" Temple stood. "I'm calling her right now. Telling her to stay at home. You have a serious injury and are in no way able to have company."

"You can't do that! She has been counting on this visit for months. You know how rough it's been with Everett out of work. And besides, I need the nursing help. You can't deny that. I promise, promise, promise," Etha said, raising her right hand, "to stay in bed. To vigilantly check the wound three times a day and to call Hinchie if it starts to look bad."

Eventually Temple said, "Let's see how this little arrangement holds up in the next twenty-four hours. If you're not improving, I'm taking you back to the hospital and calling Vadie."

Etha patted the bed. "Sit back down."

The bedsprings creaked. "I can't stay long. There's been a death in town."

"Oh no! Who?"

"Ruthie-Jo Mitchem. Cy roused me first thing this morning. We found her body near their house in a clump of weeds. Homicide."

Etha paled. "Who would do such a thing?"

"No idea."

"How is Cy taking it?"

"He's a wreck. As I would be."

Etha dropped her head. "I'm sorry for scaring you. I wasn't thinking about how the empty bed would look."

"I'm going to be firm on this. Twenty-four hours.

This old heart can't take another jolt." Temple patted his chest.

"I understand. Can you help me to the bathroom before you leave?"

After Temple departed, Etha's eyes focused on the cluster of rooftops beyond the window. The bare trees. The steeple of First Baptist. When they'd lost their boy Jack, there had been a couple of low months when she didn't want to go on. She wished she had died with him. When she finally voiced her thoughts to Temple, he'd been stunned, then frantic. After a time the deep despair dulled to an ever-present ache and she'd promised him that she would see life through. That had been fifteen years ago. Now she and Temple were growing old. There would come a time when one or the other would be alone.

Etha's last thought before drifting off was of the slow whittling down of her own mother after her father had passed away. Her mother thinning to nothing but bone-china skin, clouded irises, and tufts of fine hair.

Viviane was waiting for Temple at the foot of the stairs after he left the apartment.

"How is she?" Viviane asked, handing him a mug of coffee.

"Getting ready to nap."

"I know you and Ed have a homicide on your hands. The fellows," she said, tilting her head toward the county clerks' office, "have stepped up. Vowed to answer the phone for me. I'll stay with Etha for the rest of the day."

"Appreciate that."

Ed put aside yesterday's *Gazetteer* when Temple walked in. Claude was hunched over the evidence table, scribbling in his notepad. A gust of wind hit the windows. The radiators hissed and clanked.

Temple sat down hard in his desk chair. After the ordeal at the hospital, he was angry and preoccupied.

Ed said, "The *Gazetteer* reports that two more injured in the derailment died yesterday. Makes fifteen in all. The article includes a comment from AT&SF Detective Steele promising that the company, in coordination with Sheriff Jennings, will bring the party or parties responsible to justice within the week."

Temple laughed grimly. "Claude, you're a true optimist."

"Could be optimism or could be it's never taken me more than a week to wrap up a case. I'm that good. Think on that." Claude pulled a cigar from his coat pocket.

Temple asked, "Did Ed fill you in on Mrs. Mitchem?"

Passing a lit match back and forth across the tip of his cigar, Claude said, "Sounds as if the lady saw something she shouldn't have in connection with the wreck."

"Seems too much of a coincidence with the derailment one night and then her death alongside the tracks the next," Temple said. "I think Ed and I should bear down on the homicide."

Claude tucked the cigar into the corner of his mouth. "I'll keep at the track and train crews. Between the three of us, the man responsible should be pinned down sooner than later."

Temple ambled to the window. A couple of CCC boys were struggling to hang Christmas lights on the sparse cedar tree in the park across the street. He watched as they circled the evergreen, clipping bulbs to the branches. Christmas seemed to be coming, no matter what. "I did a quick examination of the body and looks like a strangulation to me. Not sure what with. Scratch marks on her neck consistent with struggling to breathe."

After a couple more minutes discussing Ruthie-Jo's death, Claude said, "Got to hit the road. Lot of ground to cover."

Temple turned to Ed. "You and I can start with the Mitchems' neighbors."

"Anyone around?" Ed called, poking his head into the garage's service bay.

"Over here."

Ed found Lou Harriman plunging an inflated tire into a trough.

"Can't find the leak for nothing. It's like it isn't there until you put the tube back in the tire, mount it, and it immediately goes flat." Lou straightened, drying his hands on a greasy rag. "Fill-up?"

"No. You got a minute?"

"Let's go in the office, it's warmer."

Lou's office was attached to the garage and outfitted with an old metal desk, a chair with a stained upholstered seat, and an electric ice chest of soda pop. The place smelled of gasoline and exhaust.

"What can I do for you?" Lou asked, seating himself at the edge of the desk. He was a lean fellow with an intense gaze.

Ed drew out his notepad. "Got some bad news about your next-door neighbor Ruthie-Jo."

"She on that train that derailed?"

"No. Sheriff Jennings and I found her dead not far from her backyard this morning. We're treating this as a homicide."

"You gotta be kidding! That woman was as scarce as a ghost. Barely stepped outside."

"As far as we can tell, she was murdered sometime between ten p.m. and early morning. Were you home then?"

Lou nodded. "Got home at seven. Heated up some stew. Reading in bed until maybe midnight. Got up at six o'clock as usual."

Ed made a note of the times. "Did you hear anything? Notice anything out of the ordinary from the vicinity of the Mitchems' yard?"

"Nope."

"Did you maybe get up for a drink of water or to pee in the middle of the night?"

Lou shook his head. "But you know—I did hear that dog barking."

"When was this?"

"Not sure."

"Was it directly after you got in bed? Or later?"

Lou looked past Ed's shoulder. "It seems like it was not long after one a.m. I was finishing up a chapter and dozing off when he started up. I remember getting annoyed that, you know, the dog was making a racket right when I was about to turn off the light."

Ed scribbled. "Anything else? Did you hear cries?"

"Nothing but the dog."

Temple, meanwhile, was getting nowhere fast with Milt's wife, Betty. The section foreman, Betty, and their kids lived two houses down from Cy and Ruthie-Jo. Betty answered his questions in the kitchen while stirring diapers in a pot of boiling water. She'd been at home alone with the baby and two older children the night before. Milt was working overtime. After the three were bedded down, she'd pulled out her mending but dropped off. It was not far past nine o'clock, Betty figured, when she'd jerked awake and dragged herself upstairs to bed. And no, she'd not heard nor seen anything from the Mitchems' for the entire evening. The baby woke her up at one and again at four to nurse, but Betty hadn't so much as cast her eyes out the window.

It was suppertime when Temple and Ed regrouped at the office. Viviane popped in with a cardboard box of sandwiches wrapped in waxed paper, deviled eggs, and oatmeal cookies.

"From my mom," she said, setting the box on the visitor's chair. "She knows you two are working on a big case, that I'm pitching in, and that we are all tired of the Maid-Rite's loose-meat sandwiches. She sent a jar of soup for the patient. I was just up there and Etha wolfed it down."

"Your mom's a gem," Ed said, his mouth filled with egg.

"Now that I have my own household, I see that," Viviane laughed. "I'm leaving for the day. See you at home."

For several minutes both men ate in contentment. Then the phone rang.

"Sheriff's office," Temple said.

The line was silent for half a tick. The woman's voice was muffled. "That Mrs. Mitchem got what was coming to her. She's a lousy, no-good snoop. Shakes down anyone she can get dirt on. Give those accounts books of hers a look-see." The receiver at the caller's end clicked off. Temple tapped rapidly on the hook but the connection was cut.

"I'll be damned," Temple said, turning slowly to Ed. "What?"

"Anonymous call. Said Ruthie-Jo might was putting the squeeze on some folks."

"Whoa! Any idea who it was?" After flipping through the pages of his notebook, Ed held up a finger. "You know, when I was up in the attic, there were some ledgers I couldn't make heads or tails of."

Temple tapped the eraser end of a pencil on his desk. Then flipped it and tapped the graphite. "I'm not one to put much stock in a caller who won't give her name. And I still think Ruthie-Jo's murder is tied to the train wreck, but . . ." He leaned back in his chair. "But it's worth taking a look at those books of hers. We'd be derelict if we didn't. First thing tomorrow we'll give the Mitchem place a going-over."

CHAPTER SIXTEEN

MAXINE, TROTTING THE LAST BLOCK to the Jewel, knew she was late the moment she spotted Chester pacing under the marquee.

"Where have you been?" he shouted as she approached.

Ever since August, when Maxine had pitched in to help with the first of the dreaded Dish Nights at the Jewel, her boss had been slightly more solicitous.

"What's got you in a stew?" she asked, following him inside the lobby and rubbing her mittened palms together for warmth.

"Nothing. Well . . . I need your help."

Maxine followed Chester around the concession counter. When he pointed toward a tubby dog dozing nose-to-tail on a towel, Maxine jerked in surprise. The dog seemed equally startled—jumping up on his stiffened legs and emitting sharp barks.

"Shush up," Chester said. Daddy immediately quieted.

"You got a dog?" Maxine asked, her voice high.

"I didn't *get* a dog, he snuck in when the lobby door was ajar."

Maxine studied the mutt. He had a curly coat and tufts above his brows. "And you didn't kick him out?"

Chester sighed. "Obviously that was my first instinct,

but after I got him outside he howled and scratched. I couldn't take it. That's where you come in."

"Oh?"

"Take him home with you."

"Hah!" Maxine's raspy laugh jolted Chester.

"I'm serious."

Maxine snapped her gum. "Me too. There is no way Ma would allow it. My little brother Cliff tried last year. Walked in the front door with a puppy in his arms. Ma said, 'No,' then took the dog and walked straight out the back."

"All right then, I will pay you a dollar if you can find a home for this dog and have it out of here by tomorrow."

"Deal," said Maxine, who was a practical young woman.

CHAPTER SEVENTEEN

IT WAS DUSK WHEN CLAUDE made his way back to the rooming house. It had been a long day of talking to witnesses. Everything seemed to indicate that the derailment had been purposeful, but by who and for what reason were unknown as yet.

Myra ambushed him as he started up the stairs, her long horsey face adorned with lipstick and powder.

"It's your second night in town and you haven't joined us for dinner yet."

Claude smiled. "Pleased to, but—"

"It's on the house. We don't offer board. This is an exception, seeing as you are here to help all those poor folks on the train."

"In that case, glad to."

Myra clapped her hands with flattened palms. "We dine at five thirty. In the kitchen."

Claude bowed. "I'll be there."

He stomped upstairs, his heavy boots feeling like lead. Beatrice, the landlady's daughter, emerged from the room next to his with an armload of dirty linens. She nodded perfunctorily. As she retreated down the stairs, Claude kept his eyes on her. Under that loose apron a decent figure hid. Inside his room, Claude removed the pistol and

its holster and tucked them in the top drawer of the bureau along with the brass knuckles. He stripped down
to his union suit and flopped on the bed, grateful for an
hour of quiet. He closed his eyes, thinking of all the beds
he'd occupied in rooming houses across the middle of
the country. Without exception, the standard fare was
lumpy innards covered in blue-striped ticking. He rolled
on his side, extended one arm under the pillow, laying
the other stiffly along his trunk. From the room above
came the snapping of suitcase latches. As he drifted off,
Claude pondered whether the upstairs lodger was coming or going.

At 5:25 on the dot the detective sat bolt upright. Railroad men lived by the clock and pretty near all knew the
time without even casting an eye on their pocket watches.
He pulled on his trousers, padded down the hall to the
common bath, shut the door, and peeled down the top half
of his union suit. Lathering his hands, Claude swabbed
his armpits, floppy breasts, and abdomen. Rinsed the
same way. Toweled off. He raked wet fingers through his
hair and decided a shave wasn't needed.

The kitchen table was set with a cloth, silver-plated salt
and pepper shakers, and floral china. Beatrice was yanking a roasting pan from the oven. She set it down on the
range top with a clatter.

"Something smells mighty fine," Claude offered from
the doorway.

"Rump roast. Mother will be out in a minute."

Beatrice forked the beef, carrots, and turnips onto a
platter. She whisked flour into the roasting pan for gravy.
Claude brazenly speared a carrot from the platter. When

he glanced up, he saw that Beatrice had noticed his grab.

"No harm." He grinned boyishly.

She frowned and turned away.

"Here we are," Myra announced as she entered. "What do you think, Mr. Detective?" She turned slowly, extending the skirting on her polka-dot dress.

"Very smart."

"Make yourself comfortable," she waved Claude to a chair. "Can I offer you a nip of something? I take a dose of apple brandy before my meal for digestive purposes."

Beatrice plunked the laden platter onto the table.

"I won't turn it down," Claude said.

"Oh goodie!" Myra clapped her hands. "Bea, get out two of those teensy glasses for Mr. Steele and myself."

Beatrice returned to the table with three cordial tumblers. "I'm having some too," she declared, depositing them on the table beside the brandy bottle. Myra opened her mouth, then clapped it shut. Beatrice lifted the apron over her head, brushed off her skirt, and sat down. Claude had been right about her figure.

"Let me do the honors," he said, pouring the amber liquid into each glass. "A toast to new friends!"

Myra beamed and drained her glass. Beatrice sniffed her tumbler.

"Don't be a scaredy-cat," her mother scolded, then added, to Claude, "She's a real teetotaler."

Claude knocked back the brandy. It was thick and sweet. "Well?" he asked Beatrice.

She sipped. "I like it."

Claude shifted in his chair, turning all his attention to her now. "Have some more. Loosen yourself up."

* * *

Claude began acting as the host, Beatrice noticed. Refilling her mother's and his glasses. Normally she would find this irritating but there was something likable about his confidence. Manly.

"Yes sir. Nothing like a couple of nips on a cold winter's night. That's how I look at it."

He was at least fifteen years older than she was. He had a big gut. Dried food stains patterned his vest. Yet from within her drab routine of making beds, setting Mother's pin curls, and feeding scraps to the backyard incinerator, he stood out. Cocky. An old rooster who still had spunk.

While Beatrice cleared the table, Myra sipped a cup of hot water which, she explained to the detective, was part of her treatment. In the middle of her monologue about a fibrous growth in her abdomen, the bell at the reception desk rang.

"Could you take care of the check-in, Bea?"

"I'm up to my elbows in dishwater."

Myra sighed. "All right then. Excuse me, Claude."

As the landlady's voice murmured from the front hall, Claude tipped his chair and flopped his arm casually across its back. Beatrice scoured steel wool across the bottom of the roaster.

Claude said, "I'll be heading out to the roadhouse out on Route 15 in a half hour."

"The Oke Doke?"

"Yeah. I need to talk to some of the regulars there in connection with the case."

Beatrice bore down on a burned patch that refused to come off.

"I figured you might want to come along."

She dropped the steel wool into the gray water. "You want my help with the investigation?"

Claude chuckled. "Not looking for help. Just thought you'd get a kick out of seeing a detective in action. Besides, when folks see me with a lady friend, it sometimes puts them off their guard. They are more forthcoming when I start to question them. And we can have a couple of drinks, now that you're a drinking lady, and maybe plug the jukebox."

There was a window above the sink on which Myra had hung red and white gingham curtains. They made a nice impression from across the room. But after you stood at the sink washing dishes week after week, gazing out at nothing but a couple of shingled houses and beyond those the endless horizon of dun-colored prairie, the gingham seemed silly. Pointless. Beatrice looked out the darkened window, her own reflection as drab as the view beyond.

"All right."

Myra returned at that moment, a bottle of pills in her hand. "I wanted to show you, Claude, what the doctor—"

"That'll have to wait. Beatrice and I have a bit of investigating to do." He rose. "That your Plymouth in the drive?"

"Well, yes . . . But—"

"We'll need to borrow that. I'll make sure the AT&SF reimburses you for the gas." He turned to Beatrice. "Go get yourself powdered up. We gotta go."

Beatrice walked away from the half-scrubbed roaster and tepid water, past Myra, and into the back bedroom. She didn't have face powder, but she wasn't going to admit that to Claude. Instead, she brushed out her bob and pinned a brooch near her collar. That would have to do.

Somehow, Claude had finagled the car keys from Myra and stood ready in his winter coat. Beatrice slipped hers on and off they went.

Downtown was dark. The shops were closed and the evening show at the Jewel was over.

"Right at the light," Beatrice said. "That's Route 15. We cross the tracks and then it's just a couple of miles."

Claude steered with his right index finger hooked at the three o'clock position. "Remind me to show you this here spike I just acquired."

"What?"

"Railroad spike. I collect them." And for the remainder of the fifteen-minute journey, Claude expounded on the history of railroad spikes. He'd gotten through their inception in the 1830s all the way up to the Civil War when the lights of the Oke Doke flicked into view. A dozen cars were parked, fan-wise, on the gravel lot skirting the low-slung roadhouse. A slow freight swayed on the tracks a dozen yards behind the establishment. Claude parked the Plymouth and hoisted himself out. Beatrice was surprised when he opened the car door for her. This wasn't a date, after all. Tin signs talking up Schlitz on tap and the pipe appeal of Prince Albert tobacco plastered the roadhouse exterior.

Claude opened the door and stood aside for Beatrice to pass through. She waded into the gush of warm air and steady rumble of voices punctuated by shrieks of laughter. The bar was immediately ahead. Most of the stools were occupied. It was a mixed crowd, as far as Beatrice could tell. She recognized two teachers from the high school. There was a gang of CCC boys in uniform. Three men with unshaven jaws and torn overalls clustered at the far end of the counter. Beyond the bar were tables and, in the corner, a two-person band strumming a fast dance number. A strand of colorful Christmas bulbs tacked to the wall behind them bobbed up and down.

"Get a table and I'll bring you a beer," Claude shouted into her ear.

Pushing past the bar, she found an empty table. Cigarette smoke hung thick in the low-ceilinged space. The musicians faced one another in straight-back chairs. The fiddler, in a soft collared shirt and worn trousers, stomped his work boots in time to the music. Bending over a guitar was a woman, the large brim of her hat flipped upright. She'd tucked three silk flowers on its underside. Her fingers flew up and down the frets.

Beatrice lowered herself into a chair. The tabletop was damp with rings from earlier drinks. Claude emerged from the throng at the bar with two bottles of beer in his fists. He plunked one in front of her and sat down.

"Everyone is always begging me to talk about my hobby, so I'm going to get right to it." He pulled the spike from his coat pocket. "Now this here . . ." he began. It was clear he was a learned man. As far as Beatrice knew, none of the fellows who stayed at Mayo's had a hobby. Whenever she'd taken the train, usually to Oklahoma City to visit cousins, she had never given a thought to the ties the wheels were running across, nor the spikes that held the ties in place.

"You say this is a dog spike? How many kinds are there?"

A big smile crossed Claude's face. "Glad you asked. Hundreds, at least."

Beatrice considered this. "Does the AT&SF use the same type on all its tracks? That would make sense economically."

Snapping his fingers, Claude said, "Way ahead of me. You're right. The company is working toward adopting a common spike. As the old nails wear out, they're all being replaced by the same design. Sort of sad. Really old ones were hand-forged by blacksmiths."

Beatrice sipped the beer. "Something's lost when the old ways are left behind."

"Exactly!"

Claude tucked the spike into his pocket. "Now comes the investigation. Want to come along?"

"Why not?" Beatrice said.

"Follow me."

The crowd at the bar had thinned. Claude asked a couple, flanked by two empty stools, to move down one seat. Beatrice draped her coat across the back of one, climbed up, and tucked her pocketbook in her lap. Claude ordered two more beers. Sitting to his left was the trio of down-and-outers Beatrice had noticed when they arrived.

"Here's how!" Claude said, chinking his bottle against hers.

She sipped the foam and smiled gamely. The roadhouse noises and smells spun pleasantly around her.

Claude turned to the trio. "You fellas camping in the environs or just passing through?"

The man in the middle pushed back a hank of hair. "Been here about a month. Mostly camping at the hobo jungle by the tracks. We got work taking down a barn and stacking the planks for fuel." He was older than the other two.

"Buy you fellas a round?" the detective asked, simultaneously circling an index finger at the bartender.

"Wouldn't turn it down."

Nothing more was said until three dripping bottles were delivered. The younger men chugged theirs directly. Beatrice noticed that the fellow in the middle nursed his. A wary old tomcat with oily tufts of fur. With surprise, she saw that half of her bottle was empty. Claude introduced Beatrice and himself to the trio. As soon as he said "AT&SF railroad detective," the men froze. Claude rolled quickly on.

"And I'm not interested in you three except for general information. I know you'll want to cooperate." He coolly opened his jacket. Beatrice caught a flash of metal and a leather holster. *Where is this going?* She'd heard stories about railroad bulls pummeling men and young boys riding the rails. The image of Claude as a stern lawman made her both uncomfortable and slightly titillated.

Claude continued: "What I'm wanting to know is if you three have noticed any troublemakers passing through. Busting out windows in vacant houses. Vandalizing railroad equipment just for the heck of it. Like that."

The tomcat looked to his two compatriots, who shook their heads. "Nope," he said. "Not since we've been here."

"Aw, come on. You can't tell me that every tramp in these environs is living on the side of God. Not a one is vandalizing or thieving?"

The tomcat cocked his head. "I've run into my fair share of hotheads traveling the rails. Angry guys picking fights, tossing ballast onto the rails, stomping down the shacks in a hobo camp for no good reason. But nothing like that in the past couple of months. And I'd say it even if you hadn't shown me your gun." He chugged the bottle. "Thanks for the beer," he added. And then to his buddies, "Come on, fellas." They sauntered out.

Claude scratched the coarse bristles on his jaw and turned to Beatrice. "'Course, that doesn't rule out vandalism. That is simply one man's observation."

Beatrice propped an elbow on the bar, chin in hand. "Someone derailed that train on purpose? Killed all those people for no reason? Is that what you think?"

"One possibility, but there are others." Claude tossed back his beer. "Finish up. I better get you home to avoid the wrath of Myra, which I'm guessing can be fierce."

Beatrice laughed loudly. "Who cares? What's she going to do, hand me my walking papers? In case you haven't noticed, I do all the work."

When Claude got her on her feet, her pocketbook slid to the floor. He picked it up. "Your mom might short-sheet me."

"That woman hasn't made a bed since she taught me how when I was five. If she even so much as thought about firing me, I'd fix her wagon and she knows it."

"Then how about another?"

"Why not?"

After two more beers and several sloppy twirls on the cramped dance floor, Claude boosted Beatrice into her coat and guided her out to the car. She promptly slumped against the passenger door. As she dozed off, railroad spikes occupied the tiny crumb of her brain that was still awake.

C HAPTER EIGHTEEN

CHESTER FLICKED OFF THE PROJECTOR and hurried downstairs to usher the scanty crowd through the lobby. "Move along, now," he said, making scooping motions with his hands.

Chester was of the opinion that weeknight moviegoers preferred to be home by eight thirty p.m. at the latest. That was, after all, when *he* preferred to be home.

He stuck his head into the auditorium where the squeak of the carpet sweeper's rollers could be heard.

"Almost finished, Mr. Benton!" Maxine called out.

"I need you to take the dog out before you leave," he said.

When she and the dog returned, Maxine said, "You know you can take him out yourself. He's trained. Take him outside and he'll do his business."

Chester grimaced but appreciated this information. "Just get right on finding him a home."

"I'll ask the kids at school tomorrow."

Once Maxine sauntered off, chewing gum cracking, Chester locked and bolted the lobby doors. The side exits in the auditorium got the same treatment. The dog followed him, whining.

"All right!" Chester said, his voice rising. "You will

find I do things in a specific order. Nothing willy-nilly about this operation."

The dog apparently understood, for he padded behind Chester in silence as more doors were secured and the cashbox was locked in the safe.

Upstairs, Chester was dumping scraps of ham and bread into a basin then ladling leftover stew on top, when the telephone jangled.

"Jewel Movie House," he said crisply into the receiver.

The voice on the other end did not identify himself. "I've got a deal you might be interested in."

"If this is a business matter, you will need to call during working hours. The Jewel is closed for the evening."

The man's voice was vaguely familiar but Chester couldn't place it. It sounded like the caller might be talking through a handkerchief.

"I'm giving you a chance to buy a hundred-pack box of cigarettes at half price. For seventy-five bucks you can take these off my hands and sell them. Make all your money back and then some."

"What? Are you crazy? We're talking about stolen goods, right? I'm an upright citizen with standing in this community. I'm not about to be pressured into breaking the law."

"I know who you are. You're a blind man who wouldn't know if a moviegoer stayed after the show or not."

"Are you threatening me?" The receiver shook in Chester's hands.

"This is a simple business proposition. I'll call you with a time and place. Bring the money—unless you want me turning up in your bedroom one of these nights. And don't even think about calling the sheriff's office. I got friends on your party line."

Crawling into bed, Chester flopped on his back. He didn't have the cash to pay for this false bargain. No one had any extra money like that in these times. But if he didn't produce the seventy-five dollars he'd never feel safe in his apartment again. Fully awake and anxious, any chance of sleep that night was shattered.

CHAPTER NINETEEN

LIKE A BAD PENNY.

Milt glanced up from the stack of paperwork on his desk, his stomach sinking as the railroad detective lumbered into his office.

Claude lowered himself heavily into the visitor's chair. "I'm guessing I'm the last fella you want to see . . . what with track repairs and all."

"What do you need?" Milt replied stiffly. "The baby bawled all night and I'm short on patience today."

The detective fumbled in his coat pocket, eventually extracting a cigar stub, which he shoved, unlit, into his mouth. "Went to that roadhouse like you said. Mighty fine fiddler there and—"

"Mr. Steele, you need to get to the point. The company is going to have my skin if I don't get these reports finished."

"That's exactly what I want to discuss with you. You and I talked yesterday about disgruntled crew. Guys you've had to fire. I thought maybe we should revisit that discussion. Along with the thrill of vandalism, revenge is a strong motivator."

Milt inhaled, tried to keep his voice steady. "As I told you, none of those men are around anymore. In fact—"

A knock on the office doorframe drew both men's attention to Daniel. "Sir, sorry to interrupt, but the wrecking derrick's here."

"Thank God." Milt jumped to his feet and turned to Claude. "I've gotta go."

Claude waved the cigar. "Of course. That comes first." He rose and followed Milt and Daniel out through the toolhouse. Milt shouted to three trackmen working down the line to come up and help with the equipment.

As the workers strode toward the derrick, Claude stepped in front of a fellow straggling at the rear. "I'm a detective with the AT&SF." He flipped open the cover on his badge. "Got a quick question for you."

The fellow, who went by Toady, gestured up the line. "My boss is calling."

"Only need a minute. And I'll vouch for you if he gives you a hard time."

"Who are you again?"

Saphead, Claude thought. He tapped on the metal star.

Toady squinted. "Police?"

Claude drew the man inside the toolhouse and out of Milt's sight line. "Just tell me the name of the guy that got fired in the last couple of weeks."

"Lonnie."

"All right. Progress!"

Toady stepped toward the tracks.

"Whoa! Hold your horses. How did this Lonnie take it?"

"Not good. But who would?"

"Make any threats against the foreman or the company?"

"He was kicking and swearing. Said he'd never work for the railroad again. Said he was going to head to California where folks were treated right."

Claude nodded. "And did he? Go west?"

"Guys said he did but I saw him at the derailment. Pulling out passengers and—"

"He was here! Did anybody else see him?"

"Sure! Lots of us on the crew."

Up the tracks, Milt was shouting.

Toady backed out of the toolhouse. "Gotta go."

Claude took his time lighting the cigar. He didn't want Milt to know who spilled the beans about Lonnie. After a bit, the detective strolled to the tracks. Up ahead, mounted on a flatcar, the wrecking derrick's massive hook dangled over the toppled engine. Track and wrecking crew men crawled over the locomotive, securing rigging lines. Milt stood on the ground, yelling orders to the crew.

Claude came up behind the foreman. "I need a word."

Milt pivoted with a scowl. "We're in the middle of an operation here." He turned away, making a lassoing motion at the workers. "Hurry it up!"

As Milt tramped toward the derrick, Claude shouted at his back. "Couple of weeks back you fired a man!"

Milt spun around. "That fella is long gone."

"You're wrong on that. Lonnie showed up at the wreck."

"What?" Milt froze.

"At least one of your men saw him pulling survivors out of the wreckage."

Milt slumped. "I didn't see him that night. Honest. When the train derailed I was yanked in so many directions I could hardly see straight. And everyone told me he headed west right after I gave him the boot . . . So, what do you need from me?"

"Lonnie's full name, address, description. Then I'll get out of your hair."

With a metallic screech, the crane swung slowly toward the locomotive. Two men remained on top of the wreck to guide the hook. The rest scrambled to the ground.

"Lonnie Taylor. He roomed over Mooreland way."

"What'd he look like?" The detective pulled a notebook from his coat pocket.

Milt paused. There'd been so many Lonnies and Mikes and Johnnys over the years. They came and went with the seasons—staying six months, maybe a year, before taking off to another state, another section of track. Lonnie's image came into focus. Long face, fleshy nose. Always wore one of those flat cloth caps. In his thirties. Heavy stubble. Milt gave Claude the description and turned away.

"Appreciate it," the detective called to the foreman's back. Claude moved off in the other direction, the buckles on his rubber boots clanking.

The hook was secured and the derrick's steam-powered winch screeched under the weight of the 400,000-pound engine. Claude felt the earth quaking when the locomotive was thumped into place, but he didn't turn.

Back at Mayo's, Claude wrangled the car he needed to drive to Mooreland by softening Myra up with flattery and then giving her some attaboy about civic duty to help the AT&SF and those poor souls killed in the derailment. Eventually she handed over the keys. He even had the nerve to ask Beatrice, right in front of her mother, if she'd like to go along on the ride. But Myra quickly nixed that.

It was early afternoon when Claude pulled into the Mooreland train station. He yanked on the handbrake and climbed out. The temperature had dipped lower during the day and the heater in Myra's Ford was luke-warm at best. The detective stomped into the depot's waiting room, slapping his upper arms to get the blood going. The station agent, the same fellow Claude had talked to before arriving in Vermillion, was there.

"How's the investigation going?" the man asked.

"Fair to middling. I'm here about a Lonnie Taylor." Claude leaned across the ticket counter. "Worked on the track crew on this section until he got canned not long back. His supervisor thought he was rooming somewhere around here."

The station agent shrugged. "Don't know."

"Okay. But let's say he was living in the surrounds. Where might he bunk up?"

"The bar across the road sometimes lets rooms."

The saloon was dim at midday. The clientele consisted of two fellows in dusty overalls, their skinny hindquarters planted on barstools and the heels of their boots hitched over the rungs. Cigarette smoke and the hoppy smell of beer filled the barren space. The bartender, a man who looked to be in his forties with thick hair in need of a barber, said he hadn't rented out any rooms for months.

"But a track worker did come in here every few days until a couple of weeks ago. I was thinking he rode a handcar up this way to keep his drinking habits private from the crew down in Vermillion. But maybe he was bunking here in Mooreland."

Claude cocked a finger at him. "That's helpful. I'll have a beer before shoving off."

After the drink was fetched, Claude described Lonnie. "Could he have been your visitor?"

"Could have been," the bartender said.

"Did he mingle with any other folks?"

"Nope. Only the gal that he brought with him."

The beer was halfway to Claude's lips. He paused and put it down. "You mean he had a companion?"

"Most times."

"What did she look like?"

The bartender shrugged. "Plain."

"That's it?"

Another shrug.

Claude tossed the glass back. "Appreciate your help." He snapped two nickels on the counter and walked out.

The only other business of note in the town was the grain elevator. Claude ambled toward its three towering silos where wheat from neighboring farms was stored. There was a chance the fellows working the elevator would know of a crewman living nearby.

A worker was scooping grain from atop a farm truck when Claude approached.

"How do?" the detective greeted, displaying his badge. "Got a minute?"

The worker, a teenager, paused. "What's the problem?"

Claude grinned. "No problem. Just looking for a guy on the track crew that might be living around here."

"How come?"

"He's not in trouble. I'm needing help on an investigation is all. Where's he bedding down?"

The kid jammed the scoop into the pile of grain in the

truck, pulled out a handkerchief, and blew heavily. "He's not around anymore."

"Took off, did he?"

"About two weeks ago."

"Where was he staying before he vamoosed?"

Another load of dust and snot was deposited in the hankie. "He and the girlfriend were living out of an abandoned camp car for a couple of months. We hardly spoke—*howdy, nice weather* . . . that sort of thing. The camp car is just off this spur line so I'd see them purdy regular."

"They were squatting?"

"Guess so."

"Did you take note when they moved on?"

"Sure did. They were scrapping. She lit into him about losing his job. I couldn't tell what he was saying back but then I heard maybe pots and pans or whatnot hitting the ground. I figured she was tossing stuff out of the car. Half hour later they headed right past me. She in front, gripping a suitcase and marching like a general. He behind with a croker sack over his shoulder and a sorry look on his face. They didn't say boo to me."

Claude tossed up a coin. "Here's a quarter for your trouble." The kid tucked it into his pocket. "You say the camp car is up this away?"

"Two hundred yards. Stay on the spur. You can't miss it."

Claude himself had occasionally bedded down in camp cars, alongside the track laborers, during his early years as a detective. The repurposed freight cars, which provided free lodging for section gangs, were outfitted with bunks, rudimentary tables and chairs, and stoves.

No plumbing. Traditionally the car was ruled by a crumb boss—railroad slang for the fellow overseeing the car. *Crumbs* were the gray-backed lice that infested most of the cars.

The camp car on the Mooreland spur was of the same ilk. Claude climbed up a rickety ladder and paused at the top to survey the scene. He could smell the galvanized bucket used as a toilet before he spotted it. Four sets of rusted bunks with stained mattresses, two on each end.

On the right, broken bottles of illegal hooch and a smashed chair littered the dusty floorboards. Carved into the wall was a note: *To my best pal I ever had. I'm sorry I did you wrong Glenn. From Clarence.*

The left side, though, had been tidied up. Someone had covered the table with fresh oilcloth and arranged two chairs beside a squat potbellied stove. Claude hoisted himself inside.

The top and bottom berths on the left had been occupied fairly recently. No dust on the mattresses. A pair of men's socks had been neatly hung along the bunk's cross bar. Claude sniffed one. Faint odor of washing powder. The upper bunk yielded three bobby pins. He peered into the stove. Charred ashes and the tart stink of creosote. A pan, crusted with something, sat on the iron lid.

Claude dropped into a chair. *So, Lonnie, you were living here with a lady friend until you got fired. Then what? Some said you headed west but then you surfaced at the wreck. If you did throw the switch, you're likely bunking in Vermillion. Close enough to sneak onto the tracks and then turn up within minutes after the crash.*

Claude lit a cigar and puffed in silence, shaping the glowing ash against the table's edge. Clearly the thing to do was to head back to Vermillion. Figure out where Lonnie and this woman were bedding down. The big question was—if the trackman was the vandal—why did he show up at the wreck? And not just as a spectator, the way some arsonists did. He'd pitched in to rescue survivors.

At about that same hour, Temple and Ed pulled up at the Mitchem house, its naked windows reflecting a skim of gray clouds hanging low in the sky. Minutes earlier, Mrs. Jacobs, the pastor's wife, had bundled Cy off to the mortuary to make the funeral arrangements. Cy apparently had shoveled a bellyful of coal into the furnace before he left. Heat poured from the floor registers. Temple and Ed quickly shucked off their coats.

"Yesterday you mentioned there might be something fishy with those ledgers in the attic," Temple said. "Go get them so we can take a closer look. I'll start with the paperwork on the dining room table. See where that gets us."

Ed made four trips up and down the ramshackle attic ladder transferring the account books, which he stacked against the dining room's baseboards.

"She appears to have been a meticulous woman," Temple said.

Ed snorted. "I'll say." Pressing his back to the wall, he slid down to the floor, bumping his rear beside the tallest pile.

For a time, the only sound was the rasp of pages as the two lawmen bent over the ledgers. After Ed thumbed through two of the stacks, he paused. "Got to say, I don't know who the heck the woman was keeping books for, besides her husband, that is."

"How so?"

"For one, only some of these are labeled. Mitchem's Hardware accounts are titled and include inventories, invoices, debits and credits—all related to the business. That's clear as day."

"Same here," Temple said, tipping back in his chair and rocking his head to loosen his neck bones. "Should have brought a thermos of coffee. I didn't get much sleep last night. I was scooched to the far side of the bed so as not to disturb Etha and woke up with a crick in the neck."

"Want me to make some?"

"Naw. Go on."

"But besides that, there seems to be bookwork done for other businesses too." Ed stabbed at the ledger open in his lap. "Listen to this: *glycerine, glucose, sodium salicylate, iodide . . .*"

"Sounds medical. That sodium whatchamacallit. My mother dosed with that for arthritis."

"Maybe Ruthie-Jo kept books for the drugstore?"

Temple tapped a cigarette from his pack. "But that's not a motive for strangling her."

Ed stood. "I'm making coffee." He passed into the kitchen, found a match, and lit the burner. The coffee-pot sloshed with hours-old brew when he shook it. Good enough. "And there seems to be a third set of books," he called to Temple. "Payroll lists, I'm guessing."

Temple whistled. "Our Ruthie-Jo had her fingers in several pies. What I'm seeing here, besides the hardware records, is a file on the hatchery. Seems Jess Fuller was way behind in his payments to the hardware store. There are carbons of letters she sent to the hatchery demanding payment." Four months back, the same time the itinerant rainmaker had been found murdered in the alley beside the Jewel, the Fuller family farm had been foreclosed on by the bank. Since sheriff duties included keeping the peace, Temple had been obligated to monitor the bank's auction of the family's livestock, machinery, and household goods. Enraged at the drought, the bank, and his wife, who left him that same day, Jess had taken out his anger on Temple. The man had never forgiven him.

Temple joined Ed in the kitchen. "Guess it's not unusual for a local business to go after customers for nonpayment. Happens a lot these days. Although I can't see Cy as the type for that sort of thing."

Ed handed him a cup. "But apparently Ruthie-Jo was."

Temple sipped and made a face. "This takes the hair off your chest. Where's the sugar bowl?" After spooning in a generous amount, his eyes fell on the spice box. His mother had one of those, with little alphabetized drawers for loose spices. Temple opened C, expecting the scent of cinnamon or caraway, but instead found a carefully folded strip of paper. *Tom Finny. Cheater.* The C was heavily inked in.

Temple handed the note to Ed. "What do you make of this?"

The sheriff opened more drawers. Most held spices, but he found three more notes. Each bore a name that Temple recognized and an unflattering summation. *Gambler. Spendthrift. Liar.*

Ed scrutinized the kitchen. "I'm feeling as if we're in the middle of a big old spiderweb."

The sheriff ran his fingers through his hair. "How are

we going to bring this up with Cy? Are these just crazy ramblings or something serious?"

"Like blackmail? That might rile somebody enough to permanently shut Ruthie-Jo's mouth."

"Maybe. We'll need to interview these folks—discretely. This is a ready-made list of suspects if she contacted any of them and made accusations. I thought it was her being in the wrong place at the wrong time and coming into contact with whoever cocked the train switch, but now I'm not so sure . . ."

"Jeez."

Temple stepped back into the dining room and eyed the piles of ledgers and paperwork. "This also needs a closer look. Lots to do between just the two of us. You know . . ."

"What?"

"I'm thinking to ask Etha to help with this. She has a good head for figures. Having a project might keep her still. I know she'll get bored to tears pretty quick and will be up and about too soon."

"I'll load up the car."

As Ed gathered the armloads of registers, bumping out the front door and to the sedan, Temple unfolded the notes, arranging them on the kitchen table. *What were you up to, Ruthie-Jo?*

"Busy?"

"Very funny," Etha said, putting down a shabby copy of *Radioland*.

Temple's topcoat released a billow of fresh air as he strolled into the bedroom. Etha, trapped in the stuffy apartment among the aromas of medicine and stale linens, inhaled appreciatively.

"I hate to tear you away from that serious read," he said, raising his brows, "but I've got a project for you."

"Really?" Etha sat up too quickly and immediately regretted it. "Ow!"

Temple dumped an armload of leather-bound volumes he'd been carrying on the bedside chair. "Remember what Hinchie told you about taking it easy."

Etha glared. "I hate this! So, what's this about a project?"

Temple pointed to the stack of ledgers. "These are Ruthie-Jo's account books. Ed and I found them at the house."

"Everyone knows she kept the books for the store."

"But it seems she was also managing financial records for another person or persons unknown."

"You know when Reverend Coxey reads the list of

shut-ins during the service? That's how I thought of her. Confined to the house. Sort of an invalid."

Temple snatched up two ledgers. "Seems like she might have had more irons in the fire than anyone thought. There's an outside chance that one of those irons is connected to her murder. It's probably a long shot. I still believe it is way more likely that she saw whoever cocked the signal and got killed as a result. That said, we need to investigate every angle. Ed and I started going through these when we were at the house but it's a big job and we don't have the time. We're still interviewing possible witnesses. I thought—"

"You thought that I don't have anything to do but twiddle my thumbs so I might as well be put to good use," Etha bantered. "I know how you operate."

"Will you help?"

Etha made a show of examining her hands. "Yes. But in exchange . . ."

"Here it comes."

"I want to go ahead with our Christmas plans. With Vadie and her family coming and all."

"You are a stubborn one."

"If I'm capable of helping with the investigation, I'm also well enough to celebrate Christmas with my family."

"You know damn well that sitting in the quiet of your own bed looking over some ledgers is a totally different thing than hosting a Christmas visit with your niece, her two kids, and that husband."

There was a moment of silence.

"I already asked Carmine to get a tree for us."

Temple sighed heavily. "You're way ahead of me, I

see." He leaned over and pecked her on the cheek. "Now get to work!"

"Do I get a badge?"

"Don't push your luck, lady."

As the sheriff walked into the office, Ed was on the phone. He made a squawking sign with his thumb and fingers for Temple's benefit.

"Yes, Mrs. Hinchie. We'll take care of . . ." Ed was saying.

Unsteady footfalls paused outside the office. Chester appeared in the doorway; trembling, his tie uncharacteristically crooked.

"My God, man." Temple jumped up and guided the movie house owner to a chair. "You look like death warmed over."

"Someone phoned last night. Threatened to attack me. I've been a wreck since."

"Hold on. Threatening you how?"

"Threatening to break into my apartment. Do me harm unless I pay him. I was afraid to call you. He said to keep you out of it. If I called he'd know—someone on my party line would tip him off."

"All right. Tell me from the beginning."

Chester described the call, the hint of fencing stolen goods, the demand for seventy-five dollars.

"He broke me down. It's very hard to admit, but as a blind man I'm vulnerable. There's no getting around that. But I don't have that kind of money." Chester's voice lifted in agitation.

"Did you recognize the caller at all? Was it someone local?"

"Maybe . . ."

"How is this exchange going down?"

"He hasn't said."

A point above Temple's right eye throbbed. Fires, big and small, had sprung up all over the town and there was only so much a two-man outfit could handle. "Sit here for a spell. Viviane can get you coffee and then I'll drive you back to the Jewel. I'll make sure it's secure. If this fellow calls again with details on when and where, ring me immediately. Ed or I will stake it out. Until then, there's not much we can do."

After Chester calmed down, Temple stood, shrugging into his overcoat. "Ed, I'll be at the morgue with Hinchie and then come back for Chester."

Temple turned up the collar of his coat, buried his nose in its folds, and stepped out into the frosty air.

Hinchie was already at the morgue and had rolled Ruthie-Jo's body out of its cooler drawer when Temple arrived. A sheet was pulled up to her chin.

"How's my runaway patient?" Hinchie asked.

Temple squeezed the back of his neck. "You can't reason with that woman. But so far she's staying in bed."

Hinchie chuckled. "Tell her I'll be by tomorrow. But call me if anything changes before that."

"Appreciate it. How's our gal here?" the sheriff asked.

"Better than some of those upstairs. Nothing nastier than a thermal burn. When that boiler burst it spread death and misery."

Temple noted the doctor's rheumy eyes and gray skin. "Not at your handsomest either."

Hinchie grunted. "Folks in Grove City finally got

'round to sending another doctor and some nurses. Good thing. I'm ready to drop."

"Any more deaths?"

"Not as of today. Three barely hanging on."

"What about the stoker from the train? He one of them?"

"Now, he's a question mark. Still got him doped to the gills. He could pull through. Too early to tell. Ready to talk about Ruthie-Jo?"

Temple bit into the fingertip of his leather glove and pulled. From his coat pocket he withdrew a pad and pen. "Shoot."

Someone had combed the hair away from her high forehead. In death, she was as sternly plain as she'd been in life. The ends of her lips drooped as if in disapproval of how her days had ended.

"The cause of death was asphyxia," Hinchie said. "Someone used a strap of some sort, I'd say. Managed to get it around her neck then pulled the ends in opposite directions. Closed off the blood vessels and airway in the neck. Cut off all oxygen to the brain."

"Facing her or from the back?"

"From the back. There is a large bruise on her tailbone as if someone planted a shoe or boot there and pulled."

Temple scribbled on the pad. "Can I see?"

"Sure. Help me get her on her side."

Temple removed his other glove. Hinchie leaned over the body and gripped the far shoulder. Temple wedged his hands under the buttocks and pushed toward the doc.

Hinchie puffed, struggling to keep the body balanced on its side. Temple bent. There was a mottled bruise at the tip of her tailbone. "Did you measure this?"

"Six point two inches."

"Okay." They rolled Ruthie-Jo onto her back.

"Given the size of that bruise and the powerful strangulation marks, are we talking about a male suspect?"

"Not necessarily. A strong woman with large feet could have done the deed."

"Wouldn't that be something?" Temple slipped the notepad and pen back in his pocket. "Are you thinking that she was killed late Friday night? Last time Cy saw her was when he went up to bed at ten p.m."

Hinchie pulled the sheet up over Ruthie-Jo's face and slid the body back in the cooler. "Can't pinpoint it exactly. But from your observations when you found her as to body temperature and state of rigor and seeing the stomach contents, I'd guess it was within four hours of when Cy retired for the night."

"Can't give me anything more precise?"

Hinchie shook his head.

"Personal effects?"

"On my desk."

An orderly leaned through the doorway. "Doc, you're needed in the men's ward."

Hinchie turned to Temple. "See what my life has become? An infinite string of interruptions."

C HAPTER TWENTY-ONE

ETHA HAD ONLY TAKEN one business class in high school. Business correspondence, shorthand, bookkeeping— none of it had stuck.

Now, as she flipped open the thick cover on one of Ruthie-Jo's ledgers, she prayed something would come back to her. On the front page, in blunt script, Ruthie-Jo had noted the contents—*Mitchem Hardware Store June 1 to December 30, 1935.*

The journal traced debits and credits by weeks and months. Etha assumed Temple wanted her to review the contents in a general way. He couldn't expect her to delve into every entry. For that, he'd need a bespectacled accountant like the one whose advanced accounting methods and pure doggedness had helped imprison Al Capone for tax evasion several years back. At the time, the story of the Bureau of Internal Revenue's bean counter had been splashed across every newspaper in the country, including Vermillion's own *Gazetteer.*

The ledger was arranged by customer account, rather than daily credits and debits. Many times Etha had entered Mitchem's to find the place empty except for the talkative Cy. She was now surprised to see how many accounts the store maintained. Much of the business, it appeared, depended on large orders for field fencing, lumber, and lime for whitewash. It seemed that every one of the hundreds of outbuildings in the county was white-washed with lime purchased from Mitchem's.

Riffling through the pages, Etha paused at Fuller's Chicken Hatchery. Ruthie-Jo must have spent a lot of time on this account because the ledger's ribbon marker had been left at this page. In the six months covered by the ledger, the hatchery made many purchases. Most had not been paid for as yet. Three times Ruthie-Jo had written tiny notes in the margins beside the amounts owed. Etha couldn't make out the words. She retrieved the magnifying glass from her workbasket. Even with the lens, the writing was almost impossible to read.

She got out of bed, lugging the ledger to the bright light of the window. She made out *S. cor.*

What might that mean? One of the first lessons Etha taught her piano students was the mystery of musical abbreviations. "The *p* is for *piano,* which means this part is to be played softly," she'd explain, "and *mf* is for *mezzoforte.* The volume should be more loud than soft." But if there were abbreviations used solely by bookkeepers, Etha didn't know them.

From the street came the putt-putting of a ramshackle jalopy. Etha smiled. *Maybe Vadie and her family are packing up their auto for the trip to Vermillion this very minute.*

She and Temple had driven to Vadie's house a couple of times. It was a long journey—straight across the state, through Tulsa and over the state line into Arkansas. Almost every mile of the three hundred–plus total was on dirt roads. The family lived in the small city of Spring-dale. Everett held intermittent jobs as a laborer—grading roads for the county, digging ditches. For several months he'd been the night watchman at the ironworks but got sacked for drinking on the job. When the rough years of the Depression had set in, the family depended solely on Vadie's earnings at the canning factory.

"Poor Vadie" had been the constant refrain of Etha's mother and aunts. Vadie was the youngest child of Etha's sister. A vigorous, rosy toddler, Vadie had been the recipient of tap dancing and piano lessons. Captain of the high school pep squad. But then her string of luck snapped. Vadie's boyfriend Everett, the high school athlete, became Vadie's husband, the angry brawler. Two pregnancies. Bing bing. Poor Vadie.

Etha turned back to the page and it came to her. *S. cor.—See correspondence!* That was worth checking out. Etha shuffled through the stack Temple had left and found a file thick with letters to various vendors about missing shipments and complaints about the quality of the goods. These were clipped together. Other notices had been sent to the store's account holders. It was not a surprise to Etha that the biggest bundle of letters was to the Fuller Hatchery. Etha set the rest of the bulky file aside, removed the paper clip from the letters to the hatchery, and began to read.

Dear Mr. Fuller,

This is the first notice, and hopefully the last, regarding your overdue payment of $134.16 owed to Mitchem's Hardware. Your invoice of September 18 records the shipment of chicken wire and lumber to the hatchery.

*I understand you are still in the process of set-
ting up your new venture but I want to be clear
that Mitchem's is not in the business of lending
money. That is the job of a bank and I strongly
suggest you discuss this with your banker. Please
inform me immediately if there is some piece of
information that will incline me to look more fa-
vorably on your delinquency. Otherwise, I will
look for payment in tomorrow's mail.*

Sincerely,
Mrs. Cy Mitchem, Bookkeeper

The next letter read:

Dear Mr. Fuller,
*The situation has not changed since the date
of my last letter to you.*
*You still owe Mitchem's $134.16. We still need
the money and you still refuse even to reply to my
requests for information.*
*Yes, you are gaining a temporary advantage.
Nevertheless, a continuation of such tactics will
cause you to pay rather heavily for the advantage
that you are gaining.*
*Courtesy is the foundation of all business
interchange. As of today, there is the additional
overdue amount of $56.86 for incubators and
brooder equipment you ordered through our
concern on September 27. I am not in a position
to know why Mr. Mitchem allowed you to make
further purchases when past bills remain due, nor*

to fathom why he would special order hatchery
equipment for your business, but I can assure you
that the bookkeeping department will not tolerate
overdue accounts.

Yours very truly,
Mrs. Cy Mitchem, Bookkeeper

The woman was certainly direct, Etha thought. She
flipped through the pile. The last letter read:

Dear Mr. Fuller,
    How much is enough? I have written you
twice drawing attention to the fact that you owe
Mitchem's money—now in excess of $191. Isn't
that enough?
    We do not believe it would be fair to inform
your friends that you either have no money or are
the type of man who refuses to carry out his ob-
ligations.
    But we need the money to run our business. To
stay in business we must collect our bills. There-
fore, I regret to inform you that unless I hear from
you in two days' time, we shall be forced to take
other and more drastic steps. This is your final
notice.

Very truly yours,
Mrs. Cy Mitchem, Bookkeeper

I'll be jiggered. A sly smile crossed Etha's face. *Ruthie-Jo,*
you had grit. The third letter had been written shortly be-

fore someone strangled the woman to death. It was possible there was a connection. When Temple walked in the
door after work, she'd tell him straightaway.

"Heard you got yourself up and dressed this morning." Viviane breezed into the apartment as Etha was putting Ruthie-Jo's collection of letters aside.

"That husband of mine is a blabbermouth."

"How you feeling?" Viviane asked as she moved
about the room, plucking clothes draped over the chair
and bedposts and putting them away.

"Pretty good."

Viviane paused. "Are you fibbing?"

Etha forced a smile. "Not at all."

"How about I fix you a sandwich?"

"I wouldn't say no."

Etha hobbled behind Viviane into the kitchen. The
younger woman turned on the radio and they listened to
the livestock market report while eating ham sandwiches.
Viviane's mother had sent along a tin of Christmas cookies and they each had a couple.

"I've been thinking that maybe you should hire someone to help with the cooking and cleaning. At least while
your family is here. You can't manage it all," Viviane said.

Etha frowned. "But I'm sure Vadie can—"

"Vadie will have her hands full with the boys."

Etha chewed her lip. "You might be right. But who
would I get?"

"Surely there is some needy soul in town. Maybe your
pastor could suggest someone?"

Etha snapped her fingers. "There is this young woman
who works at the hospital. Seems very sweet. Her name
is Alice."

"Can she cook?"

"She's a diet aide."

Viviane clicked her tongue as she gathered up the lunch dishes. "Not sure that means much."

"I think she would work out."

"I'll swing by the hospital later today and track her down."

Once Etha was alone again, she took up her knitting. Each of the boys, including Carmine, would receive a knitted hat and also a cretonne bag of hard candy. Two hours later she was finishing off the headband on the final cap when the phone jingled. It was Viviane.

"I'm at the hospital," she said. "Alice has a second job and can't take on any more. But another aide overheard us. Said she's willing. I told her that'd be swell. I hope that's okay."

There were, Etha knew, only two diet aides on the women's ward. Thelma was prickly and glum, not someone you'd want around your house at Christmastime—or, to be honest, ever. And it was sure as shooting that the two boys would get under Thelma's skin pronto. But rather than share these thoughts, Etha said, "I'm sure it will work out fine."

It was late afternoon when Temple mounted the stairs to check on his wife. On the second-floor landing he encountered Carmine, who was heading down. The young man stopped with a jerk. His coarse, weather-beaten face paled.

Temple's eyes narrowed. "You . . . could . . . have . . . killed . . . her." At each word he jabbed Carmine in the sternum with a crooked index finger.

Carmine's eyes filled. "I knew the minute she asked me, the instant the words came out of her mouth, I shouldn't do it. But she felt so strong others needed her bed. I couldn't say no. She's treated me like family."

Temple stepped forward—his face two inches from Carmine's. His voice was hard and low: "That's not a good enough reason."

"I'm sorry. There's nothing I'd like more than to take it back." The young man's chin and the corners of his mouth, with their sparse wisps of hair, trembled.

Temple froze. *Why . . . he's just a kid. He's not even shaving yet. Jesus. Why am I just seeing this now?* "Okay then," he said, his voice gruff.

Carmine's brows shot up. "That's it?"

"Don't get too excited." Temple continued up the stairs.

Etha started talking as soon as Temple walked through the door: "Viviane suggested I get someone to help with groceries and cooking. At least while the family is here. One of the hospital aides named Thelma is stopping by."

"Should have thought of that myself. I can't stay, but I wanted to know how you are feeling."

"I wish everyone would stop asking that."

Temple crossed the room and kissed her on the forehead. "Honey, we're worried about you. That's all."

"I don't like being pitied."

"I know you don't. It's not a permanent thing. Anything you need?"

"There is something. Get Ruthie-Jo's account books and files from the bedroom."

When Etha handed the hatchery letter to Temple he

gave a low whistle. "This is substantial. Could be a solid motive. Maybe Ruthie-Jo was killed for seeds she planted well before the train wreck. I'll get Ed on this quick."

After Temple returned to the office, Etha drifted off with the yarn and needles nesting in her lap. She was awakened by forceful knocking. Levering herself upright, she hobbled into the kitchen and opened the door. Thelma, with her round face and thick body, stood in the hallway.

Etha ushered the young woman in and offered her something to drink—remembering how hard it had been to get a simple cup of coffee from Thelma in the hospital.

"Hot tea would suit."

Etha filled the kettle. "It's hard for me to admit, but with this leg I need help around the house."

"How much?" Thelma pulled off her coat and knit cap. She was wearing her hospital uniform with the cuffs tight around the forearms. But something about her was different, Etha thought, and then realized it was the woman's hair. In the hospital, it had been smoothly combed and secured with a hairnet. Now it was a prickly nest of stiff strands.

"How much? . . . Oh, how much will I pay you?" Etha poured hot water into a cup and added the tea bag. "Dollar an hour?" She handed the cup to Thelma and brought over the sugar bowl.

Thelma spooned in three teaspoons. She stirred and slurped noisily. "All right. What needs doing?"

Etha pulled a paper from her apron pocket. "Here is a grocery list. I thought you could fill it tomorrow. What's your shift at the hospital?"

"Just breakfast." Thelma squinted at the paper, then

stuffed it in her uniform pocket, stood, and knocked back the remainder of the tea. "That it?"

The young woman was all business. Etha stuttered, "I, ah . . . So after you do the marketing I'd like you to clean the apartment. My niece and her husband and two boys are coming from Arkansas and—"

Thelma slapped a palm on the table. "I don't take care of kids."

Etha pulled back. "No. I wasn't thinking that you would. I need help cleaning and cooking the make-aheads."

"Just so we're clear on the kids. I did my share and then some with my brothers and sisters. Only six years of age myself and made to mother four shin-kickers."

Etha imagined her two great-nephews racing through the kitchen, bumping into an irate Thelma. "My niece's two are very well behaved," she lied before switching the subject. "How is your cooking?"

"Tolerable. Most of what we et at home was biscuits, sorghum, pork gravy. But I've picked up some education in the diet kitchen. I'm studying on the different meats and greens."

"Good for you," Etha said, yet her mind latched onto the dreary fare that Thelma had been raised on. *Poor man's food.* Etha figured that the woman's whole life had been hard. No one was immune from the Depression, Etha thought, but women seemed to be shouldering the worst of it.

CHAPTER TWENTY-TWO

By the time Claude motored back to Vermillion from Mooreland, the streets were jumping. Two days before Christmas, city and county folks crammed the sidewalks. Most only window-shopped, but some clutched wrapped parcels. In the small park across from the courthouse, a poster announced a Christmas Eve community program of carols and lighting of the county tree. *Maybe I'll take Beatrice to that*, he thought. Then for a drink.

At Mayo's Claude found Myra at the kitchen table. Crowding her head were dozens of tight wet curls anchored with bobby pins.

"Appreciate the loan of the car. Just add it to my bill."

She glanced at him with cold eyes. "I certainly will."

"Is Beatrice around?"

"She's working."

Claude was a practical man and knew there was no use trying to soften this hardened scab of a woman. Her back was up and that was that. He found Beatrice in the basement, feeding towels through the wringer washer, the handle squeaking at every turn.

"You ever get any time off?"

Lifting the hem of her apron to dry her hands, she said, "I do now."

Claude grinned. "That's the spirit, kid. Want to take a meander down the tracks? I'd like to show you the back end of the operation."

The late-afternoon sun glinted off the rails, rinsing the dried sumac and bluestems in tints of copper. Beatrice inhaled the fresh air—glad to be shut of the rooming house for an hour or two. Claude was describing the head markings on spikes.

"On this one here. See those marks engraved on the head?"

She bent close and their foreheads touched. "Those little scratches?"

"This one here with the *CU* indicates copper has been added to the steel. Then there's some, not this one, but others with symbols tell you where they were made."

"Like a secret code," Beatrice said with a smile.

They walked with their heads down, scouting for stray spikes. *He's intensely fascinated by all this.* Beatrice herself had never developed a deep enthusiasm. Did not know it was possible. Until now, her days had been long, dry streambeds of work and sleep and occasional outings—trips to the Jewel or a meal at the Maid-Rite. Church socials.

When the couple reached the train station, Claude proposed they sit on a bench facing the tracks. Although the air was cold, the sun warmed their faces.

"Want to hear about my biggest arrest?" Claude asked.

"Sure." Beatrice closed her eyes and listened, thinking he could tell her anything and she'd believe every word.

A jeweler, traveling with a sample case, had been

robbed of $35,000 worth of diamond pendants, watches, and sapphire rings, while he slept in the upper berth of a train traveling from Chicago to St. Louis. The theft was discovered when the train pulled into St. Louis and the jeweler was preparing to debark. He had washed up and was collecting his things from the berth. The sample case was under the pillow where he'd left it. He picked it up and all seemed as it should. But then he noticed a trickle of sand leaking from between the seams of the grip. When he snapped the catches open, the jewelry was gone. It had been replaced with sandbags. Claude had been working out of the St. Louis terminal at the time. "We turned that train inside out. Questioned the jeweler and other passengers in the sleeper. Grilled the porter. Nothing."

"Did you ever find the robber?"

Claude tapped the side of his head. "You betcha." He removed a cigar from his pocket and lit up. "After the poor little jeweler returned to Chicago, I got to thinking that maybe the answer lay up in the Windy City. So I took a trip. Found the jeweler. I asked him about the evening he got on the train. Did he leave from the shop or from home? Who knew he was going? That sort of thing. Turns out his wife and a nephew who worked in the store were the only ones who knew about his sales trip. His nephew had packed the sample case under the jeweler's direction. The jeweler had checked it over and then slipped his coat on, picked up the case, and headed for the train. When he boarded, he slipped the case under his pillow and didn't leave his berth all night.

"This is when I knew something didn't smell right. I asked if he was certain he had checked the case, put on his coat, and left immediately for the train. 'Absolutely,' he told me and then paused. He then remembered the phone in the back room had rung just as he was leaving. The nephew answered it and called out to his uncle, 'It's for you.' The jeweler took the call. It was someone with a question about watch repair. The jeweler remembered being irritated that the nephew didn't answer the question himself. But he shrugged it off and headed back to the front room, picked up the sample case, and walked to the station. I think you know where this is going."

Beatrice had been gazing across the tracks, listening with her chin propped on one fist. She turned. "The nephew?"

Claude cocked his finger at her. "You got it. After being grilled he confessed that he'd set up the phone call and used the time to swap the contents of the sample case. Very satisfying investigation."

"Why you're a regular Sherlock . . ." The remainder of her words were consumed by a passing freight.

She had taken the train to Oklahoma City five years back. At first, staring out the window, she'd watched the same level plains rolling by and felt disappointed. Nothing had changed. But then, the terrain must have begun an undulation so infinitesimal that Beatrice hadn't detected it from her seat by the window. When the ruddy Sandstone Hills rose up near Oklahoma City, she was caught unawares. The vista, as flat as an ironing board, had vanished as if in an instant.

She had lived her whole life expecting nothing but the same flat expanse from one hour to the next. But in the last few days, spending time with Claude, she sensed a change in the landscape.

After the train passed, Claude switched his cigar from

the left to the right side of his mouth. "As you're from here, I'd like to ask you something. Say someone was living near the depot. Not necessarily right beside the rails, but close. And this person doesn't have much money. Where might he hole up?"

"That's pretty specific," Beatrice laughed. "There are a couple of families that take lodgers in for extra money."

Claude brooded on his cigar. "Possibility. Where else?"

"I've heard the pool hall rents out a few of its back rooms."

"Appreciate the tip." Claude checked his watch. "Guess it's time for me to get on the stick. Let's get you back before Myra calls the sheriff on me."

They stood. He gallantly offered his elbow and, smiling, she took it.

That evening, Temple cooked up scrambled eggs, sausage, and toast for himself and Etha. Over the meal she filled him in on Thelma.

"I think it will work out, although she's rough around the edges," Etha said.

"I don't care if she's as uncivilized as an ancient barbarian. If she keeps you off your feet, I'm all for her."

The couple retired to the living room to listen to the radio. Within five minutes, Etha was asleep. Temple got her up and walked her to the bedroom, where he pulled off her shoes and hose. He peeked at her bandages. From this side of things the wound seemed to be healing. He covered her with a blanket.

Settling back into his armchair, Temple splayed another of Ruthie-Jo's account books across his knees.

Bell's Drug Store was printed across the center of the first page, along with the words *June 1 to December 30, 1935.*

Bell's Drugs on Vermillion's Main Street had been founded in 1900, not long after the city was incorporated. Two years back, when the Dust Bowl demonstrated it was here for the long haul, and the original owner had arthritis so bad he couldn't fill the pill bottles anymore, he sold the concern to Bill Donley. No one in town could figure why Donley would buy the place with shops closing left and right and folks moving out. But not only had he taken it on, he'd hired a pharmacist and added a soda fountain with a marble-topped counter and wooden stools.

Temple slowly turned the ledger's pages, studying the neatly written lists organized in columns. Inventories, items sold, items bought, store assets—the works. As far as he could tell, Donley was making a profit. His biggest seller was cigarettes—twenty to thirty packs a day, which seemed like a lot, but still . . . Temple didn't see anything that merited the somewhat secretive nature of Ruthie-Jo's handling of the ledgers. Why were they tucked away at her house instead of kept in the drugstore's back office? Not enough space?

Temple put the ledger aside. In the bedroom, he could tell by Etha's breathing that she was sleeping deeply. Amen to that. He retrieved his notepad from his suit pocket and returned to his chair. Made a note: *Fuller Hatchery, Bell's.* Both would need a visit.

There was a tentative knock on the door. Temple rushed to answer it, hoping the noise hadn't woken Etha. He frowned when he saw Carmine on the doorstep.

"Sorry to stop by this late—no one would give me a

ride to town for love or money. Anyway, I saw something today I thought you ought to know about."

Temple ushered him inside. "Okay. What?"

"This afternoon, I was clearing an irrigation ditch and spotted two men slinking into a nearby ravine. They were lugging heavy sacks that could have been sugar. I was thinking they might be working a whiskey still."

"Go on," Temple said levelly.

"I could, you know, scout it out if you wanted. I mean, I'll be desilting that ditch all week."

Trying to prove himself.

"What do you think?" Carmine asked.

When he was a kid, Temple had the same urge to earn an older man's trust. He had been eleven when a mighty flood had swept through his hometown deep in the Allegheny Mountains of Pennsylvania. Only hours after a sixty-foot wall of water thundered into Johnstown, volunteers were organizing a search for survivors. Temple's father immediately signed up. And, over his father's protests, Temple had too.

As this passed through his mind, Temple made a decision. "You'll need to clear this with Commander Baker."

"I already did—just in case you gave me the green light," Carmine said eagerly.

"Okay, kid, then show me what you're made of. But only observe from a distance. Don't engage with these fellows in any way. I'm serious about that. And call me daily with a report. Got it?"

"Yes sir. Thanks for this chance."

As Temple closed the door he hoped he had done the right thing.

Back in the living room, he resettled himself. His

thoughts turned to Vadie and Everett's visit. It had been in the works since Thanksgiving, when Etha had begged her niece to drive to Vermillion. Etha had been convinced that a Christmas get-together would lift the struggling family's spirits.

Families made you do funny things. Setting out cookies, hiding presents . . . and putting up with cussing and loutish behavior not tolerated in anyone else. Temple wondered about Ruthie-Jo's family. Cy said his wife had only a few kin left in Tennessee but there was no communication between them. Could Ruthie-Jo's murder be rooted in events that far away? It was not unheard of, but someone would have to be awfully angry to hold a grudge this long and travel so far to do the deed. He might need to push Cy harder on what had created the distance between his wife and her family. He didn't relish that thought.

Temple grabbed his notebook and added *Talk to Cy about RJ family* to the list. And what about those slips of paper in the spice box? Temple wanted to put off asking his friends and neighbors if indeed they were gamblers, adulterers, or spendthrifts for as long as possible. He'd question the suspects gleaned from Ruthie-Jo's account books first and hope he got lucky. Temple shoved the ledgers to one side, turned off all the lights, and lowered his lids.

The telephone woke him an hour later.

"He wants the money tonight! I don't have it. Jesus Christ. This thug is going to beat me to a pulp. He said so. Those were his exact words." Chester was frantic.

Temple said, "Calm down."

"Calm down? Are you . . ." Chester's voice was interrupted by a barking dog. "Shut up, will you?"

"You have a dog?"

"No. No! Some damn stray showed up. My God, my life is in shambles. This dog and now—"

"Where and when are you meeting the caller?"

"What?"

The only other time Temple had heard Chester this rattled was when he'd come upon the dead body of the rainmaker under a drift of soil and sand whipped up by a huge duster. Temple repeated his question.

"The loading dock behind the post office. Twenty minutes."

Temple checked his watch. "I'm heading over there right now. I'll lay low and catch him trying to shake you down."

"I don't know if I can do this." Chester's voice was strung tight.

"I'll be there. Remember that."

Temple leaned through the bedroom doorway. Etha was sleeping soundly. He slipped on his coat, grabbed his pistol from the kitchen pantry, and trotted downstairs and into the night. The post office was a half a block away. No one was out. The storefronts and houses were dark—buttoned up for the night. There was a scent of woodsmoke. Temple rounded the post office. The sky was cold and cloudy. Thick darkness swathed the loading dock. The grain elevator and its outbuildings sprawled directly beyond the post office. Temple slipped into a small toolshed. He left the door ajar and was provided with a clear view of the dock. He couldn't make out the time on his watch. He pulled out his pistol—the grip was cold. Temple himself was chilled to the bone. *Come on, Chester. Let's get this done so I can get a decent night's sleep.*

Minutes passed. No sounds except the creak of a rusty belt conveyor swaying in the wind. Then the barking of a dog, not far away, broke the quiet. Yapping dogs, rumbling trains, crying infants—all standard nighttime refrains. But these yowls were urgent and were coming from the direction of the Jewel. *Chester's stray!* Temple bolted from his hiding place and hurried to the theater. The marquee cast a deep shadow. Yelps issued from the passageway running alongside the theater. Temple loped down the alley. In the dim light he could just make out a crumpled figure slumped against the exit door. The stray, standing to one side, growled at him.

Temple recognized the dog immediately. "It's okay, Daddy. Settle down." He knelt beside the huddled form. Chester's right eye was swollen shut. "You okay?"

Chester moaned.

Temple gently squeezed the man's arms, ribs, and legs. Nothing broken. No blood matted the back of his head. After a few moments Chester got himself seated fully upright and tenderly touched the closed lid.

"What happened?" Temple asked.

Chester exhaled heavily. He had gathered what cash he had on hand—thirty-four dollars—and left for the post office through the side exit. The minute he walked outside, someone stepped toward him. The crook demanded money. Chester admitted he only had less than half of the seventy-five dollars. The man slugged him in the face so hard the theater owner's head was thrown backward into the doorframe and he had slumped to the pavement.

"I felt the man's hands searching my coat pockets and removing the bills."

Temple studied a stack of four cardboard boxes

shoved against the theater's outer wall. There seemed no reason for the thug to deliver the goods when clearly he'd be able to muscle money from the blind theater owner without dressing it up as a sale.

"Let's get you inside. Did you recognize anything about this guy? Smell? Voice?" Temple slipped an arm around Chester and got him on his feet.

"I'm too rattled to think straight right now."

"Give it some time," Temple said, and then whistled. "Come on, Daddy."

Chester frowned as he stumbled inside. "What?"

"The stray. It's Ruthie-Jo's dog. He's been missing since she was murdered."

Chester halted. "Oh my God. I had no idea."

"Let's get you upstairs."

In the kitchen, Temple applied a wet cloth to Chester's eye and fed Daddy.

As Chester climbed into bed, he said, "You know, I remember the voice now. I'm fairly certain it was Bill Donley."

Temple raised his brows. "You sure?"

"Yes." Chester flopped back on the pillows.

"I'll be damned."

CHAPTER TWENTY-THREE

EVEN THOUGH HE WAS EXHAUSTED from the events of the night, Temple slept fitfully and woke too early. Beside him, Etha was awake too.

"You were up late," she said.

Normally he would have told Etha everything about Chester—the threats and mugging and the huge shiner on a blind man, which seemed particularly awful. But now she was fragile in his eyes—still recovering. Examining his wife's pale face, he didn't want to risk upsetting her. "I couldn't sleep so walked around town for an hour or two."

"That sounds fishy. You don't need to coddle me, you know. I'm not an invalid. Were you out on a call?"

"No. I really was just walking."

Downstairs, Temple found Ed standing at the file cabinet with an open folder in his hands.

"I wanted to read your report on the foreclosure auction on the Fuller farm in August," the deputy said. "Seems like Jess Fuller was blaming you and the banker for it in equal measure until the other farmers hijacked the affair by refusing to bid."

"Hard to hold that against him. His whole livelihood was on the block and then his wife took the kids and left anyway."

Ed crammed the file back in the cabinet. "Got a chip on his shoulder."

"Keep that in mind—I want you to drive out to talk to him about those collection letters today. In a lot of situations, a lawman needs tact more than a gun. Use it when you get to the hatchery. Now, let me fill you in on what happened to Chester last night."

After Temple finished, Ed frowned. "Do you think Donley nicked a shipment of cigarettes and was trying to offload some? Or was he only a middleman passing off stolen goods?"

"Good question. Before Chester called me last night I was studying Ruthie-Jo's ledger for Bell's Drugs and noticed that their sales in cigarettes jumped big-time in the last couple of months. Maybe Bill took some thieves up on an offer to sell stolen merchandise and then, for some reason, tried to muscle Chester into the action."

Ed emitted a low whistle.

"One more thing. Carmine DiNapoli's going to be our eyes and ears on that still operation. His crew is working in the area and so shouldn't arouse the moonshiners' suspicions."

"You're going to let him take that on? He's just a kid."

"I have my reservations but I decided to give him a chance," Temple said. "Took you on ten months back when you were fresh out of the CCC, didn't I? Let's see what he does with this."

Ed stayed silent, then pulled on his coat, palmed his hat, and left for the hatchery.

Temple dialed up Ned Harris, sheriff in the adjoining county.

Ned said, "How you holding up? Train wreck and a murder. Tough going." He was an old-timer who'd begun his career as a city marshal in Guthrie, before Oklahoma became a state. Temple often called on Ned for advice and to chew the fat.

"Got a couple more items to add on. One I wanted to ask you about. Anything happening out your way with the selling of stolen goods? Specifically cigarettes?"

"Yes indeedy. A wholesale grocery outfit was robbed a month ago. That raised the fur on the back of my neck, and after a bit of digging around I found out that, sure enough, a local market was selling cigarettes at below cost. I broke the grocer down and arrested him for receiving stolen property. Your man's likely part of the same ring."

"Right with you, Sheriff," Bill Donley called out from the cash register.

Temple swung his leg over a wooden stool at the soda fountain and readied Ruthie-Jo's account book on the counter.

Donley punched the cash register's keys and turned the crank. A bell rang and the drawer flew open. Two teenage girls, the only other customers, paid up and sauntered out. That left Donley, Temple, and Tim Ryan, the pharmacist in the back.

"What can I get you? On the house. Ice cream soda? Don't that sound good?" Donley's dulcet tones undulated in the direction of a huckster . . . or even a con man.

"A soda with cola syrup might hit the spot. But I'm paying."

Donley chuckled. "You're a straight arrow for sure."

The owner of Bell's was a tall, lumpy guy with a profile straight out of the Sunday funnies. He had a stiff tuft of hair on top of his head and a big schnoz that gave the impression of a friendly lug. But immediately after buying out Old Man Bell he'd installed the soda fountain and filled the shelves with an array of faddish merchandise. Shower caps, eyelash curlers, a twirling rack of comic books, boxed chocolates, stationery. A go-getter in a hurry.

He pulled the tap, filling a glass with carbonated water, added a squirt of syrup, stirred, and slid the works over to Temple. Then, leaning on folded arms, he asked, "What's cooking?"

"Ed and I are knee-deep in Ruthie-Jo Mitchem's murder." Temple took a swig from the tall glass.

"Geez, what a shame that is." Donley shook his head.

"That's why I stopped by. You knew her, right?"

"By name only. She never stepped foot in here. You know how she was."

Temple slid the ledger toward Donley. Tapped the cover. "But she kept books for you, right? So I'm thinking you might have known her better than you're saying."

"Guess I should have mentioned that. She helped out some. She didn't want it broadcast that she was working under the table. No big deal. But I do have something cooking that *is* a big deal. Give me a minute."

Donley rushed off before Temple could respond, then returned with a rolled-up blueprint. "This is confidential, but I have plans to buy another pharmacy over in Wayne. Walter Darnell at the bank has given me the verbal go-ahead. He's seen what I've done here. The place in Wayne has more square footage. I can put in booths." He unfurled the plans on top of the open ledger. "Now see here, this is where the booths—"

Temple laid his palm across the proposal. "I'm not here to talk about booths or display counters. I'm questioning you about a murder. Tell me how you came to hire Ruthie-Jo."

"To be honest, she called me not long after I bought the place. This was my first time owning a business and I was feeling that I'd bit off more than I could chew. She offered bookkeeping services. That's all. I don't know a thing about her private life."

"Where were you last Friday night?"

The bell jingled over the door. Donley paled when Chester stepped in, asking for an ice bag. "Far right aisle, top shelf," Donley called out.

When Chester returned to the front counter, he removed his dark glasses. A blue-black shiner glared from the sightless eye. He said, "You know, I've had an unsettling phone call and the voice on the other end sounded like yours. Was it you?"

Temple scrutinized Donley's mug. A scowl momentarily passed over it before an outraged expression appeared. "What? No!"

"Sorry. My mistake," Chester said, then strolled out.

Turning back to Temple with a falsely jovial expression, Donley said, "Don't know what that was all about." He rotated an index finger beside his ear. "Anyway. Nice chatting but I've got some inventory to—"

"We're not quite done here." Temple tossed back the remnants of the soda. "I was asking for your whereabouts on Friday night."

"You're making me mighty uncomfortable, Sheriff. If you are thinking—"

"Where were you?" Temple pulled out his notebook.

"Okay. Well, took my wife to dinner at the Crystal Hotel. It was our anniversary. Eight years. Then home. Paid the sitter and put the kids to bed. Listened to the radio. Then we called it a night." Donley tapped the marble counter hard with his index finger. "God's honest truth."

"Mrs. Donley will vouch?"

"Of course."

"I'll check on that. Meanwhile, I am curious why Mrs. Mitchem stored your account books at her place."

"Well, uh, that was just her way. Like I said, this is my first business and it sounded—"

Temple held up his palm, removed a cigarette pack and matches from his pocket, and drew out a smoke. "I took the time to scrutinize this ledger. Seems like all of a sudden you're selling lots more cigarettes. Camels in particular." He gestured toward the tobacco counter adjacent to the soda fountain, then struck the matchbox and lit up.

Donley wiped his palms down his thick torso. "You know how it goes. Sometimes a certain brand becomes all the rage."

"Sheriff Harris over in Woodward County says a large quantity of cigarettes was stolen from a wholesale house a month ago."

"What? You're accusing me of robbing a . . . what? A wholesale place? That's—"

"No. But maybe you bought some of that stolen property at a lower-than-market price." Temple took a drag and the smoke twisted silently toward the ceiling.

"Maybe the reason Mrs. Mitchem had your account books stored at her place is because you're keeping a second set here. A set she doctored—falsifying the price you paid for the cigarettes. I'd like to see those books."

Donley opened his mouth but no blandishments rolled out. He stomped toward the back of the store and returned with a ledger. Temple began comparing it with Ruthie-Jo's.

"Doesn't look good," the sheriff said. "And in case you didn't figure it out, Mr. Benton just identified you as the person who put the squeeze on him to come up with seventy-five dollars and then mugged him outside the theater."

Donley pressed a handkerchief into the corners of his eyes. When he looked up again he was bawling. "I don't know what I was thinking. I got wrapped up in the idea of a second store and the cigarettes seemed a way to help pay for it. Then the carpenter at the new place wanted to be paid up front and that's when I tried to get Chester involved. I'll make good. I promise. On my word. My wife can't know about this, though. It would kill her."

Temple stood and snapped a dime on the counter for the soda pop. "Mr. Donley, I'm taking you over to the courthouse for questioning. Get Tim to mind the store."

At the sheriff's office, Temple asked Donley if he wanted a lawyer present. The merchant shook his head. Temple took his time checking the phone messages Viviane had left on his desk. *Let the man stew.*

Finally he settled in across from Donley and offered him a cigarette from his pack.

Donley shook his head. "Don't smoke."

"Now that's sort of ironic. Anyway, tell me how you came to obtain the stolen property."

"It was a slow night back in November. These two fellas come in with hats pulled low."

"Recognize either one?"

"Never saw them before."

Temple, who was taking notes, glanced up. "Guns?"

"Didn't see any but they acted like they had them."

"Then what?"

"I was at the soda fountain. They sat down on stools like they were going to order something. One pulled out a pack of Camels. Said he had a proposal I wouldn't want to turn down. That he and his buddy had happened upon a load of cigarettes that weren't spoken for. That's the words he used, 'weren't spoken for.' They offered them to me at a huge markdown. For a small outlay, I'd be able to cash in big-time. All the while he talked, the fella kept tapping on the pack in front of him."

"Did he say why he'd come to you?"

Donley laughed grimly. "Yeah. Heard I was an up-and-coming businessman who might be in need of extra cash for a second commercial project."

"How'd he know about that?"

"No idea."

Temple understood how word got around among the scattered towns of the panhandle. Likely someone in Wayne had sniffed out Donley's plan to buy the pharmacy. "Go on."

Donley told Temple that he'd agreed to the arrangement right on the spot. The talker had motioned to his partner to bring in the goods. The merchant had taken the last of the cash he'd set aside for the Wayne operation

and handed it over. "I figured I could double my invest-
ment by pocketing the difference between what I paid
and what I sold them for." He paused. "I can't believe I
got mixed up in this. Jesus!" He dropped his head into
his palms.

"And Chester?"

Donley pounded his fist against his forehead. "Stupid,
stupid. I never wanted to hurt him. Just thought I could get
seventy-five bucks to keep the Wayne project alive. Then
he shows up with thirty-four bucks. How pathetic is that?"

The Depression seemed to bring out the worst in
men—cases of fistfights, petty theft, and public drunken-
ness in the county had all risen in the past several years
as families struggled to hold on to their property and
feed their children. But there were also men who were
now looking for easy ways to make an extra buck by
going against the law, when ten years back that would
have been the furthest things from their minds. The hard
times were corroding people's scruples. Folks started
taking chances they never would have normally. When
Temple and Hinchie had their twice-weekly confabs at
the Idle Hour, Temple had witnessed a fair number of
church folk come in—not necessarily to drink but to play
the punchboard. They'd put down a dime and eagerly
take up a stylus to push a tightly rolled paper out of the
covered board. Most of the papers were blank but some
were printed with prizes of five or ten dollars. Temple had
even seen a couple of ministers indulging in what many
considered gambling.

Temple felt a brief pang of sympathy for this fellow,
but there was no ignoring the man's lawbreaking. "Bill
Donley I'm arresting you for receiving stolen property,

attempted extortion, and assault. While I fill out the paperwork, you can stretch out on a bunk in the jail and think about where you went wrong and how you're going to explain this to your wife. And who you can get to represent you."

As Ed was driving out of town he considered how best to interview the fractious hatchery owner who had no love for the sheriff's office. Pulling up to the farm, Ed noted the new tin sign reading *Live Chicks!! Fuller's Hatchery* in red letters. He spotted Jess's battered truck parked in the corner of the farmyard and pulled alongside it. He climbed out, calling Jess's name. All was quiet.

The house, barn, and corn crib gave off the musty smell of vacancy. No lights, no woodsmoke, no bellowing heifers. Ed marched to the house and knocked. Nothing. He entered the barn, calling out, "Hello there!" Two feral cats glowered from atop a beam.

The silence began to prey on Ed. Since he'd come on as deputy less than a year before, there had been three suicides by farmers in the county. All due to money troubles and the family upheavals that came with them. Next to the barn, behind the corn crib, were low-roofed buildings built of new pine. Ed figured this was the hatchery operation. The door at one end stood ajar so he stepped inside. The shed smelled of dust and feathers. Hens milled in an open area, clucking and commenting as they picked at the dirt floor speckled with their own droppings. One pecked at Ed's shoestring until he toed her away. In wooden nesting boxes built against one long wall, a dozen or so hens turned their heads to train their button eyes on him.

Ed noticed splashes of water leading to a galvanized watering trough. Jess must be around. He'd watered the hens. At the opposite end of the shed was a low door, partially closed. Ed waded through the clucking poultry and into the adjacent room.

"Stay right where you are." Jess stood to the right of the doorway, a shotgun pointed at the deputy's forehead. "You're trespassing, you dirty son of a bitch."

Ed opened his mouth.

"Don't say nothing."

Ed stared steadily at the farmer despite his quaking innards. Above Jess's shoulder was a wide pen, alive with a carpet of yellow chicks jostling around a small coal stove, their tiny beaks opening and closing in urgent, incessant peeps.

"You got a warrant? Just nod yes or no."

Ed shook his head.

Jess laughed. "Thought not. You lawmen can't stand it to see someone get ahead, can you? Someone who had to pick themselves up from nothing, thanks to your kind, and start a new enterprise." He lowered the shotgun. "If the sheriff had his way, this whole place would have been auctioned off and then—"

"You know it wasn't the sheriff's choice. Just doing his duty."

"You're going to tell me it was the bank. The bank. The bank. Yeah, but the banker wouldn't have even considered holding the auction without knowing the sheriff would be there with a shotgun."

Ed was aware his hands were shaking. He balled them into fists. "You know that isn't so. No one could be sorrier—"

"Hah." Jess spit in the dust. The peeping of the chicks got louder, a cacophony of high-pitched notes— overlapping, crawling on top of one another, crowding the air of the low-ceilinged outbuilding. "No one could be sorrier? That my wife left? Took my son? That this farm we poured sweat into is slowly falling apart? *I* am. I'm sorrier!" Jess yanked the shotgun back up so that the muzzle's eye pointed directly at the deputy.

Ed slowly lifted his hands. Sweat rivered down his spine. "I'm gonna take a step backward. And then another. Then another."

Jess laughed again. "You do that. You drive back to town and tell Temple what I said. No one's going to trespass on my property anymore. Ever again. Tell him that for me."

Ed nodded and inched his right foot back. Then his left. He stared steadily at the muzzle, at Jess's finger hooked in the trigger. The peeping of the chicks crashed against his eardrums. Jess said something. His mouth opened and closed but Ed couldn't hear anything except the relentless chirping. As he slowly shuffled backward, Jess followed. Light from a window skimmed the gun barrel. Now they were passing through the first section of the hatchery. Ed shoved the feathered bodies aside as he crept backward. The urge to turn, sprint into the barnyard, and dive into his car was almost overwhelming. He willed his limbs to slow. An unconscious flick of Jess's eyes told Ed he was nearing the outside door.

"When I get outside, I'm going to turn and cross the yard and drive away."

"You're banking I'm not a man to shoot someone in the back."

"I know you're not."

"You don't know nothing about me."

Ed's backside jounced into the door. Every limb in his body shook. He slowly turned and stepped outside. He was a dozen feet away from the sedan. Ed exhaled unevenly and forced himself forward. A door slammed. Had Jess gone back inside? Or was the farmer only a couple of feet behind? Ed couldn't chance finding out. Thinking of Viviane. The baby on the way. What if Jess was, at this moment, sighting up to send a slug ripping through his back? Then what would happen to Viviane? Their child? *God, get me out of here.*

He gained the car and climbed inside with painful slowness. When at last he looked up, the barnyard was empty. His hands shook so bad he could barely turn over the ignition. The inside of the car was still warm. Had it been, what, only ten minutes since he'd driven up the lane?

He motored a mile, made sure he was out of site of the farm, and parked beside a wire fence. Once, when he'd been on the road, an ancient tramp had pulled a knife on him. Ed was younger and stronger and could easily overpower the vagrant. He'd known he could take the tramp down. Yet he'd run. The fear had funneled straight to his legs. Now, he dropped his head on the steering wheel and sobbed. *What the hell am I doing? I'm not cut out for this. What made me think I could be a lawman?*

After a time he collected himself. Right now this was the job he had and he'd have to live with it. He drove back to town and when he turned into the courthouse lot, he spotted Temple sitting on the back step smoking a cigarette.

"You look like hell," the sheriff said.

"Thanks," muttered Ed.

"How'd it go at the hatchery?"

"Can we talk inside?"

The lawmen entered the office. Ed dropped into his desk chair with a thud.

"So?"

"Jess pulled a shotgun on me."

"You on the up-and-up?"

Ed flopped back, finger-combing his hair. "Said I was trespassing. Asked if I had a warrant."

"A warrant?" Temple guffawed.

"I didn't even get a chance to explain why I was there. He was going on about how we—well, you—were the reason his wife left with the kids, the farm went bust."

"Criminently!" Temple said. "He can't let that go. And it's not even true. We'll go back out there together and if he won't cooperate, we'll bring him here for questioning. That letter Ruthie-Jo sent him was nothing less than gasoline to a man like Jess who believes he has been wronged and is looking for a fight. I'll get a warrant so we can search the premises if needed."

"Right now?" Ed's voice wavered.

"We'll give him a day to cool off."

Ed lit a cigarette with shaking fingers.

Temple asked, "You okay?"

After a deep draw, Ed said, "Couple of times I thought Jess was going to pull the trigger. He was wild. All I could think about was dying on a dirt floor in a chicken house. And Viviane. That we wouldn't even have one Christmas together."

Temple walked over and laid a hand on the deputy's

shoulder. "I've faced down more of those types of situations than I care to remember, but look, I'm still kicking. Part of being a lawman."

"I sort of knew that, but it hit me square in the face today. I hope I'm up to it."

"No question in my mind," Temple said, turning to his paperwork.

Ed smoked his cigarette. Paced around the office and then smoked another.

Temple sighed and handed him two envelopes. "How about you deliver these summonses? Work the kinks out of your joints?"

Up in the apartment, Thelma had not yet arrived and Vadie and family were, presumably, motoring westward. Etha settled in on the davenport with a manila folder from Ruthie-Jo's papers. None of its contents were labeled in any way to suggest the client's name or business. Ruthie-Jo's tightly formed script covered both sides of a hundred or so pages, arranged chronologically with the most recent on top. Thumbing through, Etha grasped that the file tracked an ongoing bookkeeping project dating back six years. Most of the pages simply listed tasks completed, with check marks alongside. *Material inventory. Monthly repair report. Inventory of tools and supplies.*

"Bingo," Etha murmured when her eyes fell on an entry labeled *Weekly track crew payroll*. Ruthie-Jo was keeping books for the railroad. But it all seemed secretive— the notes did not name who exactly at the AT&SF she was working for, or any other specifics.

Etha turned back to the last completed page. It was dated the day someone strangled the life out of the reclusive bookkeeper. Rather than a report of tasks completed or materials inventoried, this entry was merely a payroll statement. And in the margin, Ruthie-Jo had written, *Discrepancy in figures. Purposeful?* Two lines down she had answered her own question: *Yes.* What had occurred in the empty space between those lines? Had Ruthie-Jo confronted the client with her suspicions and gotten an answer? Had that same client waited in the dark to put a stop to her questioning? What could be heinous enough in those bland inventories and payroll lists to merit murder? More items for Temple to chew on.

Etha never imagined that Ruthie-Jo would have amassed such a heap of secrets. Not long back, the *Gazetteer* had run a piece about a woman in Arkansas who'd gotten a blackmail letter. The sender had claimed that he had plenty of stuff on this woman and her boyfriend, who was the type of street-corner gigolo known as a "drugstore cowboy." The writer threatened to share the information with the woman's husband if she didn't supply five hundred dollars in hush money. The Arkansas matron had immediately contacted the police, who had her set up a false drop-off and arrested the extortionist—a dry goods owner. Now it seemed Ruthie-Jo might have been up to something similar.

At best, Etha had encountered the woman maybe half a dozen times, and each time she'd been reminded of the stern face of the angel Gabriel depicted on a colored plate in her Bible. Tight jaw. Grim eyes.

Having gone as far as she could for the day with Ruthie-Jo's accounting papers, Etha pushed herself to wrap her small collection of Christmas presents, although her bed beckoned. She was covering tubes of shaving cream with the funny papers when there was a knock on the door. Etha took in the kitchen clock. Thelma was a half hour late.

"Door's open," Etha called.

Thelma strode in, her usually pale cheeks flushed from the cold. "Afternoon," she said, hanging her coat and hat on a hook and dropping an apron over her head. Etha was relieved to see that Thelma had covered her frizzy hair with a net. Etha didn't want stray strands falling into the food.

"I'd like you to start with the pies. There are jars of stewed apples and peaches in the cupboard over the icebox." Etha smiled tightly. She was uncomfortable giving orders, and judging by the stiff expression on Thelma's face, the young woman resented taking them. "But first, would you like a sandwich?"

"I already et."

This was going to be a slow go. "You're from Tennessee?"

Thelma's sturdy forearms swelled as she prepared dough for the pie crusts. "Yes'um." She smacked the ball of dough. "When I was thirteen, I packed up and got as far from the hills as I could. Came from nothing and didn't want to die that way."

Etha was taping Vadie's gift when the paper ripped. "Damnit."

Thelma turned, smiling slightly.

Reddening, Etha laughed, "Caught!" She pushed the present aside and rested her head on her hand. "I don't know if I'm ready for all the company that'll be stepping through the door in a couple of hours."

"In my opinion, families are nothing but trouble.

Especially if the man is weak. If the man is weak, if he ain't providing, ain't using the smarts God gave him, then there's a problem."

"You married?"

"Me? No!"

"Boyfriend?"

"More or less."

Dorothy Dix's advice column, which ran Thursdays in the *Gazetteer*, was filled with teary pleas from young women whose husbands or boyfriends cheated on them, stole their nest eggs, or abruptly left town on a passing freight. Etha had noticed more of these letters were showing up in Mrs. Dix's column as the soup lines lengthened and the drought bore down.

She pulled on her lower lip, thinking of Vadie, wondering if Thelma was in the same boat. "I hope he treats you right."

"He tries. I'll give him that. Maybe that's why I've stuck with him—even after a fight I always go back. No one else in my life has ever tried to do right by me. Not my pa or ma. Nobody. But he does." Gripping the rolling pin in both hands, Thelma muscled the ball of dough into a circle. "A good fella but not much in the brains department. I do the thinking for both of us." She tapped her head. "Horse sense. Which is funny since when we first met I was fourteen. He was pumping gas. Older guy. I thought he was real slick. Eleven years later and I know who's the slick one and it ain't him. But that's okay. I know he'd go to the wall for me and he knows I'd do it for him."

"You're only twenty-five?"

Thelma laid the rolling pin aside. "Always been grown

up. Ma needed me to take care of the young ones and, sometimes, her. Never was a child, I'd say."

"That's sad."

Thelma shrugged. "Way it was."

It was dusk when the young woman finished up the cooking, washed the pots and bowls, and made up the various cots and pallets to accommodate the family. From her purse hanging by the kitchen door, Etha removed three bills and handed them to Thelma. She started to say that she was glad they'd gotten to know each other better, but at that moment the stairwell echoed with the excited screech of children and Thelma's mouth tightened into the same rigid line Etha had seen on the hospital ward.

Thelma grabbed her coat and hat, escaping down the stairs as two kiddies sprinted up, running straight at Etha standing in the doorway.

Homer, ten, and Leland, eight, grabbed Etha around the legs. She grimaced. "I've got a boo-boo there. Be careful."

The two stepped back. Homer said, "Can we see?"

Etha laughed. "Maybe later. Where's your ma and pa?"

"Slow as molasses," Leland said, running to the head of the stairs and shouting, "Hurry up!"

"Maybe they need help. Homer. Go down and see if you can't carry something." Etha prodded his back.

"Ah, nuts."

"Go!"

The next to emerge from the stairwell was Vadie, lugging a suitcase bound with twine. "I thought we'd never make it," she announced, dropping the luggage on the floor and hugging her aunt.

Etha held her tight. "How was the drive?"

Vadie stepped back, fingering the bobby pins in her brown hair. "Had the usual couple of flats. Radiator overheated outside of Oklahoma City."

"You must be exhausted. Go right on in. Leave your suitcase in the dining room."

"Come on, Leland," Vadie said, grabbing his hand and shuffling into the apartment.

Breasting the top step was Everett—once slender and handsome, but now jowly with bags under his eyes. *For God's sake*, Etha thought, *he's only in his early thirties and he looks fifty if he's a day.* He smelled of cigarettes and unwashed armpits. He'd lost two teeth since Etha had last laid eyes on him.

"Auntie, ain't you a sight for sore eyes. Where should I put these suckers?" Everett lifted the two suitcases he was carrying. Homer trailed behind with a paper sack in his arms.

"Everything in the dining room for now." Etha shepherded them into the apartment. "Temple should be up directly."

"We seen him downstairs," Vadie said. "I sure could use a bath. Nary a paved road between here and Oklahoma City."

The two boys raced from the kitchen to the bedroom and back again. Vadie and Everett seated themselves on the living room couch beside the Christmas tree, which Carmine had set up the day before.

"Oo-ee, that is sure enough a pretty cedar!" Everett exclaimed. "See that, Vadie? She's got those shiny balls."

Vadie crossed her legs, pulling her skirt over her knees. "We used to have some of those kind, Ev. But they all smashed when you fell into the tree last year."

Everett turned to Etha, who was leaning heavily against the doorway. "I make it a point never to refute the wife. She's got a better memory than I'll ever have. If she says I knocked the tree down . . ." He shrugged, and then added, "I get a little rowdy sometimes."

"There's community caroling at the park across the street tonight," Etha said. "I thought we could take the boys. Santa may be making a surprise visit."

"That sounds swell," Vadie responded. "I hope he knows to come down your chimney tonight. Otherwise I'm afraid the boys' stockings will be mighty skimpy."

"I got a few things for them," Etha said.

"How about your old nephew? Got something for him? It is Christmas Eve, you know. God rest ye merry gentlemen." Everett stood, stretching his arms. "Mighty cramped from that long trip. I could use something to loosen up the joints."

"We don't have any booze, if that's what you're hinting at." Etha looked at him sharply.

Everett held up his hands. "No, no! 'Course not. I know this is a law-abiding household. But I do believe I'll take a quick walk around the block before dinner. Try to chase this charley horse out of the barn." He shook his right leg and then limped out through the kitchen.

Etha dropped into an armchair. "Why do I feel like a whirlwind just blew in?"

Several minutes later Temple appeared—kissing Vadie and hugging the boys. When Etha got dinner on the table, Everett had not yet returned.

"He'll turn up. He always does," Vadie declared.

Damn that man, Etha thought. *On Christmas Eve?*

Temple and Homer had two helpings of the creamed beef on toast. The first of the apple pies disappeared. Vadie stacked the dishes, shooing Etha away and dumping too much dish powder into the sink. From the park across the street, several horn players ran through their scales.

Etha checked the clock. "Boys, get your coats. It's almost time for the tree lighting."

Settled in his overstuffed chair in the living room, Temple lifted the *Gazetteer* in front of his face, mumbling, "Well, would you believe that?" when Etha stuck her head in the room.

"Put that paper away, mister. You're coming too."

By the time Temple escorted Etha down the stairs, the flying heels and bobbing caps of Leland and Homer had already disappeared into the crowd. Six high school kids, with trumpets pressed to their lips, tootled a shaky version of "Jingle Bells."

Stars quivered in the chill night sky. The sharp scent of woodsmoke mingled with the wooly lanolin of hats and mittens.

The mayor stepped out, said a few words, and gestured at the tree, which was plugged in by a high school musician to cheers from the crowd. In the twilight, the red, blue, and yellow bulbs blazed, defying the drought and the hard times.

The children were herded into a line to receive candy canes from a man with a cotton beard and a loose one-piece red suit with a black felt band around the middle for a belt.

"Can you see the boys?" Etha asked Temple.

He twisted for a better view. "Yeah. Middle of the line."

"Merry Christmas!" a voice bellowed from behind Temple. Grinning mightily, Claude stood with his elbow linked with Beatrice's and a cigar tucked in the corner of his mouth. "Good thing I caught you, Sheriff. Several things I need to run by you, if the ladies don't mind."

"Not at all," Etha said.

"What's the story?" Temple asked, stepping away, but keeping an eye on Etha. Beatrice squeezed in beside her on the bench.

"Still haven't tracked down that Lonnie. My next step is to check out if he's holed up in town."

"Could be. I'll put the word out."

"Appreciate it. What's going on with the murder investigation?"

Temple shook his head. "Got one lead with a fellow heavily in debt to the hardware store. Could be a motive. The more we uncover about Ruthie-Jo's bookkeeping activities, the more I think her murder is something she brought on herself instead of it being connected to the derailment." The sheriff cast his eyes across the kiddies lined up to talk to Santa, the high schoolers stowing their instruments, the older citizens stomping their feet in the cold. "Either way, let's keep one another posted on what's what."

"Sure thing. And Merry Christmas to you."

C HAPTER TWENTY-FOUR

ON CHRISTMAS MORNING Etha was jolted awake by the boys jumping on the bed.

"Stop that this minute," Temple snapped, roused from a deep sleep and sitting up. "Your great-aunt is on the mend."

Homer and Leland froze, then crept away with stricken faces. The younger boy whispered, "But Santa's been here."

Etha checked the clock: four a.m. Beyond the window was velvet darkness. "Boys, it is not yet morning. Go back to bed. There is a clock in the kitchen, Homer. Don't come back until the little hand is at six. You understand?"

"Yes'em. Come on, Leland." Their bare feet slapped down the hall.

Giggling quietly, Etha and Temple flopped back on the pillows.

"That caught me flatfooted," Temple said.

"Don't you remember? Jack did the same thing. He was up before the crack of dawn. Then every twenty minutes he'd be back and I'd stall him off. 'Put on your socks.' 'Brush your teeth.' 'Comb your hair.'"

"How long do you think we've got?"

"Twenty minutes."

They rolled to their respective sides of the bed.

As Etha limped into the kitchen to make coffee, she heard Temple announce, "Go at it, boys."

Homer and Leland tore into the wrapping, yipping with delight at the bags of cat's-eyes and shooters. Temple brought out two pairs of roller skates he'd hidden in the bedroom closet.

"Boy oh boy!" cried Homer. "These are swell!"

Vadie, handing a gift to Etha, said, "Say thank you, boys."

The morning's activity ended with a satisfyingly messy pile of crumpled funny papers and ribbons. Etha, wearing her new fur collar, retired to the kitchen. Vadie poured her aunt another cup of coffee. The boys flopped on their bellies in the hallway, shooting marbles.

Temple and Everett were alone in the living room.

"Vadie said you might get called back to the iron-works. Said that she convinced the super there that you've turned over a new leaf."

Everett stood. Shook out his legs. Bent backward with his hand gripping his lower spine. "Your dining room floor is mighty hard."

"You want a mattress from one of the cells?"

Everett waved him off. "Forget it."

"So, what's going on with the works?"

"Nothing. There is no way I'd go back. They pay chicken feed. Maybe eighteen bucks a week."

"Better than nothing. Together with Vadie's pay, I can't believe that wouldn't cover food and rent."

Everett lit a cigarette. "You might think I'm foolish,

but I'm a proud man. I'm not going to take pennies when I'm worth a whole lot more. I'm college-educated."

Temple said nothing. *Not getting anywhere with this.*

In the kitchen, Vadie stirred the pancake batter. From her seat at the table, Etha saw tears dribbling down her niece's cheeks.

"What's wrong, honey?"

Vadie dabbed at her face with a dish towel, abandoning the wooden spoon, which quickly sank into the batter.

"Did something happen?"

"No," she sniveled. "Nothing. That's just it. No steady job. No mind paid to the boys. Only thing I can count on is him drinking every night."

Etha patted the chair beside hers and Vadie sat down.

"Ever think of leaving? You and the boys can stay with us until you get on your feet."

Vadie shook her head.

"Even for the good of the children?"

"I can't. He needs me. I see those old tramps sleeping in doorways and think, *That could be Everett.* I can't let that happen." Vadie scoured her face with a dishtowel. "I don't know why I'm bawling like this. It's Christmas Day. And you gave me those lovely soaps and all." She inhaled shakily.

"Just so you know, if ever—" Etha's throat thickened.

"He's really a good man," Vadie said, returning to the stove.

CHAPTER TWENTY-FIVE

THE NEXT DAY, Jess Fuller was up early. Beyond his window, the sky turned from black to indigo. He knew they'd be coming. When the sun finally bubbled on the horizon, Jess shouldered his shotgun. He'd make a stand at the start of his lane where it met the main road. Leaving the house, he snatched a kitchen chair. Might as well be comfortable.

An hour later, Temple and Ed motored up the road to the hatchery. Temple spotted Jess and let up on the gas.

"He's expecting us."

Ed craned toward the windshield. "Got a gun across his knees."

"I'm going to pull up a couple of yards away. We'll step out. Everything nice and slow. I'll show him the warrant. Explain why we need to talk to him."

Ed reached back to grab the shotgun.

"Leave it."

Ed blanched.

"Jess is a good man. The times have warped him some but I'm betting the good is still there."

"Hope you know what you're doing."

"So do I." Temple inched the sedan forward, turned it off, and set the brake. They climbed out slowly.

Jess's features were granite. He stood with the gun loosely gripped in his hands. His hat was tipped back. His eyes met the sheriff's. "If I was you, I'd not get closer."

Temple held up his hands. "No intention. We're investigating the death of Ruthie-Jo Mitchem. Need to ask you a few questions."

Jess laughed sourly. "Find that hard to swallow. You can't stay away. Pecking at me about one thing or another. Stripped me of my family, tried to strip me of my farm, and—"

"You know that's not so. And I'm none too pleased that you greeted my deputy with a shotgun before even knowing what he wanted." Temple's voice rose: "Don't push your luck with me right now."

Jess's eyes reduced to slits but he kept silent.

"Let's move on to the topic at hand. I do have a warrant," Temple said, deliberately removing the paper from his pocket and showing it to Jess, "and we can go into town if you want to do this at the courthouse, but I see no need."

"Let's get this over with right now. I can't think what I have to do with Mrs. Mitchem's death, but—"

"My deputy here will take notes. So first, to be clear, you do know Mrs. Mitchem?"

Jess shrugged. "Seen her once or twice."

"You've had correspondence with her in connection with your overdue bills from the hardware store?"

"Starting up a hatchery, you gotta have certain pieces of equipment. The business is only now taking off. I've got orders from five farmers in the area. Cy knew I'd pay when I could."

Ed, who had been scribbling mightily, flipped a page.

Temple said, "That may be so, but it was clear his wife felt different. We found copies of the letters she sent you in her files. The last in particular was extremely direct. I happen to have it here." He withdrew the letter from an inner pocket of his coat. "Let me read this one bit." He put on his spectacles. "It says here, *I regret to inform you that unless I hear from you in two days' time we shall be forced to take other and more drastic—*"

"I know what it says."

"Do you recall that this letter was sent two days before she was murdered?"

Jess frowned. "No." He paused. "You're saying you suspect me of killing her? Because of that letter?"

"It is clearly a threat with a deadline attached," Temple said. "Where were you between ten p.m. Friday and six a.m. Saturday?"

Jess stepped toward the sheriff. "You're joking."

"Where were you?"

"At the Oke Doke until two a.m. Dorothy Schutte and I play there weekdays. At least a dozen folks at the place. Ask any of them. And Sam Flynn. He was tending bar."

"Take any breaks?"

"Once or twice to use the men's."

"Then you came home?"

Jess looked away. "Yes."

"Know anyone who can vouch for that?"

"I live here on my lonesome, thanks to you and the banker. So no. No one to vouch for me."

"Then I can't rule you out as a suspect just yet."

"What the hell!" Jess shouted. "I don't know a damn thing about the Mitchem woman. I barely remember what she looked like!"

Temple removed his hat, ran his fingers through his hair. "I understand that, but until—"

"All right! I spent the night with Dorothy at her place. Spend most nights there these days. But that's not for public consumption. On paper, I'm still married."

"That's all I needed to hear." Temple resettled the Stetson on his head. "We'll check this out with Sam and, discretely, with Dorothy, but you likely won't hear from us on this again."

Jess snorted, shouldered the shotgun, snatched the chair, and ambled back up his lane.

Ed shut the notebook and shoved it in his coat pocket. "That son of a bitch. Scared the living daylights out of me the other day. And for nothing! If he'd even let me say why I was—"

"That's the way it is sometimes. A possible suspect will clamp down before you even explain what you're after. We need to confirm Jess's alibi and then dig in on those other leads."

While Temple drove, Ed jotted a couple of notes for his guidebook project. He'd add another chapter about how to face down a man pointing a loaded shotgun at you. How to lower the temperature and talk some sense into him. Temple handled it first-rate. Take it slow. Show the man you're operating in good faith. Ed remembered Temple's voice. Calm and low. He made a note about that too.

When he was a kid, Claude had trailed his pops to the billiard parlor many a Saturday. Off-duty cops spent their afternoons sipping from steins with their names painted on them, lounging on the raised spectator chairs, razzing the players, telling dirty jokes, and filling up the spittoons with dark-brown juice.

Over the years, as Claude had traveled around with the company, staying a week or so in a strange town on an investigation, he'd gotten into the habit of stopping in the local pool hall. He never played. He just went for the atmosphere—to have a few beers, gab with the regulars.

Now Claude was mounting the steep stairs of Mick's Pool Hall, his shoes scuffing the decades-old layers of grit. At the top, he turned the knob on the frosted-glass door and lumbered inside.

The sharp click of pool balls brought a smile to his face. He inhaled the cigarette smoke and smell of stale beer. He took in the squeak of chalk against the tip of a cue and players calling out shots. *Ace in the side. Fifteen in corner. Three in the side.* The sweet rattle of a ball rolling down the chute.

Everything was as it should be on this day after Christmas. Six or so men shooting with another dozen occupying chairs. To the left, inside the cashier's cage, lounged the manager. Below the rolled shirtsleeve on his right arm, a tattoo of a hula girl posed wearily—as bored as he was. Claude settled his forearms on the shelf where money and tickets were exchanged.

Emanuel Stricker had managed the hall for eight years. The owner, a gentleman out of Oklahoma City, trusted him with the daily operations, to the point that Stricker hadn't set eyes on the proprietor since he had been hired.

Claude displayed his badge. "I'm investigating last week's derailment."

"Terrible," Stricker said.

"Tragic. I'm questioning folks running boarding-houses and such. Trying to get the lay of the land. Strangers in town—that sort of thing. Someone told me you sometimes let out rooms?"

Stricker cleared his throat. "I do. There are two in the back, and with times being what they are, I have let them out on occasion."

"What about now? Is this an occasion?"

"You could say that. The owner doesn't know I've got this setup. You know, helping folks out who need a place. So . . ."

"I'm not interested in squealing on you. Tell me about your lodgers."

"There's just the one. Came in about two weeks ago asking about a room. I don't know where he was staying before. Fellow by the name of Lonnie Taylor."

"That so?" Claude made a show of pulling out his notebook and jotting down Lonnie's name—as if hearing it for the first time. "Is there a woman living with him?"

"I don't let rooms to women."

"So Lonnie is by his lonesome?"

Stricker nodded. "What is all this about? Is Lonnie involved with the wreck?"

"Can't comment on that. Which way's his room?" Claude tucked the notepad in his pocket.

Stricker motioned to the back of the pool hall. "Through there. First door on the left."

Claude stomped through the door in the back, fingering the pistol holstered under his arm, then knocked.

The door swung open. Wiping his face with a wet wash rag, the occupant, a droop-eyed man in his thirties, said, "Yeah?"

"Lonnie Taylor?"

Lonnie squinted. "Who are you?"

Claude drew out his badge. "I'm doing some investigating for the AT&SF."

"I don't work for the railroad no more."

Over Lonnie's shoulder, Claude spotted a laundry line crisscrossing the narrow room with yellowed underdrawers, work shirts, and misshapen socks. There was a sour stink of boiled cabbage.

"Mind if I come in?" Claude stepped through the door. "Naturally, I've been questioning the track crew, and since you worked the rails here not long ago, I thought I'd swing by. Find out your general opinion about the wreck and such."

Lonnie shrugged and stepped back. "Make yourself at home."

Claude straddled a wooden chair. Lonnie sat on the narrow bed. The detective pulled out his notebook. "So, what's your general take on the derailment?"

"I don't know. Ain't that *your* job?"

"Right, but you're familiar with that stretch of track." Claude drew out a cigar, wet it in his mouth, and lit up. "What do you think? Were there regular problems there?"

"Not particularly. Maybe the train was going too fast on the approach. Or had bad brakes."

"Or problems with the switch stand?"

"Yeah, I guess. That too."

"Why'd you get the axe?"

Lonnie grimaced. "I was living a ways out in Mooreland at that time and sometimes I was late for work. The foreman closed his ears when I told him it weren't easy to find a cheap place nearby. So after a couple of times I got canned."

"Bet that riled you."

"He was hitting below the belt. Not like I was feath-erbedding. I did my hours and then some. When Milt handed me my walking papers, I told him off. Right to his face."

"You had words?"

"You bet. Told him he was lower than ditch water. Didn't know jack about how to handle a crew. I slammed my tools and keys down on the son of a bitch's desk, pardon me, and hoofed it to the Idle Hour. That's it. Sure I was hot at the time, but that's only natural."

"Rumor was you headed out west right after."

"I was gonna, but I got a job spreading gravel for the county so I stayed."

Claude studied the cigar smoke snaking around the undergarments. "The day of the wreck, where were you?"

Lonnie jumped up. "Hey! I had nothing to do with that."

"Doing my job. Asked the same to a load of fellas this week." Claude poised a pencil over the notebook. "So?"

According to Milt, the switch had been cocked between Daniel's 3:44 p.m. inspection and the derailment itself, at 7:34 p.m. A four-hour window.

Lonnie lit up a cigarette. "Worked a full day. Two of us were filling holes out on Liberty Pike. Clocked out at four, came back here and had a beer, and shot a couple rounds of pool."

Claude showily flipped the pages of his notebook. "Then what?"

"Then I came back here and boiled dogs for dinner."

"What time was that, would you say?"

Lonnie rubbed his chin. He looked like one of those

fellows who, by the end of the day, had heavy blue-black stubble covering the lower half of his face. "Guessing around five? Something like that. I washed up, ate, lay down. Listened to the radio."

Claude brightened. "Yeah? I do the same after a long day. What were you listening to?"

Lonnie hesitated. "Whatever was on."

The pencil wriggled across the detective's pad. "Continue."

More chin scratching. "Then I sort of drifted off until the explosion."

"What'd you think it was?"

"I knew what it was. A locomotive. Work around the railroad as long as I have, you just know. I hustled into my clothes and sprinted to the station. As soon as I got there and saw it was a passenger train, I knew it would be bad. I jumped right in to help."

"Must have been a nasty scene."

Lonnie's eyes fell on the wash line's wilted socks. "The screams were something terrible."

"Seared into your skull, I bet." The detective pushed on his knees and stood. "I'll be checking out your side of things with Milt and Stricker."

The laborer stood, began pacing around the small, windowless room. Something was clearly eating at this man. Claude decided to let it chip away at Lonnie overnight and come back the next day. Meanwhile, he would check with Milt to see if Lonnie did in fact turn in his key. Claude didn't yet have enough for an arrest, but he was making headway. "Don't go nowheres."

Lonnie had lit up another cigarette before the detective had his notepad tucked away.

On his way out, Claude pigeonholed Stricker. The man remembered Lonnie hanging around the pool room in the late afternoon on the day of the wreck. But the manager wasn't so certain about when Lonnie retired to his room. Claude questioned him about a back way out of the pool hall. The manager said there wasn't one. The frosted door at the top of the stairs was the only way in or out.

Chester hurried along toward Mitchem's Hardware. He had an early evening show to set up and wanted to get this errand over quickly. The bell jingled as he and the dog stepped through the door. Something wooden clattered to the floor in the back. "Right with you," Cy called out.

The scramble of paws and nails as Daddy raced toward Cy sent Chester's guts plummeting.

"Would you look-it who it is! Where'd you find him?"

"He turned up at the Jewel," Chester explained. "I thought he was a stray. Maxine, my cashier, asked around town and couldn't find the owner. It was not until the other day when Temple recognized him that I understood he is your dog."

Cy must have knelt down because there came the sound of Daddy flopping on his back for a belly rub. "My Ruthie-Jo would be mighty pleased you've taken care of him all this time."

"I've never had a dog. Didn't know what to feed him."

"He'll eat anything. Won't you, fella?"

"He certainly favors popcorn."

"You don't say! Who would have guessed! Ruthie-Jo probably knew. She doted on him. He was her dog . . . Hey, what happened to you? Quite a shiner."

Chester gently prodded the flesh around his eye. "Someone socked me when I stepped outside the other night."

"In town here? Sorry to hear that."

Chester stooped to pat Daddy on the head. "You've got a good dog here."

"Daddy is top rate. I'd keep him if I could, but being in the store all day . . ."

"You're not going to keep him?"

"How would that work? A hardware store isn't any place for a dog. And to be honest, I never had much use for one. My great-aunt had this nasty hound who bit me one time, and after that, well . . ."

"Understandable. As a matter of fact, Daddy and I have settled in very companionably these few days. And if you are certain you don't want him, I would—"

Cy grabbed Chester's hand, shaking it vigorously. "Sold, to the man in the black overcoat!"

"I never expected this outcome, but I am extremely pleased."

"Swell! So am I."

Chester cringed. He disdained slang in general and "swell" was particularly egregious.

Cy continued: "Ruthie-Jo's graveside service is at noon tomorrow, if you care to come."

"We will be there," Chester said, relaxing.

Out on the sidewalk, Chester leaned down to scratch the dog's head. "That was very kind of Cy to allow us to stay together. But to be clear, this is not just any black overcoat. It is a Chesterfield."

C HAPTER TWENTY-SIX

DRIVING BACK TO TOWN after the encounter with the hatchery owner, Temple said, "We'll need to check with Sam at the Oke Doke, but I'm figuring that Jess's alibi will hold."

"Like as not," Ed responded. "What's next?"

Temple contemplated the landscape. Past the sedan's windows spread plains as flat as a dried cowpat. Brown. Beige. Russet. Snuff. One tint merging into the next, stitched together with an unbroken line of telephone poles. The cedar poles, riddled from the cleats of linemen, had been planted thirty-five years earlier. Some listed in the sandy stuff left behind after the prairie grasses were plowed under and the winds carried off the topsoil.

"We've got to finish following up on the leads from Ruthie-Jo's little side jobs and then take a crack at those notes from the spice box. I'm beginning to suspect Ruthie-Jo had a nasty streak bordering on blackmail."

The sedan bumped over the tracks as Temple pulled into town.

Ed brought out his notebook. "Most of her victims aren't going to want to talk about the poison she was stirring up. How we going to handle this?"

"No idea. Maybe Claude will come through on this

track hand. Maybe the guy who cocked the switch killed
her, like we first thought. That would make life easier."

"I'm with you. But just in case he's not the one, why
don't you drop me off at the train station and I'll ask
about those books Ruthie-Jo was keeping for the railroad. See what that was all about."

The station was jammed with folks traveling home after Christmas. Ed waded into the sea of harried women,
squalling red-faced toddlers, and men overburdened with
suitcases. He caught a glimpse of Herschel's frantic expression behind the ticket counter. Sweat trickled from
under his agent's cap. *Shoot.* Ed gripped the accounting
reports. Maybe Milt, the section foreman, would be less
busy. He found Milt in the shop, talking to a couple of
the hands about replacing bolts on a half mile of track.

The burly foreman spotted Ed. "With you in a minute."

After the two crewmen left, Milt strolled over.

"Nice Christmas?" Ed asked.

"The kiddies did. The wife and I were able to put a bit
aside for a couple of toys. Not much, and thank goodness
the baby isn't old enough to know any better. What you
needing?"

Ed handed him the reports. "We're investigating Mrs.
Mitchem's death. Found this among her papers. Appears she
was doing some bookkeeping for the AT&SF. We're looking
for some help on who she might have been working for."

Milt leafed through the papers. Coughed. "Excuse me
a sec, I need my specs." He hustled into his office and Ed
strolled to the open doorway. A crowd surged onto the
platform—a train was due in.

"Let's see what we got here," Milt said upon return,

chest slightly heaving. "Sorry, I think I might be coming down with something." He adjusted his glasses. "This is the type of report our roadmaster, Tom Fetner, compiles. Purchases of ballast, tar . . . whatever needed for his section."

"And payroll."

"Oh. Yeah."

"Is this type of work normally farmed out to a local bookkeeper?"

"I really don't know. Sorry I can't be more help. I'd be glad to keep this and run it by him when he's in the area."

Daniel tramped in and nodded at the two men on his way to the tool bench.

"Fetner's not around?" Ed asked.

Milt sighed heavily. "He oversees a hundred miles of track so he could be anywhere in that vicinity."

Daniel spoke up: "Just saw him. Couple of miles down the rails inspecting that ballast work."

Milt snapped his fingers. "Slipped my mind. Trying to catch up after the derailment has got me a bit cockeyed."

"Understandable. Can someone get me to this Fetner? And I'll take those back." Ed pointed to the paperwork.

Milt hesitated. "Is this urgent? I mean, inspecting the rails is a big part of accident prevention. The AT&SF drills that into us. Fetner plays a big role in that, and I'd say if you could come back next week—"

"This is a murder investigation, man!" Ed barked. "I need to talk to Fetner pronto."

Holding up his hands, Milt said, "I get it. Okay. Daniel, take the deputy down the track on the handcar."

Together, Milt and Daniel pushed the handcar, parked outside the shed, onto the tracks. Ed followed and climbed aboard.

"Deputy, you mind working the hand pump with me?" Daniel asked. "We'll get there faster."

The two men faced one another, grabbed the T-shaped handles, and began pumping in a seesaw motion. The car moved forward. Within minutes Ed had to ask if they could stop so he could take off his overcoat.

Daniel chuckled. "Harder than it looks."

When they reached the roadmaster, Ed's shirt was stuck to his back.

"Hey there," Ed said, jumping off the handcar and striding up to Fetner. "Can we talk? I'm Deputy Ed McCance."

Fetner, who was a tall man with pale-gray eyes and a loose mouth, started. "What?" He stared at Daniel, who shrugged slightly.

"It's related to a murder investigation."

"Murder? Who?"

"Mrs. Mitchem. Somebody strangled her last week. You knew her, right?"

Fetner pivoted to Daniel. "How about continuing to check the grade while the deputy and I talk." He passed the tamper and gauge to Daniel, who moved up the rails.

Fetner planted one boot on the splintered platform of the handcar, crossed his arms, and rested them on his thigh.

From the inside pocket of his overcoat, Ed pulled out Ruthie-Jo's folded reports. Fetner examined the paperwork.

"Any of this look familiar?" Ed asked.

"Weekly material purchases and payroll for my section." Fetner handed the papers back to him.

"How did this end up among Mrs. Mitchem's account books?"

The roadmaster removed his hat, pushed his hand

through his hair. "Because I hired her to do my reports. My clerk quit and the railroad didn't replace him. Ciphering was never my strong suit. She'd do the figures and I'd swing by her place once a week. She'd show me a copy, then she'd fill the calculations in the official ledger and off I'd go."

"Did you take notice of Mrs. Mitchem's memorandum here?" He pointed to the scribbles in the margin.

Squinting, Fetner shook his head.

"Says, *Discrepancy in figures. Purposeful?* Do you know what she meant?"

Fetner pulled a cigarette pack from his pocket and lit up. "Not really. Maybe something in the materials list was off. Let me see that again." He ran his eyes over the figures.

Ed peered up the track. Daniel raised the tamper and brought it down with a mighty blow. The deputy turned back to Fetner. "Find anything? If not, maybe this is something to bring to the attention of your bosses?"

"Well, sure. I don't think it's anything, but—"

"With a murder case, everything has to be checked. Who is your supervisor?"

Fetner sighed. "It's the payroll. That's where the figures are off. I've been carrying a dead man for a couple of weeks."

"What?"

"A dead man. We fired a trackman but kept his name on the payroll."

"You pocketed his wages?"

"Most."

"Split it?"

"With Milt."

"Christ Almighty. And Mrs. Mitchem sussed this out?"

"Last time I was at the house, she asked me direct. I told her what was going on and gave her something extra to keep quiet." The rail master sat abruptly on the handcar platform, head in hands. "What the hell was I thinking?"

"When did you have this exchange with Mrs. Mitchem?"

"The day she was killed," Fetner said in a low tone, quickly adding, "But I had nothing to do with that."

Ed jotted a couple of notes. "Where were you between ten p.m. last Friday and six a.m. Saturday?"

"Come on! I'd never—"

"Where were you?"

Fetner ground out his cigarette. "I was back home in Enid. Stopped at a bar. Then went to the house."

"Anyone to vouch for that?"

"Lots of folks."

"How long were you there?"

"Left at closing. Two o'clock."

"Anyone at home?"

"My wife. Look, Enid is a healthy three-hour trip from Vermillion—in a car or train. I'd be hard-pressed to get down here and then back up to Enid at six a.m. when my wife poured me a cup of coffee."

Ed tucked his notebook away. "You'll need to make a statement down at the courthouse. Get your gear."

"Now?"

"Yep. And then I'll be talking to Milt."

CHAPTER TWENTY-SEVEN

WITHOUT SWITCHING ON the kitchen light, Cy arranged two slices of bread on the counter, smeared each with mustard, and slapped on two slices of bologna. He didn't bother with a plate. Every dish in the house, including the teacup Ruthie-Jo got at the Jewel's Dish Night, was submersed in the kitchen sink's scummy water. Cy ate standing up in the lavender twilight. Musgrove, the undertaker, had telephoned earlier.

"Pick out a dress, shoes, hose, and jewelry. A brooch is always a nice touch," the man had said. The funeral was two days away.

Cy wasn't even sure Ruthie-Jo had a brooch. He dreaded going into the chill bedroom. He dreaded rooting around her things. After he ate, Cy ran his hands down his thighs to brush off the crumbs and mounted the stairs. To the left was his bedroom. He'd hauled the radio cabinet there, along with the parlor's overstuffed chair. After work and a sandwich, Cy would spend the rest of the night hunkered in his bedroom.

Now he turned right. Ruthie-Jo had never been one for gewgaws. No pictures on the walls or pillow covers on the swayback bed. Hanging from hooks at the back of her closet were a number of droopy house wraps. On hangers were her three good dresses that she wore on rare outings. Cy plucked out the blue frock and laid it on the bed. She'd had a fondness for blue—he knew that much. There was only one pair of dress pumps, which made things easier. What else had Musgrove said? Hose. The bureau yielded thick beige stockings and plain drawers. Below the undergarments, Cy found a cookie tin.

Maybe the tin contained some jewelry. He sat on the bed and lifted the lid. Inside was a jumble of miscellanea. Cy poked around with an index finger and recognized the compass that the banker's son had lifted. How had she gotten ahold of that? An invoice from their store for a packet of nails. A hankie with the initials *L.H.* Most surprising, a girlie-show flip-book. Cy ruffled the pages, turned crimson, and stuffed it back inside. At the bottom were a couple of sewing needles but no brooch. He started replacing the lid when something wrapped in white tissue paper caught his eye. Plucking it out, he unwrapped the small package. A key. Not a house or padlock key. *AT&SF* was engraved on the head. Where had she gotten this? He'd never know. Ruthie-Jo was secretive, no doubt about that. He rewrapped the key, slipped it in his pocket, thinking to return it to the train station, and put the tin back in the drawer.

From under the bed, Cy pulled out the empty suitcase she'd carried with her all those years ago when he'd first brought her to Vermillion as his bride. He flipped the latches and folded and laid the dress and underclothes inside. He tucked the shoes in the elasticized side pockets. She'd just have to go without jewelry, but that suited her better anyway.

Ed had awakened that morning to discover his bride bent

over the garbage can in the shared kitchen of their room-ing house. For the past few days he'd stirred to the sound of Viviane upchucking in the bathroom. She'd assured him this was all in the course of a normal pregnancy. On this morning he'd assumed it was more of the same. But instead he found that she was tearfully scraping off the burned bottoms of a batch of molasses cookies.

"I hate this oven!" she cried.

"Hey, it's okay," Ed said, drawing her into his arms. Not minding the smell of burned sugar. Not minding the scattering of crumbs under his bare feet. "We'll have our own place someday soon and you can pick out whatever oven you want. I promise."

An hour later, showered and dressed, they saun-tered to the courthouse—Viviane toting a tin canister of burned cookies and Ed a bundle of file folders with notes on the Mitchem killing. When Ed entered the office, the evidence table had been cleared and Claude sat at the far side, smoking a cigar.

"Viviane baked some cookies," Ed said, unloading the tin and his folders on the table.

Temple was at his desk studying a notebook. "Be right with you, boys."

Ed pried the lid off the container and took a seat.

"Appreciate you calling this confab, Sheriff," Claude said, reaching for a cookie. "I got some significant findings."

"Sorry for the delay." Temple rolled his desk chair up to the table and propped his long legs on the top. "So, what you got, Claude?"

Pulling a jotter from inside his suit coat, Claude flipped through the pages. "The latest on the derailment is that I hunted down that trackman who was fired. Lonnie Taylor rents a room in the back of Mick's Pool Hall. I interviewed him yesterday. He gave me an alibi for the times when we suspect the switch was cocked. Leaky, I'd say. The pool hall manager is fairly certain he saw Lonnie during some of that time, but then Lonnie went to his room and we only have his word on that. Also, Lonnie claims he was one of the first at the scene of the wreck. That he was prying open doors and risking life and limb to save passengers."

Ed frowned. Something tickled at the back of his mind but he couldn't figure out what it was. "What about that lock and chain I found?"

"I'm getting to that. Lonnie says he turned in his switch key and tools to Milt when he was canned. I'll check that out after we finish here." Claude settled back in his chair. "I'm closing in on building a tidy case against Lonnie, and in the meantime he can stew."

Nodding at Ed, Temple said, "You're up."

After smartly tapping the bottom edge of his folder on the tabletop, Ed opened the file. "The sheriff and I inspected the Mitchem house. Clearly Mrs. Mitchem was not only keeping the books for her husband's store, but also for others on the side. From those ledgers, we zeroed in on three possible suspects." He carefully turned the page. "I attempted to interview Jess Fuller, a local farmer trying to start up a hatchery, and got a shotgun pointed at my forehead for my trouble."

"Hothead!" Claude exclaimed.

"Exactly. Two days later Temple and I again visited the hatchery and Fuller then provided an alibi. Seems he plays fiddle at the Oke Doke every night and—"

"Hey, I think I saw him there," Claude interrupted. "Lanky guy in his forties?"

Ed nodded. "I have since confirmed Jess was playing at the bar, and afterward . . . well . . . he stayed with a lady friend who vouched for him."

"I'm betting it was that gal singer," Claude said.

Temple broke in: "Did you interrogate this woman in person? Think she can be believed?"

"I swung by the Oke Doke around dinnertime yesterday," Ed said. "The singer was there running through a couple of songs. I talked her up and got around to asking did she know where Jess went after the gig. At first she said she didn't, but was blushing to beat the band. Finally she admitted that he stayed the night, and many nights, with her. If she'd been coached to cover for him, I don't think she'd have been so hangdog about it. She was genuinely mortified."

"Okay. What else?"

"Another lead based on the account books turned out to be the roadmaster, Tom Fetner."

Claude leaned over the table. "You don't say."

"When I interrogated Mr. Fetner, he readily admitted that he paid Mrs. Mitchem to do his accounts. Said he was bad with figures. I questioned him more closely about a notation Mrs. Mitchem made in the margins of the last report. Fetner broke down and stated that recently a trackman had been fired—likely that fellow you're hot on, Claude. Fetner confessed that he hadn't yet removed the man's name from the payroll list."

Claude pounded the table with his fist. "A dead man! Goddamnit. I'd like to use your phone. I need to call this into the higher-ups right away."

Temple said, "Hold your horses. Ed had Fetner come in and write it all down. Then we brought Milt down here. He was apparently in on it too."

"Holy Christ," Claude mumbled.

"We're asking you to hold off reporting these two men for a bit. Both have solid alibis for Mrs. Mitchem's murder, but we're not ready to exonerate them altogether. I'd like them around and cooperative for a bit longer."

The railroad detective was up on his feet, pacing. "Those no-good bums. I'd like to give them a what-for."

"One more update and then we can wrap this up," Temple said. "I talked to Bill Donley at Bell's. He was another lead from Mrs. Mitchem's moonlighting activities. There was something irregular about his accounts. Before I stopped by his place, I made calls. I was thinking if he was up to something criminal, he might have killed her to cover it up, especially if she was blackmailing him. In the end, he did admit he'd received and sold stolen goods and, in addition, tried to extort money from Chester Benton. As of this moment he is cooling his heels up on the third floor. His lawyer is due in thirty minutes for the arraignment. Donley's wife gave him an alibi for the night of Ruthie-Jo's death—after she calmed down enough to put a few words together. Not airtight, but I don't think he's a killer."

Claude said, "Lot of cards in play."

Temple chuckled grimly. "What I'm hoping is that we can nail this Lonnie for the derailment *and* for the homicide. Straightest line between two points."

Claude said, "Do my best but I need to finish connecting the dots. More evidence, like that key, pointing to him would be a huge help."

Temple rose, shook his trouser legs down over his boot tops. "Let's get to work, then."

* * *

Daniel was in the toolhouse when Claude marched inside, his cheeks burning and nose running from the cold.

"Boss in?" he asked.

Putting aside the splitting wedge he was sharpening, Daniel said, "Should be back in five, sir. He's up the track checking on a couple of ties."

"I'll wait." Claude hoisted himself on a stool beside the workbench. He blew his nose raucously—following up with several dainty dabs around his nostrils. "Lonnie told me he turned in his switch key and tools. Do you happen to know if he did?"

"You're going to need to ask the foreman about that."

"Okay. I was wondering—"

A blast of chill air rushed in. "What exactly where you wondering?" Milt asked, walking through the door.

"Just the man I wanted to see," Claude said.

Claude and Milt retired to the foreman's office. Milt dropped into his chair with a grunt. "You're like a dog with a bone, aren't you?"

"Nature of detective work," Claude replied. "I'm closing in on this one, I tell you true. Tracked down that Lonnie Taylor you fired. Matter of fact, I have a reputation for relentlessly sniffing out workers who do wrong. Nothing gets by me."

Milt dropped his gaze.

Claude continued, "I'd say Lonnie is bitter about losing his job. Confidentially, he's my prime suspect on the derailment. Lonnie told me he turned in his switch key."

"Absolutely. I made sure of that. Company policy." Milt turned to draw a ring of keys from the front pocket in his workman's jacket. He leaned over and unlocked a side drawer, extracted a small envelope, and dumped out three keys. "Two are extras and this one here," he pushed it across the desk to Claude, "was Lonnie's. He'd scratched his initials on it. See for yourself."

Claude examined the brass surface. "So he did. That desk drawer always locked?"

"By the book."

The detective shoved the key back and rose. "Any other extra switch keys around?"

"Herschel, over at the station, always keeps two extra."

"All right then. You'll be seeing me again. You can count on that. Yes sir."

When Claude stepped inside the station, he heard the halting rhythm of one-fingered typing coming from the ticket office. He stuck his head through the ticket window. "Afternoon."

Herschel, concentrating on the typewriter keys, snapped his head up, eyes wide. "Jeez. You startled me."

"Got a minute?" Claude reached through the window, appropriating a paper clip from the station agent's counter and straightening it to clean his nails.

"What are you needing?" Herschel asked from his side of the grille.

"I understand you keep a couple of extra universal keys here."

"Besides my own," Herschel jingled the chain looped from his vest, "I've got two for emergencies." He reached to the right of the ticket window where several cup hooks studded the wall, then frowned. "Should be two keys here."

Claude pushed his bulk through the window. A cup hook with a single key was only three inches from his nose.

"Give me a minute," Herschel said. "The other must have fallen." He stooped and patted the floorboards. When he stood his forehead was ridged with worry.

"Who else besides you has access to this office?"

"You think it was swiped?" Herschel's eyes widened. "That's grounds for dismissal if I can't account for all the keys!"

Claude put up his hands. "Slow down. Right now I'm more concerned with when this might have happened and who might have done it than your piss-poor security measures. When was the last time you saw both keys on the hook?"

"I don't know."

"Think, man. Take your time."

After a couple of ticks of the station clock, the ticket agent said, "I'm almost 100 percent it was last Wednesday. I remember Mrs. Klein, that Jewish lady whose husband owns the clothing store, she was buying a ticket and remarked that business at the store was slow even though Christmas was only a week away. When she was walking out the door I saw she'd left her car keys on the counter and called her back. She made some remark about always misplacing her keys. It made me think of the universals. To be honest, I'm in terror of those things. That I will lose one and get the boot. That's when I took note of the cup hook, and both were there."

"So we're talking about the day before the wreck?"

Herschel studied the AT&SF wall calendar behind him. "That's right. December 18."

"Okay, so sometime between then and now, one's gone missing. Tell me about your security routine for the ticket office."

"It's locked tight every night. During the day, Milt comes in and out to pick up notices from headquarters and such. So does the roadmaster if he's here. But they have extra switch keys themselves and wouldn't be using these extras."

Claude tapped the narrow ticket counter with the paper clip. "What about when you're on duty and need to use the gent's? Or are on the platform taking a shipment? You close the ticket window and lock the office door?"

"Absolutely!"

"I'm not here to write you up. Be honest. There must be times when you get in a rush."

Herschel ran his tongue over his prominent front teeth. "Not often. But yeah."

"And who might be knowing about where you hung those keys?"

"Besides Milt and the roadmaster? No one."

"But that key is not hard to spot by someone leaning in, like I just did. And if you were a railroad man, you'd know right off that they were universals. I'm wondering if you recall a railroad man doing just that in this past week? Standing right where I am, shooting the breeze, maybe with his arms folded on the counter?"

Herschel thought on this. "It's a rarity when a crewman stops by the ticket office to gab. They work straight through and then head direct to the Idle Hour. But you know, one of the guys did swing by late last week. Guess he wasn't officially a railroad man anymore. He'd gotten the boot. Anyways, he showed up and we gabbed for a bit."

The railroad detective had moved on to apply the paper clip to the nails of his other hand. "Interesting. Name of . . ."

"Lonnie Taylor. Not a talkative fellow, so I was surprised to see him. At first I thought he wanted to buy a ticket."

"Now think closely. When you and he were gabbing, did you have a need to leave the window unattended?"

The station agent blanched. "You think Lonnie took it? Jesus. You know . . ."

"I'm just covering all the bases in this investigation. Go on."

"Mrs. Price was trying to squeeze through the door with a couple of parcels. She was traveling to Alva with Christmas presents for her grandchildren. I think it was that same day Mrs. Klein was here. I left the counter to help Mrs. Price. He could have palmed the key then."

"I'm casting a broad net for this inquiry, but certainly this Mr. Taylor might be a person of interest down the line," Claude said. "You've been a big help. I'm going to need you to write all this down."

"Typed?"

"Handwritten is fine. Sooner the better," Claude said on his way out the door.

In was late in the day when Claude left the station. After talking to Herschel, he had to fight the urge to barrel over to the pool hall and arrest Lonnie on the spot. The station agent's story pointed directly at the former track hand, but everything was still circumstantial. He'd have to soften the man up with the indirect findings to break him down.

Claude hoofed it to Mayo's. No one was hanging around in the hallway, thank you Jesus, and he found Beatrice on her knees, scrubbing a ring of brown scum from the communal bathtub. The smell of cleanser filled the air.

"Howdy there, girl," he said, leaning on the doorframe.

Beatrice rocked back on her heels, pushing sweat-frizzled hair from her forehead with the back of her wrist. "You look happy about something."

"I'm closing in on a suspect on the case. I think I'll have him cornered in another day or so. Want to celebrate with me at the Oke Doke?"

A cloud seemed to pass over Beatrice's face. Then she said, "That'd be swell."

"I got to go write up some notes on the investigation. Meet you downstairs at seven o'clock?"

Earlier that afternoon, while Homer and Leland careened up and down the block on roller skates and Everett snored on the living room sofa, Etha and Vadie had gossiped at the kitchen table.

A few feet away, Thelma was plunging her strong fingers into a bowl of ground beef, breading, and onions. Etha couldn't tell if Thelma's lack of expression was purposeful—in that Thelma was actually soaking up every word of the conversation flowing around her—or if she was indifferent to the chatter.

As Vadie prattled on about a distant relative who had run off with a lumberman from Oregon, Etha tried to bring the conversation around to her niece's own situation. Since the family had arrived, Etha noticed that worry lines were permanently etched on Vadie's thin face. Everett's drinking was taking a toll on the boys too, and they seemed to sneak away whenever their father entered a room. This was one reason Etha had invited Carmine over for dinner that night. Homer and Leland worshipped the young man. Nearly every sentence Homer uttered began, *Carmine says . . .*

When Vadie paused to light a cigarette, Etha said, "I don't know how else to bring this up, but I'm truly worried about you and the kids."

Vadie's brows rose. "How so?"

Etha thought, *Oh, we're playing* that *game?* Before she could respond, Thelma slammed the ground meat in the bake pan and turned to Vadie. "You know what she's talking about. That no-count man who's attached to you like a tapeworm."

A deep flush spread across Vadie's cheeks. "That's not . . ."

Thelma turned back to the meatloaf as if nothing had happened.

Vadie faced Etha, her voice shaking. "Is that *your* opinion of Everett?"

"I wouldn't put it exactly like that, but his drinking has brought down a heap of sorrow on you. Temple and I can find you work here in Vermillion and a place to rent. I could watch the boys after school."

Vadie shook her head. "I would never do that. It would kill Ev. I think this trip has truly changed his thinking. He's here with family. Sees how good life can be. He only went out on a real bender the first night. The last two nights he cut back to one or two drinks. Told me so."

Across the room, her back to the two women, Thelma snorted. Giving the meatloaf a final slap, she turned. "If you think that, you're living in dreamland. My pa was a nasty drunk. But my ma was always saying the same about him. *He's going to change. He's going to turn this around.* And now she's dead. Beat to death. You think you can fix this, but you can't."

Vadie and Etha froze. Etha shifted her eyes to her niece. Blood had drained from the young woman's face. Thelma coolly turned to the sink and began washing the mixing bowl.

Vadie lurched to life. "Ev would never do that," she hissed at Thelma, then leaned toward Etha. "And you need to stop sticking your nose in where it don't belong."

"I am not meddling," Etha countered. "Or if I am, it's because it's needed. What if you lose your job at the canning factory? Is Everett all of a sudden going to step up? Put the bottle down? I don't think so. There are stories in the paper every day about parents who have to give their children up to orphanages because they can't provide food or clothing. Is that what you want to happen to Homer and Leland?" Etha held up her thumb and forefinger. "You are *that* close. You may not see it but you are."

"You're just trying to take my boys. You lost Jack so now you want mine. Everett and I can provide for them just fine, thank you very much." Vadie stomped off down the hall. The door to the bathroom slammed. The Mason jars rattled in the cupboard above Etha's head.

"That's not the truth and you know it!" Etha yelled.

"She's not hearing you," Thelma said dryly.

Inside the Oke Doke, visibility was limited. Smoke hung low over the bar. Above loud laughter, Jess Fuller's voice rose, singing an Uncle Dave Macon tune:

> *Whiskey is the one thing sure people's gonna make*
> *But when they get you on the chain gang, you better*
> *   seen your mistake*
> *All night long and I couldn't get away*

All night long and I couldn't get away
Break my neck and I couldn't get away
Couldn't get away and I couldn't get away

Everett stuffed his cold-stiffened fingers under his armpits as he waited his turn at the bar. It had taken an uncommonly long time before anyone stopped at the sight of his hooked thumb. He bought three beers with the coins Vadie had given him earlier in the day. They were meant to buy liniment for her chafed hands. He downed one immediately and carried the other two away from the crowded bar to a spot near the musicians. Leaning against the wall, he took long pulls on one of the bottles. The fiddle player wasn't bad. Of course, Uncle Dave played it on the banjo. But this fellow was not bad at all.

Tomorrow he, Vadie, and the boys would pile into the jalopy and head back to Arkansas. The trip home couldn't come fast enough. Sleeping on the floor, even with cushions, tweaked his back up something fierce. There were also the loaded glances observing his comings and goings. Oh yes, he knew. He'd heard Etha bad-mouthing him. He saw the disdain on Temple's face. Hell with them! So high and mighty. A regular workingman didn't have a chance in this country. It was easy when you had a government job like sheriff. Hard on the workingman, though. *Ain't it the truth?* When they got back to Siloam Springs he'd go straight to the relief office and get on the dole. He'd been fighting against it for months, but they couldn't go on living in that filthy room with only the cookstove for heat and no hot water. Now, just thinking about signing up for the relief, having his finances poked and prodded, shamed him bad. He chugged the third bottle.

After another trip to the bar, Everett got comfortable. Faces and bodies swam close and far. A couple darted past. It was that woman who was helping Etha with the meals. A man had his arm around her shoulders. Maybe it wasn't her. The faces swam away. A foursome at a table near him stood and shrugged into their coats. He dragged one of the vacant chairs against the wall and sat with a thud. The woman musician was singing a snappy tune. Couples swayed up to the small open space in front of the players. Feet shuffling, they bounced to the rhythm. Arms were extended and hands clasped. Everett's head dipped up and down. As another pair swirled past him, the woman's skirt grazed his knees. Her partner, tubby and wearing unbuckled rubber boots, was surprisingly light on his feet. The man had removed his suit jacket and rolled up his sleeves. The woman, a brunette with a weak chin and a nice figure, kept pace.

The music slowed. The dancers clutched each other. Everett had a sudden desire to spin the brunette across the floor. He rose, wobbled, then steadied himself.

Vibrations from the stomping feet jiggled a string of Christmas lights. A drunk staggered toward Beatrice. She ignored him. The pressure of Claude's fingers around her waist gave her the shivers. She nestled her cheek on his shoulder and they circled around.

Claude pulled away. "Go on," he said to someone. "This woman's taken."

Then it all fell apart. Over Claude's shoulder, Beatrice glimpsed a slack-jawed man weaving unsteadily.

"Just asking to cut in. Give her a twirl." The drunk made a stirring motion with his finger.

"Ignore him," Claude said to Beatrice, guiding her farther into the crowd.

This time the drunk tapped on her shoulder. "Honey, let a younger man show you—"

Claude stepped between Beatrice and the drunk.

"Hey!" the drunk shouted, then staggered backward into a table crowded with three couples. Bottles rolled and smashed on the floor. An ashtray flipped over, showering the air with ashes and butts. The boozer found his footing and approached Claude with fists raised. Beatrice screamed.

"Fella, you don't want to do this," Claude said in a low voice.

Beatrice watched as the man swung loosely at Claude's head. For his trouble, he got a crack to the nose. He came back at Claude with a sloppy jab that managed to land on the right eye before Claude clocked him with a left jab. The man went down in a heap.

"Had enough?" Claude shouted.

Beatrice tugged on his arm. "Please stop. Please." Her voice shook.

Claude turned. It was almost as if he'd forgotten she was there.

The drunkard was still slumped to the floor, cradling his bloodied face, when Temple and Ed arrived on the scene.

"What's the problem?" Temple asked Claude, who had stuck around to make sure the drunk didn't cause more problems.

Claude mopped his face with a bandanna. "This bum made unwanted advances on my lady friend."

Temple pondered the fellow crumpled at his feet. Blood dripped through the man's cupped hands. "Get up." The man stood, swaying and moaning. When he dropped his hands away from his face Temple said, "Oh jeez. What the hell, Everett?"

Everett squinted at the sheriff. "Beat the crap out of me. For nothing."

"Not so," Claude.

"Shut up. The both of you. Where's Sam?"

From across the crowded room, the bartender extended his arm.

"Be right there," Temple called, then turned to Ed. "Stay with these two."

The bartender was rubbing out a cigarette with the toe of his boot when Temple got to him.

"What's the story?" the sheriff asked.

"Sorry to telephone, but I was afraid the railroad dick would beat the guy to death. He's capable, I'm sure."

"Probably," Temple sighed. "The other fellow is family. He's the husband of Etha's niece."

"Christ."

"So what happened?"

"Not sure what started it. I was behind the bar. They were going at it pretty good by the time I got a look. Your kin is blotto. He walked in . . . maybe two hours ago? Downed four beers real fast. The railroad dick and his girlfriend came in after."

Temple stroked his jaw. "Damage to your property?"

Sam took in the room. "Just two broken chairs."

"All right. I'm going to take them both down to the courthouse and get their stories. You want to press charges?"

"No. Happens all the time."

The combatants protested loudly but Temple stood firm. "Ed, you and Everett get in the backseat. Claude, you're up front with me. And I don't want any squawking."

"But my lady friend . . ."

Temple held up his hand. "I asked Walt and Sally Bramley to drive Beatrice home. The Bramleys were, by the way, celebrating their anniversary with a couple of drinks and a bit of dancing, until you two started acting up."

During the ten-minute drive, Everett passed out.

"I'm too old for this nonsense," Temple said when he pulled into the lot. "Okay, boys, I need your help."

Grunting and swearing, Temple, Ed, and Claude maneuvered Everett's rubbery body into the courthouse. In the foyer Claude stopped abruptly, hands on his knees. "I'm winded."

"Wait here. We'll take him the rest of the way," Temple said.

Above their heads, the courthouse clock released a single note. On the cusp of the third-floor landing, Ed asked, "In there?" He nodded toward the sheriff's apartment.

"Nope. Drunk tank. Etha's going to set on me like a wildcat, but I don't care. Everett is a mess. And he participated in and probably initiated a public disturbance."

"Agreed."

The second cell on the right was reserved for drunks needing to sleep it off. Temple and Ed hoisted Everett onto the rough woolen blanket of the cot. The man didn't even twitch. Temple positioned a bucket nearby just in case and locked the cell.

"Ed, escort Claude to the office," Temple said. "I'll be right down."

* * *

The deputy was making notes on a pad and the railroad detective was lighting a cigar when Temple stepped in with a lump of ice wrapped in a dishtowel. "For your eye," he said, handing it to Claude. Then he told Ed to head on home.

"Glad to stay . . ."

Temple waved him off. After the door closed behind Ed, Temple settled into his chair and took up a notepad and pencil.

"So, fill me in on your side of things."

Claude snorted. "My side is the only side. That relative of yours tried to cut in when I was dancing with Beatrice. He was drunk as a skunk and wouldn't take no for an answer."

"So you slugged him?"

"Hell no. Not at first. I pushed him away. He came back and took a swing at me. I warned him not to but he did anyway. It became a question of self-defense."

"We are not talking about a fellow with all or even a modicum of his faculties coming at you with a weapon. From what I observed, Everett was pie-eyed. I'm willing to bet he didn't even hear your warning."

Claude examined the glowing tip of his cigar.

Temple continued, "I could charge you with assault and disorderly conduct. You know that."

"You're funning me."

"Nope. Said I *could*. But I'm not. Stay away from him until the derailment investigation is wrapped up and you're back in Kansas City. I've got enough going on. This is the last thing I need. I hope you understand."

Claude dipped his head. "I do and I'm sorry. Not that I'm in the wrong, but I'm sorry for the trouble."

The two men strolled outside, pausing at the top of the courthouse steps. In the distance, the thick chords of an approaching train thrummed across the plains.

Claude cocked his head. "Beethoven, Berlin, Sousa. None can hold a candle to the music of a locomotive."

The sheriff chuckled. "Etha might think different, being a piano teacher and all."

Temple closed up the office and headed upstairs. He stuck his head inside the jail, where Everett was snoring heavily. He unlatched the door to the apartment and sat at the kitchen table to pull off his boots. All was quiet except for the heavy breathing of Homer and Leland in the corner cell. He washed his face and neck at the bathroom sink. Brushed his teeth. Confirmed that his face was as haggard and weary as his innards. Etha was turned on her side, covers up to her chin. He slowly removed his shirt and trousers—leaving them in a heap on the chair—and climbed into bed.

For some time he stared at the ceiling, ruminating on the events of the evening—trying to figure how he was going to tell Vadie that he'd locked Everett up. Eventually his eyelids closed.

Vadie's sniveling woke Temple abruptly. "Everett's not home. It's on four a.m." She leaned into the bedroom doorway and sobbed.

"You and I need to talk," Temple said, and crawled out of bed.

They sat side by side on the davenport. Before Temple got a word out, Vadie said, "You know what happened to Everett, don't you?"

"What do you think? He got pickled. No surprise

there. But then he provoked a fistfight. Two chairs were broken at the Oke Doke. He's passed out here in the drunk tank."

Vadie gasped. "You put him in jail?"

"Drunk-and-disorderly."

"Hurt bad?"

"Broken nose. Maybe a rib. Likely not the first time, though."

The young woman doubled over. "You put him in jail? I can't believe it."

"Maybe it's time to make sure your boys don't ever have to see something like this again."

Vadie jumped to her feet. "You mean *leave* him? Etha keeps saying that. *Everyone* keeps saying that. How can I leave when he's down and out and can't take care of himself? The father of my children?"

"Settle down. Things will look better in the—"

"First thing in the morning we're on the road."

Vadie retreated to the pallet in the dining room. Temple heard her bawling and blowing her nose. He grabbed his pillow and Everett's quota of the sofa cushions and retired to the davenport, pulled up the crocheted blanket, and stretched out. He didn't want to disturb Etha's sleep. The sofa was not long enough and half its cushions were missing. His legs hung over the side. No matter, he knew he'd be awake the remainder of the night.

CHAPTER TWENTY-EIGHT

AT DAWN TEMPLE STIRRED. It would take a good forty-five minutes to limber himself into working order—forty-five minutes he didn't have. As he shambled into the kitchen to get the coffee started, he heard Vadie moving around the dining room.

He spent awhile in the bathroom, waiting for a weak dribble of urine to finally make its way through his pipes.

When he returned to the kitchen, Vadie was stirring a pot of sticky oatmeal for the boys.

"Morning," Temple said. Homer and Leland grinned at him.

Vadie said nothing.

"Ma says we have to go," Homer whined.

"Don't back-talk me," Vadie snapped, banging the edge of the pot with a thick wooden spoon.

"Do as your mother says." Temple ruffled Leland's shock of hair.

The rank smell of vomit and piss greeted Temple as he strode inside the cellblock. "Still among the living, Ev?" he asked brusquely.

Everett swayed to his feet and wiped a hand across his mouth. Crusted blood caked his nose and upper lip.

"Brought you a towel and washcloth and clean clothes," Temple said, handing the pile of linens through the meal slot. "Coffee?"

"Sure," Everett said weakly.

"Get yourself cleaned up. Vadie is set on getting on the road as early as possible."

Temple returned in five minutes with a coffee mug. Everett had gotten himself dressed and was scrubbing the crust from his face. Temple pulled a chair up to the cell.

"You've got a wife and two little boys next door who need you. Straighten up and start acting like the man of the family. Vadie is sticking with you. Why, I don't know. But she is. Don't let her down. Go back to Arkansas. Take any job you can get. Take it and keep it and lay off the liquor. You hear?"

Everett lowered his head of shaggy black hair. "Yes sir, but these are hard—"

Temple stood abruptly. "I don't want to hear about no work, hard times, or any of that." He unlocked the cell door. "Pull yourself together."

"It ain't easy as you think, old man!" Everett shouted as Temple walked away.

While Vadie packed, Temple roused Etha. "How you feeling today?"

"Stronger. And look." She flipped the blanket aside, pulled up her nightdress, and gently removed her bandages. "It's healing up."

"Best news I've heard all week," Temple said. "But now I got to tell you something you don't want to hear. I had to put Everett in the tank last night. He was loaded and got in a fistfight with Claude Steele. He slept it off over in the jail and—"

"You *what*? Everett's in the lockup?"

"He was in no condition to bring into the apartment. Now Vadie is hopping mad—packing and taking off within the hour. I'm sorry."

Tears brimmed in Etha's eyes. "I thought having everyone together over Christmas would straighten him out."

"He's the cause of his own troubles and Vadie's. She knows that she and the boys can settle here in Vermillion anytime. She knows we'd put her up until she finds a place and job. But she doesn't want to do that."

The family's suitcases were in the hallway. Vadie sent Homer and Leland in to say their thank-yous and farewells to Etha.

When the boys reappeared, Vadie said, "Boys, go with your father. Take these bags with you."

Etha brightened when Vadie walked in. She patted the bed but Vadie remained standing.

"I'm guessing you know Temple locked Ev in the tank."

"He told me Ev picked a fight and was too drunk to defend himself."

Vadie's lips contracted into a tight kernel of scorn. "Temple could have brought him in here as easy as to the jail. I'd have taken care of him—same as always."

"Temple and I don't think that's a good arrangement for the boys. Or you. And we'd—"

"This is going nowhere fast. You're not hearing me. I've got to believe that Ev will come around. There's no other way."

Etha sat up abruptly. "Not yet, young lady. You are acting like all that matters is that lout you married. You know your mother, bless her soul, was against the marriage. Knew he was a bad apple from the get-go. What do you think she'd say now? Seeing you and the boys living in fear? Praying it wouldn't be one of those nights when the booze makes him rough? You've got two sons to think of. They should come first. If you don't take off those blinders and stand up for yourself and your kids, you'll be the one responsible. Not Everett. *You!*"

Vadie's eyes narrowed. "Quit butting into my life." She tramped out of the bedroom and through the kitchen, slamming the door behind her.

CHAPTER TWENTY-NINE

IT WAS EVENING; Vadie and family were long gone. Temple was heading to the courthouse with a greasy bag of Maid-Rite sandwiches—supper for the still-jailed Donley—when the frantic honking of a car horn followed by the screech of brakes on the next block stopped him midstride. He dropped the bag and bolted toward the hubbub.

A rusted jalopy was stopped in front of the Idle Hour. An irate driver leaned out the window, screaming and beating his hat against the car door. Swaying side to side while clutching the car's radiator cap was a lanky fellow with trousers drooping across his skinny backside.

Idle Hour imbibers swarmed the sidewalk. Temple recognized the two county clerks, a waitress from the Crystal Hotel, and Thelma among them. Some egged the driver on: "Run over the rummy!" Others rooted for the stew-bum.

The driver, the high school science teacher, opened the door and began to step out.

"Please stay inside your car for now, sir!" Temple shouted, then turned to the spectators. "Show's over."

It didn't take long for the crowd to break up. It was a cold night and the Idle Hour was snug. Holding fast to the radiator cap, the drunk sang incoherently in a mournful tone.

Temple approached the motorist. "What happened?"

"I was driving home from church council when this guy stumbled out right in front of me. If I hadn't applied the brakes I'd have hit him for sure." The teacher rubbed his forehead. "Jesus. Scared me half to death."

"Okay. Give me your name and phone, then I'll take him in." Temple turned to the mournful singer who was still standing, but listing badly. "What's your name, sir?"

The pale-blue eyes slipped past the sheriff's. "Done nothing wrong."

Temple gripped the fellow's arm. "Not so. As a matter of fact, I'm going to arrest you on drunk-and-disorderly."

The fellow's knees began to buckle. Temple held him up.

"I'm Lonnie Taylor."

Temple's brows rose. "Mr. Taylor, I've been hearing things about you. You can sleep this off in jail without scaring more law-abiding citizens like this fellow here."

It was coming up on nine p.m. when Temple got Lonnie into the tank, toed a bucket close to the man's head, and locked the cell.

"Got some company," Temple said to Donley, who was two cells down. Donley hadn't been able to make bail and was lodging with the county until his trial. "Sorry, but it will be bologna sandwiches for dinner tonight. I got waylaid on my way back from the Maid-Rite."

Donley moaned—maybe in despair about the fare or about his situation or, likely, both.

As Temple locked the cell door after delivering Donley's meal, he heard Lonnie heaving into the bucket.

In the apartment, he called Claude at the rooming house, told him he had Lonnie in the lockup for drunk-and-disorderly and tomorrow morning would be a good time to grill the guy. He'd be sick as a dog and maybe feeling the walls closing in. Temple ate a bologna sandwich and climbed into bed with Etha.

The next morning he got up early, telephoned Ed, and asked him to get to the office as soon as possible. "I've got Donley and that Lonnie in the cells and I need to check on something."

By the time Claude turned up at the courthouse, Temple was back and Ed was out on an errand.

"So you got our fella?" Claude grinned. "Good work."

Temple poured two cups of coffee. "See where this takes us. Right now, all I've got him for is drunk-and-disorderly."

"Got ourselves a toehold. Two old dogs like us can work that, right?"

When Temple led the prisoner into the office, the room filled with a sour stench. The sheriff sat him down at the evidence table. He and Claude settled in opposite.

"Good to see you again, Lonnie," the railroad detective said. "I thought since you were bunking here for a while—with the drunk-and-disorderly charges and all—we'd talk some more about you getting the heave-ho from Milt."

"I told you all that. I told you I had nothing to do with the derailment." Lonnie rubbed his stubble. "Got a cigarette?"

Claude smiled. "Just humor me. There are a couple of things that don't smell right. So, let's see." He paused, flipping through his notebook. "You said you turned in your switch key to Milt."

Lonnie lifted his chin. "Ask him."

"As a matter of fact, I did. He confirmed your story. See here, I've even got the evidence." Claude pulled a key from his vest pocket and held it before Lonnie's face. "You've scratched your initials on it. *L.T.* Seems like you went to a lot of trouble to make sure the powers that be would know you'd turned this key in."

Shrugging, Lonnie said, "Lots of the fellas put marks on their keys. Sometimes you got to loan it out to someone who forgets theirs. If yourn initials are on it, it improves the chances you'll get it back."

"Fair enough. But maybe you managed to get your fingers on another switch key after turning this one in. Herschel says you showed up at the station to gab the day before the derailment. At some point, he stepped away from the office to help a passenger. Remember that?"

"Guess so."

"You guess so? Can't you remember? It's not all that far back."

"Okay. Seems right."

Claude stood, pinched a second key from his vest pocket, and laid it aside the first. "Herschel . . . well, he used poor judgment. He hung the duplicates just inside the ticket window. This here is one of them. Not the one you swiped and used to cock the switch. I haven't found it yet. But I will. And when I do and your prints are on it—then you'll be charged with first degree murder. Premeditation. Something you planned out ahead."

"I don't know what you're yammering about. I didn't steal a key. I didn't cock the switch. Answer me this: why in the hell would I be pulling passengers out of the crushed cars after the wreck? Climbing inside, risking my own life to help, if I'd caused it all in the first place? It don't make no sense."

Claude strolled to the window facing the street. "Good question. I'll admit I don't know the answer quite yet. Might take awhile but I'm a patient man. I've found Vermillion to be a very hospitable place. I made me a lady friend, as a matter of fact. By the way, what about *your* lady friend? Is she involved in this too? It would be a shame because then she'd be charged as an accessory to murder."

"She don't have nothing to do with nothing."

Back at the evidence table, Claude leaned close to Lonnie. "We'll be talking to her, that's for certain. What did you say her name was?"

"I didn't." Lonnie licked his lips. "I'd like a smoke."

"In a bit. You were saying?"

"She's not here. Went home to see her folks."

"Where her folks at?" Claude asked.

"Tennessee."

Claude made a note. "What's her name?"

"I ain't giving you that. No need 'cause she ain't done nothing."

"When will she be back?"

"When I make enough money to send her a train ticket. Said she'd come back to me if I got the dough."

"Okay. I'll let that go for now. Sheriff, you want to jump in?"

Temple, who had been sitting silently, cleared his throat. "I'd like to go over where you were Thursday last between three thirty and seven thirty p.m. The day of the derailment. Sometime in those hours, the switch was thrown."

Lonnie flopped back in his chair. "I already done told Mr. Steele. I got off work at four p.m. I had a beer at the hall and two or three rounds of pool. Then I went to my room and made dinner. I had dozed off when, *bang!* I heard the crash and ran to the station."

Claude cut in: "Not all that time was accounted for. Stricker vouched for you until maybe five o'clock when he saw you heading back to your room."

"But there ain't no other way out of there except through the pool hall. Did he see me walking out? Nope. Because I didn't."

"As a matter of fact," Temple said, "I visited the pool hall just this morning to check on that. Seems there *is* another way out. There's a storeroom at the end of the hall with a window that opens real easy. And it's not more than three feet above the tar roof of the building next door. The building that directly abuts the pool hall. Easy to shimmy down to the back alley with that workman's ladder bolted to the brick."

"Stricker led me to believe there was only one entrance and egress," Claude said.

Lonnie opened and closed his mouth. Then said, "I didn't go out like you're saying. I stayed in my room until—"

Ed stomped into the office, cutting off Lonnie's words. The deputy's face was crimson from the cold, his nose dripping. "Sorry I'm late."

"Mr. Taylor, this is Deputy McCance," Temple said. "He's joining us."

Ed's eyes narrowed. "Hey, I remember you. From the night of the wreck. Dragging folks out of that coach."

"You're right! See, I was just explaining to these lawmen that I was helping folks, and why would I do that if I cocked the switch?"

"Sure! I boosted you up on that tipped car. People were screaming something terrible. We managed to get some out, but—"

"So Ed," Temple interrupted, "you want to show Mr. Taylor those pictures?"

The deputy hung his overcoat and fedora on the coatrack and blew his nose, then sat down at the table with a pile of photos. "The coroner's assistant takes snaps of the bodies in the morgue. I picked these up from the hospital file room just now." He pushed the photos one by one across the table.

The prisoner shuddered as each passed into his line of vision.

"Anything to say?" Temple asked.

"Tried to save as many as I could."

"So you still deny causing the wreck?"

"Yes, I do."

Temple lit a cigarette. "All right. The night after the wreck, a local woman was strangled to death. Her house backed up to the tracks and we believe there could be a connection between her murder and something she witnessed."

Lonnie stayed quiet.

"Tell me about the day after the wreck," Temple said.

Licking his lips, Lonnie said, "The day after the wreck I worked my shift on the highway. I washed up in my room, had a bite, and tried to sleep, but couldn't. After a whiles I gave up, wandered over to the Idle Hour, and started drinking. Then I stayed on after hours and joined the all-night poker game in the back room there. That's the Lord's truth."

"What time did you get to the bar?" Claude asked.

"Something like eight o'clock. Stayed through until seven in the morning."

Temple said, "That account is neatly tied as a Christmas bow."

Lonnie shrugged.

Temple stood. "I think we're done for now. As of today, the only charge against you stands at drunk-and-disorderly, which in this county carries a ten-day jail sentence." He cocked his head toward the door. "Let's go."

Back in the office, the three lawmen huddled. Temple shook his head. "We need more evidence to charge him for throwing that switch. Finding that missing switch key would help . . . depending on where it turns up. Or a witness, of course. Someone who saw him in the act or at least glimpsed him in the vicinity. Ed, you reinterview the track and station crews. They're on the spot and most likely to notice if Lonnie was skulking around. I'll give the ground along the tracks another close search for the second duplicate key."

Claude flipped through the morgue photographs, then pushed them aside. "Lonnie is holding back on us about his woman. I know it in my bones. She might very well be involved—knew about his plans to sabotage the train. I'm going to make another trip to Mooreland. See if that wheat scooper can't give me a better description of her."

The three men buttoned up their overcoats, settled their hats.

"All those folks dead and because of what?" Temple said. "Because a man got sacked? What a waste."

CHAPTER THIRTY

AFTER THREE HOURS HUMPING up and down the crossties in his dress shoes, tracking down various crewmen and getting the same negative shrugs to his questions about activity in the switch area before the wreck, Ed loped back to the office. *Beating my head against a wall,* he thought.

The sheriff lumbered in with a similarly discouraged expression. "Nothing but a sack of trash for my trouble—rusted tobacco cans, yellowed newspapers, apple cores. No key."

The two turned to their typewriters to catch up on paperwork and rest their feet.

For a bit, all was quiet. Then Temple's phone rang—it was Carmine. "Last night I was staking out the ravine and I think the bootleggers are moving their operation. Maybe they spotted me earlier. I caught sight of three men carrying crates out of the gorge and toward the road. They made at least a dozen trips. Not long before dawn, two trucks headed out."

"Good work. I hate to let these fellows slip through our fingers. Let me think on this. Call me back in ten." Temple turned to Ed. "I think it's time to raid that whiskey still off Route 15."

"With two cases hanging fire?"

"Carmine thinks the moonshiners are packing up. This sounds like a big operation to me. I was considering deputizing him. How do you feel about going out there with him tonight and raiding the still?"

Ed blanched at the thought of having another shotgun pointed at his head. "Well . . . ah. Do you think Carmine is up to snuff?"

"I do. He's got sharp eyes and street smarts. And these old legs of mine aren't up for clambering around a ravine in the dark. But two young men can handle it no problem. I wouldn't send you out if I didn't think so."

The phone rang again and Ed listened with a sinking stomach while Temple filled Carmine in on the plan.

By late afternoon the deputy had more or less resigned himself to the assignment. He motored to the CCC camp with two shotguns and a Bible bumping along in the backseat. As he pulled up the gravel drive, Baker and Carmine were waiting outside the commander's office. Ed grabbed the Bible and stepped from the sedan. Snow flurries peppered the air. He secured the top button of his coat.

"Commander Baker," the deputy said, striding forward with his hand outstretched. "Thanks for the loan of your man."

"Absolutely. He's come a long way since joining up in August. I recall what a fast study you were too. The best ones sometimes come to us pretty rough but catch on quick."

Carmine stared at the ground while Baker talked, seeming both embarrassed and proud.

Baker continued, "He's a first-rate shot too. I've observed him on the camp's rifle range."

Ed sent up a small prayer of thanks and lifted the Bible. "Carmine DiNapoli, please place your right hand on the Bible while I administer the oath of office, deputizing you on this day of December 29, 1935."

Carmine laid his palm on the leather.

Ed said, "Repeat after me: *I, Carmine DiNapoli, do solemnly swear that I will support and defend the Constitution of the United States and the Constitution of the State of Oklahoma and that I will well and faithfully discharge the duties upon which I am about to enter.*"

Ed remembered when Temple had administered the oath to him ten months back. They'd stood on the courthouse steps with Mrs. Jennings as the witness. This was before Viviane, before their wedding, before he'd truly understood what being a lawman meant. And he hadn't really known that until Jess had pointed that shotgun at his forehead. Temple had been his guide all these months. Now Ed looked into Carmine's eyes and felt the weight of responsibility.

After the oath was sworn, Baker shook both men's hands and wished them luck.

As they motored down the drive, Carmine said, "I'm obliged to you and Sheriff Jennings for giving me this chance."

Ed mustered a smile. "I'll be honest. It has been a long day, a long week, and I'm not all that excited about raiding a still in the middle of the night."

Carmine studied Ed's profile. "You're not seeing yourself as Eliot Ness? Jeez. I'm on top of the world. You know, like the song." He snapped his fingers and hummed.

"Stop it!" Ed barked. "This isn't a game. The bootleggers aren't going to welcome us with *Howdy, fellas, do your worst!* They'll be armed and mad as hornets."

Carmine sank into his jacket. Neither spoke for the remainder of the ride until Carmine said, "Slow down and park behind that old barn. We're a couple of miles from the still. The moonshiners enter and exit at the other end of the gorge. We won't be spotted if we hike in from this side."

The sedan jounced into an abandoned farmyard. It was coming on sunset. Specks of snow blew past but none stuck.

"What's the setup?" Ed asked.

"The head of the ravine is at that stand of trees." Carmine pulled a hand-drawn map from his pocket. "We can hike in along the creek."

"There's enough brush to cover us?"

"Yep. But it's hiding the still too. I'm not exactly sure where it's at."

"All right. Once we think we're close, we hunker down and wait awhile to see how much coming and going there might be. Then we creep up on them."

The wind blew strong and cold. The men shouldered their shotguns and moved off toward the trees in the dimming light. Ed took the lead.

The drought had reduced the creek to nothing but a narrow trickle running along the rocky streambed. The farther into the ravine the two men trod, the darker it got. The setting sun meshed with the dense branches of cottonwoods crowding both sides of the gorge. Off to the left a spark of light flickered. Ed turned and pointed. "That's it," Carmine whispered.

Ed scuttled to the right, moving up the steep side of the ravine and toward a clump of cottonwoods. The trees there had grown sideways—stretching their branches out and over the creek, their roots gripping the incline. Ed grabbed at roots, pulling himself upward. At one point he halted, thinking he heard voices across the way, but all was quiet. He moved along with Carmine on his heels.

Inside the small thicket, the two men tried to make themselves comfortable on the narrow perch of roots and rocks. The air among the cottonwoods was biting. Ed wondered if the moonshiners sensed the lawmen's presence and were lying low. He checked the time: just past nine o'clock. "Let's give it an hour," he said.

The minutes passed slowly. Ed's legs cramped. A spider crawled across his neck and disappeared inside his shirt. There was no action across the way.

"Time?" Carmine whispered.

"Close enough. Let's go."

Down in the creek bed, it was pitch black. Carmine, smaller and more nimble, had stepped around Ed and was now in the lead. The creek bubbled faintly. Soon the muffled voices of the moonshiners could be heard. Maybe fifty feet away at most, and likely with guns at the ready.

Ed laid his hand on the boy's shoulder, cocked his thumb for Carmine to step behind. Close by, a wood fire hissed. Thick brush walled off the streambed. Behind the brambles and up the slope Ed spotted movement. The deputy turned. Mouthed, *On three.* Overhead the stuttering rhythm of an owl sounded. *Hoo-h-hoo-hoo. Hoo-h-hoo-hoo.*

The two men tucked their shotguns into their shoulders. Ed lowered his head, hurtled past the barricade of scrub, and scrambled up the incline. Someone shouted. From ahead came the sound of boots scraping across rocks. Ed emerged into an open area. At the far end, about one hundred yards away, was a three-sided shed.

The roof was covered with concealing branches. Inside, a kerosene lantern glowed. Ed caught a glimpse of a large man lowering the still's copper condensing coil into a crate. Packing up, as Carmine had suspected.

"Sheriff's office, hands up!" the deputy shouted. Two fellows broke from behind the shack and dashed up the steep slope. Carmine took off after them.

Ed drew closer to the open side of the shed, his finger on the trigger. Inside, standing astride a dismantled apparatus, was the older of the two Johnson brothers. Neither of the two who took off up the incline was the younger Johnson but Ed knew he would surely be close by. The bachelor farmers were known throughout the county for keeping to themselves. No one even knew their first names, although they ate dinner at the Maid-Rite six days a week. The elder, with the paunchy face of Charles Laughton, raised a hunting rifle.

Ed inhaled and willed his voice to keep steady. "Mr. Johnson, you're under arrest for distilling grain alcohol. Put the gun down and push it over this way."

The bootlegger remained stone-faced. He leveled the rifle at Ed's chest.

The deputy planted his legs apart to keep them from visibly shaking. "You know what you're doing is against the law."

Brush crashed underfoot from the rocky hillside above. Two men emerged, arms raised, with Carmine coming up behind. Then someone else entered the picture. The younger Johnson materialized in back of Carmine and aimed a pistol at the young man's head.

"Down!" Ed shouted.

Carmine jumped to one side. He must have lost his

footing because there was a thud and he snorted as if the wind had been knocked out of him. Heavy footfalls down into the ravine told Ed that Carmine's two captives had bolted.

Ed thought quickly. He was not going to let Carmine go down with a bullet to the skull. The deputy stared the older brother straight in the eye and slowly lowered his rifle. Laid it on the ground. The older brother chuckled. Ed unhurriedly turned and called out to the younger man: "I'd like you to put your gun down too!"

"Oh you would?" the man responded.

"There's nothing you or your brother will gain if this ends badly with two lawmen dead. I'm guessing you are on the fringe of a city outfit run by big shots. You take all the risks and get peanuts." As he talked, Ed spied Carmine crawling slowly forward. "What do you take in?" the deputy asked calmly, nodding at both brothers to make sure he had their ears. "If you don't mind my asking."

"Enough for us to—" the younger brother was saying when the deputy saw that Carmine was within six inches of the man's leg.

"Now!" Ed shouted.

Carmine sprang up, grabbed the moonshiner's shins, and brought him down. There was a sharp crack as the outlaw hit his head on a rock. A gusher of blood spurted out.

In the same instant, Ed whipped around to fully face the older man in the shed. "Put that gun down."

"Why should I?"

"So we can tend to your brother. A head wound is nothing to fool with. That looks like a bad one. And even if you kill us, there is no way you can make a getaway with him bleeding all over the place. He needs a doctor."

The rifle barrel remained pointed at Ed's chest but the bootlegger leaned to one side, trying to get a look at his injured brother.

"I'm going to start walking toward you one step at a time." The deputy raised his foot and took a step. Then another. By the third, he saw the man's eyes dart again to his brother. Ed forced himself to keep up the slow pace although his brain was screaming, *Rush him!* He stopped within a foot of the bootlegger's muzzle.

Behind Ed, the injured man moaned.

The older brother tipped his head back. "If'n I surrender, you'll tend Saul?"

Ed nodded.

"All right then." The bootlegger laid his gun down and extended his wrists.

Ed handcuffed him. "Carmine, walk Mr. Johnson here to the car and wait for me there. I'll bind up his brother's head."

"Let's go," Carmine said. They picked their way down to the creek bed as Ed approached the injured man.

The deputy quickly shook off his heavy jacket, removed his shirt, and ripped it into strips. He bound Saul's skull, then got his own coat back on. "Can you walk?"

"Think so."

"Then let's go." Ed helped boost the man up and the two staggered to the bottom of the ravine.

Saul stank of sweat and woodsmoke. And despite his skinny limbs, he had heft. Still, Ed felt light inside. The fear he'd carried since that first trip to the hatchery had washed away. It would be back, he figured. It was part of the job. But now he knew he could shoulder it.

CHAPTER THIRTY-ONE

WIND GUSTED THROUGH the high grasses fringing Vermillion's small cemetery—a rustling chorus rising into the tall sky.

Temple strode down the gravel path to join the small cluster circled round Ruthie-Jo's plot. The graveside service was already underway. Most of the eight mourners kept their eyes lowered, gazing abstractly at the pine casket in the bottom of the grave, or at the heap of red soil beside it. Reverend Jacobs's message was sparse as the landscape. Like most in attendance, he had only spoken to the deceased once or twice—on one of those rare occasions when she stepped outside her house. The worn platitudes were trotted out. "Ruthie-Jo was a good Christian woman who was devoted to hearth and home. She never had an unkind word about anyone." At this last point, Temple intently studied his boots.

The sheriff was sandwiched between Mrs. Jacobs, in her standard black coat, and Chester, with Daddy on a leash. Three women from the Methodist Ladies' Auxiliary were doing their part—willing and able to see the deceased off with the same utilitarian briskness with which they served chicken dinners at the church rummage sale. Cy stood at the head of the grave.

Swatches of scrub grass separated most of the head-stones at Elmhurst Cemetery. It was established only forty-two years back, when the Cherokee Outlet was opened to the rush of white settlers. A pioneer graveyard with room to stretch out. Temple reckoned Ruthie-Jo would be satisfied with this arrangement. A loner in death as in life.

After Reverend Jacobs concluded with "Ashes to ashes, dust to dust," and tossed in a handful of loose soil, the gathering broke apart. Chester approached Temple. The sheriff bent down to offer the dog a head scratch. "Hello there, Daddy."

Chester smiled paternally. "He's a good dog. I have renamed him. He is now McTavish."

"Really? Isn't he too old for a name change?"

"Not at all. In fact, he's grateful. He knows Daddy wasn't suitable."

Chester and McTavish moved toward the Jacobs's se-dan for a ride back to town. Cy remained by the grave. Temple offered his condolences. Snuffling, Cy embraced the sheriff.

When they pulled apart, Cy asked, "Any headway?"

"We've got a strong lead. This is not for public con-sumption, but we have a former rail hand as a person of interest."

"You thinking he might have killed Ruthie-Jo?"

Temple nodded.

"Then maybe I should give this to you." Cy dug into his pocket and extracted something tightly wrapped in tissue paper.

Temple recognized the key immediately. He tried to keep his voice level but excitement threatened to bubble up. "How did you come by this?"

"I found it the other day when I was looking through Ruthie-Jo's things. I was going to turn it in at the train station but it sounds as if you might need it more."

"This will be a huge help." Temple held out his palm. "Did you touch the key or just the wrap?"

"Just the wrap."

"I'm expecting we'll find Ruthie-Jo's prints all over it, but maybe we'll get lucky and find the killer's too."

"And listen," Cy said, "thanks for giving me her wedding ring so she could be buried with it. Meant a lot to me. When do you expect I can have the rest of her effects?"

"Soon as possible. Ed and I are working to close the case. Then, after the trial and sentencing . . ."

"All right. I'm a patient man." Cy peered over his shoulder at the gravestone. "I'm going to stay a bit longer."

Temple patted him on the back, hustled to his car, and then gunned it to the courthouse.

"I think we've got the nail in the coffin that connects the Mitchem case to Lonnie and the derailment," Temple announced as he strode into the office.

Ed was at this desk typing a report on the busting of the still and the arrest of the Johnson brothers.

Temple unrolled the key and showed Ed. "Look what Cy found in Ruthie-Jo's things. I'm betting it's the duplicate universal key. I think she must have witnessed the perpetrator toss it and the lock. Maybe she got a glimpse of the man—or more than a glimpse. Maybe she could have identified him. Or at least he thought she could."

"Wouldn't that be something."

"Yes sir. So let's get this shipped off right quick to the state lab for fingerprint analysis. I have hers from the autopsy report and you run upstairs and get Lonnie's."

The two lawmen swung by the train station to drop off the express package to the state lab in Oklahoma City.

"Now to the Idle Hour. We're going to test the strength of Lonnie's alibi."

The scent of stale beer hung heavy in the bar's narrow confines. The place was empty except for Ike Gradert, his back to the door, counting coins from the till.

"What can I get you fellas?" he called over his shoulder.

"Couple of beers," Temple said.

Ike carefully funneled the change back into the cash drawer and drew two glasses.

Temple lit a cigarette, inhaled slowly. "So, we're working on the Mitchem case and need to ask you something."

"Whatever I can do," Ike said, drawing a beer for himself.

"We've got a fellow claiming he was here the night of her killing. Came in about eight p.m. and then got involved in an all-night poker game. Name of Lonnie Taylor. Know him?"

Ike rubbed the bristles on his cheek this way and that. "Think so. One of those mopey faces? Worked on tracks?"

"That's him. Was he here that night?"

"You're asking an awful lot. The place was packed. But yeah, I do remember him at the poker table later on."

"What time was that?"

"After closing. Two o'clock. Around then." Ike gazed past Temple's shoulder. Coal hissed and snapped in the stove. "Lonnie was here. He was talking about pulling folks out of the colored car. He kept rambling on to the point where the other card players had to remind him to play his hand."

"And he stayed through until dawn?"

"I know for sure he was here at sunup."

A couple of shop clerks hustled in and Ike got busy at the other end of the bar.

Ed rotated his empty beer glass clockwise and then counterclockwise. "The all-night poker still seems too perfect. Can't Hinchie give us a tighter window for the time of death?"

"I'll need to push him on that. But also I'm thinking Lonnie might have been at the Idle Hour when he says. That someone told him to hurry over there for an alibi. Maybe there was someone who cared enough about him that she would kill for him."

"The girlfriend? Is she even in the picture? I mean, no one's seen her."

"Exactly. Maybe there's a reason."

C HAPTER THIRTY-TWO

AS HE AWOKE EACH MORNING, Henry Bluett experienced anew the vast and desolate cavern that was his grief. All day it would burrow into his waking hours, until the widower could no longer keep his inflamed eyes open and surrendered to a false sleep.

After Cleo's death, he'd accompanied her back home to Cozine. Her coffin was loaded into the baggage car and he'd sat beside it the whole way. The railroad had killed his wife and yet he was forced to use it—and pay!—for the funeral conveyance. Several of Cozine's farmers, his son-in-law among them, had offered to fetch Henry and Cleo in their trucks. But Henry was a stubborn man. He was determined to make the AT&SF acknowledge its culpability. Charging the widower for a return ticket and baggage handling would strengthen his case, he believed, and he had saved the ticket and invoice as proof.

Now, nine days after Cleo's death, Henry was returning to Vermillion. He steeled himself to step inside the colored coach. The unventilated car was nasty with slimy wads of chewing tobacco and peanut shells scattered across the floor. Henry spread his handkerchief across the wooden seat and arranged yesterday's edition of Cozine's *Weekly Progress* in his lap. The train pulled out slowly—

rolling past the bank with its white marble steps, the An-
tioch Baptist Church, the clapboard post office, and the
bottling plant. The train picked up speed quickly beyond
the village limits. Tidy farms, with generous barns and
shady front-porched houses, all owned by colored families, flashed past the windows.

Henry's daughter Corrine had tried to talk him out of
making the trip.

"Wasn't it enough your letter addressing the Corporation Commission was printed on the front page of the
Weekly Progress?" she'd asked.

Now, as the colored car jolted over a rough piece
of track, Henry unfolded the newspaper. The headline
shouted, "An Open Letter About Jim Crow Injustices.
Not Equal in Point of Safety." *No, Corrine, it's not
enough.* He'd bet cash money that not a single member
of the commission had heard about, let alone read, his
letter. That was why this trip was necessary.

When the train pulled into Vermillion, Henry buttoned his overcoat and settled his hat. A biting gust of
wind nipped at his legs. He marched directly to the *Gazetteer*. The tall plate-glass windows of the newsroom, occupying a former storefront, revealed only a single occupant bent over a desk. Inside, the place smelled sharply of
ink, old newsprint, and heat rising from dusty radiators.

The publisher raised a finger without glancing up,
and continued marking up copy with a red grease pencil.

"Okay then," the publisher, a man named Stowe,
finally said, pushing back from his desk. "Placing a
classified?"

Henry stepped forward. "No sir. I'm Henry Bluett,
postmaster in Cozine. I'd like to submit a letter to the

editor." He removed an envelope from the inside pocket of his suit coat and passed it to Stowe.

"Come in and have a seat." Stowe gestured to the low gate that separated the newsroom from the public. "Let me see what you've got."

The editor settled behind his desk. Henry arranged himself stiff-backed in the seat opposite.

The three-page letter was a carbon copy of the one Henry had submitted to the *Weekly Progress*. Stowe read the first page. Then he purposefully laid the remainder aside. "I think this might be better suited for the Cozine publication. You make some strong . . . well, I was going to say 'accusations,' but let's say 'contentions.' Many are unsubstantiated. And, honestly, none of this bears directly on my readership."

Henry's jaw tightened.

Stowe ran his finger down the first page. "This here, for example. You write, *Just a few days ago, Most Honored Gentlemen, there happened one of the most damnable crimes of the age in the town of Vermillion. For in the snuffing out of the lives of fifteen helpless black men and women, whose brains, arms, and eyes were scattered like cattle dung, the vile sort of 'equal accommodations' furnished to black people by the railroads of Oklahoma was brought to light.*"

The publisher tilted back in his chair and folded his hands on his stomach. "You are accusing the AT&SF of murder when it is widely known that the switch was sabotaged. And when the perpetrator is found, as he will be, that is who will be put on trial for murder."

Henry had expected this response and tried to keep his voice steady. "If you would read a bit further, sir, you will see my argument. Of course the man who cocked the switch is directly responsible for the fifteen deaths, including my wife, Cleo Bluett."

"My condolences."

"Thank you. However, if the colored coach had not been at least twenty years old and constructed solely of wood, and if it had not been placed directly behind the baggage car, it would not have ripped apart. It would not have taken the brunt of the steam. As you well know, the coaches for white travelers are steel-plated and have been so for some time."

Stowe snapped his chair's front legs back onto the floor, leaned forward, and said. "You make a point. But the *Gazetteer* is not the place to make it. As I mentioned—"

Henry held up the copy of the *Weekly Progress* he'd brought with him. "I'm not, of course, expecting your paper to print my letter on the front page. But I respectfully believe it should appear in your paper. The derailment occurred here. The survivors were treated at Vermillion's hospital. The dead where embalmed here. I understand your sheriff's department is conducting an investigation."

"Okay. Look. I'll consider printing your letter, though you're going to have to limit it to two paragraphs and cut out the allusions to a crime, to cow dung, and the other provocative wording. Tomorrow's paper goes on the press at seven tonight. Get me the rewrite by five. This doesn't necessarily mean I'll publish it, but let's see what you come up with." He handed over a red grease pencil.

Henry stood abruptly. "I'll be back." He strode outside, barely containing his anger. *Provocative wording*— as if the railroad's criminal actions didn't deserve such strong words.

* * *

As Henry passed through the courthouse and into the lawman's office, Temple was hanging up the phone with a clatter.

Temple gestured for him to take a seat and said, "Pardon me," as he dumped a packet of headache powders into a glass of water. "Everybody's calling wanting something."

"I won't take much of your time," Henry said, removing his hat and setting it on his lap. "Our wives had adjoining beds in the hospital. I'm Henry Bluett."

"Of course. Etha mentioned your wife." Temple extended his hand. "My condolences."

"And how is Etha?"

"On the mend."

"Glad to hear that. You tell her I appreciate her kindness to Cleo."

"I will certainly do that."

"Now, I'd like to know where the investigation into the derailment stands."

"Unfortunately, I'm not at liberty to share any details, but I am hopeful we will get to the bottom of this."

"I've heard that you are working the case along with a railroad detective."

"That is correct."

Henry's voice rose: "I have serious concerns about that arrangement."

"It's standard procedure in cases like this," Temple explained.

"That may be so, but here I'd say that the railroad itself is also complicit and so should not be making inquiries into the matter. Conflict of interest."

"How so?"

"If the colored car had been built of steel, as the white cars are, and if it was not positioned near the locomotive, I don't believe there would have been many, if any, passenger deaths. Even in the case of a derailment."

"Well, sir, you make a valid point," Temple said. "You do. But it's pure speculation. I don't see how it can be proved. And regarding a conflict of interest, you are surely entitled to your opinion, yet neither I nor the county commissioners nor the State of Oklahoma see it that way."

"In that case, I would like to lodge a complaint with the Jackson County Board of Commissioners stating that these types of arrangements between county agencies and private concerns are unethical."

After several moments of silence, Temple said, "And you have every right to do that. If you write up your complaint, I will see that it gets to the county officials and is addressed at their next board meeting."

"Thank you. I will send you something by the end of the week. Meanwhile, I have a favor to ask. I composed a letter to the editor that I'm hoping the *Gazetteer* will run. The editor wants some changes. Mind if I sit over there and work on it?" Henry pointed to the evidence table.

"Go right ahead and—" Temple started to say when the phone rang.

Henry moved to the table and ran his eyes across the letter. Cutting it down to two paragraphs seemed impossible.

An hour later, Henry was back at the *Gazetteer*. After deleting half of the wording, it still wasn't anywhere near two paragraphs. If he cut anything more, all his

points would be diluted into a watery pap. He decided
if the publisher didn't accept it as is, he'd walk away.

Stowe glanced at the pages and handed them back.
"Still too long."

It was clear that the man never intended to publish
any part of the letter, even if it was cut to the bone. Henry
tucked the paper into his suit coat pocket and walked out
the door, his face rigid with fury. He'd find another way
to lay the deaths of Cleo and the rest at the feet of the
AT&SF. *I promise you, Cleo, I'll keep fighting.*

C HAPTER THIRTY-THREE

"FRESH AIR WILL DO YOU GOOD," Temple said, settling Etha into the passenger seat of the county's sedan. The sky on this particular morning was high and clear. The air reminded Etha of one of Hinchie's spring tonics—a syrupy liquid of obscure ingredients that he swore rejuvenated every organ of the body.

Another reason for the journey was so Temple could respond to a complaint by Mrs. Harvey, who lived at the far edge of the county. She was irate after turning into her driveway and running smack into Joe Melampy's Gwendolyn. Mrs. Harvey's radiator was busted, her tire punctured.

As they topped a slight hill, Etha spotted Mrs. Harvey's stout figure not more than a hundred yards down the road, planted beside the family's Model T. The Harvey farm was just beyond—up a long drive and surrounded by oaks.

"Looks like she's still fuming," Etha said.

"Mrs. Harvey or the car?"

Etha laughed. "Both."

Temple pulled up behind the Model T and yanked the handbrake. "You stay put." He climbed out and strode over to the angry matron. The wind was brisk enough, and blowing in the right direction, that their voices carried. Etha heard every word.

"That damn Gwendolyn stepped right out in front of me at the last minute!" Mrs. Harvey shouted. "I blew my horn but couldn't stop fast enough. I rammed into her flank. Couldn't help it. The ornery thing kicked my radiator in."

Temple walked around the front of the wounded car. Strolled back. "I'd say she did."

"What are you going to do about it?"

"About the radiator? I don't think you want me messing with it."

"No, about Melampy. His cow has done nothing but scare the wits out of drivers for years. Not to mention the property damage. Gwendolyn should be fenced and he should be fined."

Etha watched Temple's jaw tighten ever so slightly, though when he spoke again, his voice was steady. "I will talk to Mr. Melampy and let him know he is responsible for repairs to your car."

"And for a new pair of hosiery." Mrs. Harvey stuck a leg out from under her overcoat. "My stockings are full of burrs after chasing the cow off the road and into the pasture."

"Stockings too. Where is Gwendolyn, by the way?"

"She can go to hell for all I care. After I ran her off she headed east. Likely wanting to do more damage."

"Can we give you a ride up to the house?"

"No need," Mrs. Harvey replied, marching off.

"Well, that was a waste of time," Temple said, climbing into the car.

Motoring back toward town, they passed the cemetery. Etha spotted the fresh mound of bright earth covering Ruthie-Jo's grave.

"Did the reverend do right by her?"

"Good wife," Temple said. "Helped run the business. What else could he say? The fact is, she didn't mingle. And she seemed to make a point of rubbing the folks that she did come in contact with the wrong way."

Etha wondered how the clergy managed eulogies for those you might call the *difficult departed*. "How did Cy hold up?"

"Fair to middling. He appreciated having her wedding ring for the burial. Asked about the rest of her effects but that may take awhile."

"Those couldn't amount to much. She was just out walking the dog."

"Nightgown. Coat. Boots. Hairnet. Flashlight. Hose."

Etha frowned. "Wait. A hairnet?"

"So?"

"You don't mean a cap, like the one I wear at night to keep my set?"

"No, a net. I know what a hairnet is."

"The two times I laid eyes on her I'm sure she wasn't wearing one, that's all. There are certain types of women who use them."

"Actually, the hairnet was *under* the body," Temple said. "I couldn't say if she had been wearing it at some point or not. What types of women use them?"

Etha shrugged. "Women who have jobs that require them. Vadie has to wear one on the line at the canning factory. And waitresses. Anyone serving food."

Not far away a freight was running parallel to the road—its boxcars swaying under the blue sky. There was a faulty joint in the track and the wheels pushed through the air. *Shush-shush*. *Shush-shush*. But when they had crossed over the broken joint, the metal squealed. *Clink-clink*. Pause. *Clink-clink*. Call and response, Etha thought. Like when a baby wails and his mother scoops him up. Like when a man does wrong and his woman rushes to cover for him. To make things right.

She turned to Temple. "It's Thelma. I'd bet money she's Lonnie's gal. She told me herself she'd go to the wall for her boyfriend. That's exactly how she put it, 'I'd go wall for him if he needed me to.'"

"Maybe so, but that's not really enough—"

"And she wears a hairnet. I know you're skeptical but it's possible it's her."

"You may have a point. It's worth checking out."

Etha was now deep in thought. "I believe I may have seen Thelma just hours after the killing. That was the morning she was late with the food trays. Looked like something the cat dragged in. Hair tangled. Socks bunched up around her ankles and covered in burrs. I remember thinking, *Where did she pick up all those prickers?*"

"Is she coming to the apartment today?" Temple asked.

Etha checked her watch. "She said she'd be by after lunch."

The pair rode along in silence. Etha's excitement at possibly helping to find Ruthie-Jo's killer began dissolving at the edges. Despite Thelma's gruff ways, Etha admired the young woman for speaking her mind—most especially for calling out Vadie. As they bumped into town, Etha was hoping her theory about Thelma was wrong.

* * *

When they arrived at the courthouse, Temple accompanied Etha upstairs—he didn't trust her to take the steps slowly.

Once she settled in on the sofa with her knitting, Temple said, "I'm going to make a couple of calls in the office. And I'll stop Thelma for questioning when she walks in."

He hurried downstairs. Ed was at his desk.

"We've got a possible suspect for Ruthie-Jo's murder," Temple said.

"Not Lonnie?"

"Thelma Bennett. She could be Lonnie's girlfriend. Thelma's been helping Etha out these last couple of days and according—"

"The suspect has been working in your apartment all this time?"

"*Possible* suspect. Thelma is due upstairs after lunch. I'll waylay her. Bring her into the office for questioning. I need you to start calling around to the surrounding counties. See if anyone has heard of her. I'll find out if Claude connected with that scooper in Mooreland. Might be the kid could identify her as Lonnie's girlfriend."

Temple dialed up Mayo's and Myra answered. Claude's name was shouted out. Temple felt the pressure of time. Minutes ticked away.

Finally Claude got on the line. Temple filled him in on Thelma as a potential suspect. "Were you able to chat with that grain scooper?"

"Just got back. Mike, that's the kid's name, is sharp-eyed. Gave me a solid description of Lonnie's companion. Sturdy build. Brown hair cut short. Round face."

"All fits for Thelma. I'm going to send Ed over to pick up Mike. See if he can identify her."

After Temple replaced the receiver, Ed jammed his hat on his head and plucked his coat off the rack. "Talked to two sheriffs so far. Neither had anything on a Thelma Bennett."

The wall clock said one ten. So did Temple's watch. He opened the office door and moved his desk chair against the far wall so that he could spot Thelma the moment she strolled into the courthouse. He stuck a cigarette between his lips and, cupping his hands around the flame, lit up. It was an old habit acquired during an abundance of stakeouts. Crouched in the merciless wind hour after hour. You sheltered the match to keep it lit. And then you waited.

When his phone rang an hour or so later, Temple glanced at the door. All was quiet. He quickly crossed to his desk. Mrs. Harvey. Had he done anything yet about Gwendolyn? Not yet, but he promised he would. Temple returned to his post. Nothing had stirred.

Not two minutes later the phone sounded again. Temple decided to let it go this time. Whatever it was, it could wait. But it kept on and on—reaching fifteen before he gave in.

Etha was breathing heavily. "She's got the keys to the cells. I heard someone tiptoeing around the kitchen, so I peeked out and spotted Thelma. She took the keys off the hook. Just left."

"Oh my God. Lock yourself in. I'm on my way," Temple said.

He bolted out of the office, taking the stairs two at a time and berating himself the whole way. *She must have slipped by when I was on the phone with Mrs. Harvey.* The steel door to the cellblock was ajar. Lonnie's cell was empty. Temple paused. They couldn't have gotten far. Probably not even out of the courthouse. He rang the office from the cellblock phone, praying that Ed was back from Mooreland. The phone buzzed in Temple's ear for what seemed like an eternity. What if Lonnie and Thelma had holed up on the first floor? Were holding Viviane hostage? He was about to disconnect when he heard Ed's voice in the receiver.

"It's me," Temple said. "Thelma broke Lonnie out of jail. They might still be in the building. Make sure Viviane is locked in and then post yourself at the back door and that scooper at the front. I'll check the second floor."

One floor down, Temple silently turned the knob on the courtroom door. Dust motes floated in front of the tall windows. The state and federal flags stood motionless. He was slowly treading toward the jury box when Etha shouted something from upstairs. Temple ran to the stairwell and heard her yell, "They're in the parking lot!"

"Sweet Jesus," Temple muttered under his breath. He sprinted down the steps, calling for Ed. By the time the two lawmen burst out the back door, Thelma was behind the wheel of Judge Gibson's Ford. Lonnie was in the passenger seat and they were gunning across the gravel.

"I'll grab the shotgun, pick me up out front," Temple said.

Ed tore to the county sedan and careened out of the lot as Temple hustled past the wheat scooper, who stood unmoving in the foyer with a terrified expression on his face.

As Temple slid into the passenger seat, Ed said, "I think they're taking Route 15. I spotted them heading that way as I was running to the car. That Ford V-8's got as big an engine as we do. We might have trouble catching them."

"Do your best. Those two are nerved up, so we've got that on our side."

There were two main roads out of Vermillion. Route 20 went north and south. The other, Route 15, traveled east to west. The Texas border was only fifty miles away. If the pair crossed the state line, they'd be out of Temple's jurisdiction. And with 26,000 square miles in the Texas panhandle alone, Lonnie and Thelma would be almost impossible to track.

For several minutes, the view through the lawmen's windshield was empty. Then Temple spied a speck on the horizon that slowly grew larger.

"It's them! Inch up—but not too close. I don't want a Clyde Barrow and Bonnie Parker–style shootout."

Another three minutes clicked past on the sedan's dashboard clock. The V-8's rounded silhouette came into sharper focus.

Ed glanced at Temple. "Speed up?"

"Hold off a bit. We'll get them at the next left."

Route 15 zigzagged toward Texas in a series of ninety-degree lefts and rights, at regular intervals. Temple had lost count of how many drivers had missed one of these turns and flew straight into a wheat field or tipped into a gulley. At least a dozen had been fatalities.

An abandoned gas station, with weathered gray siding and a partially collapsed canopy over its rusted pumps, marked this particular hard left. From his vantage, Temple calculated that Thelma was continuing to push the V-8 even as the turn came into view. "Slow down, sister," he muttered.

At the last second, the Ford jerked tightly to the left and veered toward the station. A spray of gravel flew up. The rear of the jalopy swung around, slamming against the pumps.

Ed braked twenty yards back. Thelma's tires spun then lunged forward, regaining the road.

"She's not going to be able to stick it," Ed said.

As he spoke, the getaway car fishtailed wildly and overshot the road, then somehow straightened for half a tick before both right wheels slipped down a slight embankment. The Ford skidded a few feet on its side before rolling three times and landing on its roof. *Bang. Bang. Bang.* The lawmen scrambled out of the sedan and tore toward the wreck.

Thelma was already out of the car and crouching outside the passenger window, yanking on Lonnie's arm. "You son of a bitch! You louse! You dirty louse!" she screamed.

Temple shouted, "The car's going to catch! Get her out of here!"

Ed snatched Thelma around the waist and hauled her across the road. Temple knelt by the Ford. Lonnie's face was a bloody pulp. One eye stared vacantly. The other was closed. His arm was as limp as a dead fish.

"Make tracks!" Ed yelled.

Temple reached in, closed the open eye, and then dashed away, diving at the last second. Flaming debris burst from the engine, then rained down on the sandy, sterile field.

Ed, gripping Thelma by the arm, strode toward Temple.

The woman continued cussing out Lonnie as she tried to break free of the deputy.

"Thelma, listen to me, Lonnie is gone," Temple said, shaking her by the shoulder.

"What?"

"I'm sorry."

Her face froze for a moment. Then she shouted, "I wouldn't care if the son of a bitch drowned in his own blood! The stupid jackass! Wrecking that train."

She raged on until Temple said, "Quiet down."

Thelma's lips pinched together and her eyes narrowed.

The sheriff continued: "Thelma Bennett, I'm charging you with aiding and abetting the escape of Lonnie Taylor from the Jackson County Jail. You will be housed in said jail until arraigned by the judge. And we'll be questioning you about the murder of Ruthie-Jo Mitchem."

"I had nothing to do with that woman's death. You can't prove a goddamn thing."

Temple nodded at Ed, who fastened cuffs around Thelma's wrists.

"You're both—"

"Yeah, louses and jackasses. Same as Lonnie," Ed said.

"Ed, give Hinchie a call, will you?"

The deputy loaded the suspect into the car and drove back down the dusty road to the courthouse. Temple tramped over to a bench under the gas station's slumping canopy and smoked a cigarette. After a while, Hinchie showed up to examine Lonnie in his final resting place. Then the two men pulled the charred remains from the still-smoldering passenger seat and covered them with a rubberized sheet from the back of Hinchie's car.

"I've seen enough incinerated bodies this past two weeks to last me a good long while," Hinchie said dryly.

"We're on the same page. Could you drop me at the courthouse before heading to the morgue?"

Back at the courthouse, Ed stopped Temple as he was heading upstairs. "I put Thelma in the cellblock. Didn't think using the ladies' cell in your kitchen was a good idea."

"You thought right."

"When I got her in from the parking lot, Mike was still at his post at the front door. Shaking like a leaf and pale as milk."

"Understandable."

"I told him to wait in the office. I'm going to take his statement now. He got a good look at Thelma and says she was the woman living with Lonnie in the camp car."

"Good work. Viviane okay?"

"She seems fine."

"I'm going to check on Etha."

When Temple strode into the kitchen, Etha was leaning against the sink with a worried expression. "Are you all right? I've been a mess," she said.

He wrapped his arms around her. "All fine."

She murmured into his chest, "I was praying there wasn't going to be a shoot-out. Then when Ed came back without you, I was thinking the worst."

Temple kissed the crown of her head. "Thelma wrecked the judge's car. Lonnie was killed. Hinchie and I were taking care of that."

"What's going to happen to Thelma?"

"She's certainly doing time for springing Lonnie from jail. But as you know, it might be way more serious than that."

Through the apartment walls came muffled bellowing from Thelma.

"That's one angry woman," Temple said.

THE NEXT MORNING, December 31, Claude woke feeling sorry for himself. Last night, Temple had dropped by and filled him in on Lonnie's demise and Thelma's arrest. Although Claude wasn't going to be bringing Lonnie to trial, it was a fairly satisfactory ending to the case—for Claude and the railroad. Not for Lonnie, of course.

Things had turned out well, Claude thought. *So why am I so glum?* He'd be back in Kansas City, sleeping in his own bed, that very night. No worries about waking in the early hours to pee and finding another boarder had beat him to the toilet.

Although he was slow to admit it, Claude actually knew the source of his blues. It was Beatrice—he was going to miss her.

He rolled out of bed. Showered and shaved with care. Digging into his suitcase, he unearthed a balled-up shirt and sniffed the armpits. It would do. Clomping downstairs with suitcase in hand and boot buckles rattling, he passed into the kitchen where he knew he'd find her at this hour.

Beatrice was hunched over a sink of suds, her back to him. It was impossible that she hadn't heard his steps or felt his presence. Yet she did not turn.

He cleared his throat. "So today's the day. The company is expecting me back in time to ring in the new year," he announced, aware that his voice sounded falsely jolly.

When Beatrice turned, her eyes were rheumy as from an attack of hay fever. She rubbed her nose with a damp wrist.

"Hey, sugar, I'll be back. Honest to God." Claude lifted his right hand.

"I can't stay in this place another hour!"

Claude studied the floor. "I don't have an answer to that quandary right this minute, but we will figure something out. Work takes me out this way pretty often. And look here. There's a two-week excursion for railfans next July." He opened his suitcase, pulled out an issue of *Railroad Magazine*, flipped to a page with the corner folded down, and read: "*Special train travels from Chicago to Oakland, up to Seattle, then back to Chicago. Includes chances to photograph railroad equipment, stops at Pike's Peak, Golden Gate Bridge, and inspection of a narrow-gage line.* What do you say?"

"You know I can't run off with you for two weeks. Mother would have a fit."

Claude thought on this. She was right. "Well, how about if this was our honeymoon? What would you say then?"

Silence fell solemnly across the plain linoleum, then Beatrice burst out laughing and spread her palms. "I accept."

Hinchie and Minnie rapped on the Jennings's door at nine p.m. on the dot. Ringing in the new year together was a tradition among the four.

"You two look swell," Temple said, swinging wide the door.

The pair bustled in, bringing chill December air and a box of assorted chocolates. Tucked under Hinchie's arm was a bottle of medicinal whiskey that, as a doctor, he was licensed to dispense in limited amounts. Between the derailment and murder, Hinchie figured they all could use a curative pick-me-up.

Temple poured everyone a stiff drink and then raised his glass. "To 1936! May the trains stay on their tracks and may the rains be generous and long."

"Here, here," Hinchie said, tossing back his portion.

The phone rang as the four glasses clinked. "Damnit," Temple and Hinchie said simultaneously. Both were expecting it to be some emergency that demanded their response. While Temple took the call, the other three moved into the dining room and began setting up for pinochle.

"I'll be damned," Temple said, taking his seat at the table.

"Who called?" Etha asked.

"The singer from the Oke Doke. The woman Jess Fuller took up with. She confessed she was the anonymous tip from last week. The one that accused Ruthie-Jo of putting the squeeze on folks in town."

Minnie slapped the tabletop. "Good for her. Should have been done a long time ago."

The four drew cards for partners. Etha and Minnie were paired.

Hinchie laughed. "The mens against the womens. We got to be at the top of our game, Temple."

While the sheriff shuffled the deck, Etha set up a score pad. By ten p.m. the women had won four out of seven games, and the chocolate box held nothing but a half-bitten fruited nougat nobody wanted.

"Hel-lo!" Ed leaned in through the kitchen doorway. "Got anything for three thirsty travelers?" The wind-stung faces of Viviane and Carmine peered eagerly over his shoulder.

"Come on in," Temple hollered, striding into the kitchen. "Give me your coats. Hinchie and I just got soundly trounced at cards by the ladies."

Viviane entered the dining room clapping. "Hooray for the girls!"

Temple came around with Hinchie's bottle and three more glasses.

The *ting-ting-ting* of Ed tapping a glass with a fork interrupted all conversation. "Viviane and I have an announcement to make. She's—"

"Having a baby?" Minnie rushed in.

Hinchie swatted her on the arm with the rolled-up tally sheet. "Let the kids tell it."

Etha burst into tears, waving her hand in front of her face. "I'm sorry! I seem to be boohooing at the drop of a hat these days . . ."

"Mrs. Hinchie is right and we are very excited," Ed declared.

Temple and Hinchie pounded Ed on the back.

"Your ma must be all smiles," Etha said to Viviane.

"She wants me to name the baby after my pa, if it's a boy. But I think Edward McCann Jr. is swell."

There began a discussion of possible names for girls. Temple drew Carmine aside. "Can you help get that broadcast from the Roosevelt Hotel on the radio?"

As Carmine squatted beside the cabinet, twisting the

dial, Temple coughed, then said, "I . . . Shoot. I want you to know that the way you handled yourself in the bootlegging operation is duly noted. I've had doubts about you since August but you've now proved yourself to me."

Temple extended his hand and Carmine jumped up. The sheriff gripped the young man's forearm and the two shook.

"Boy, you don't know how much that means to me," Carmine said.

From the dining room, Etha called, "Goodness, look at the time!" She passed into the kitchen with Minnie at her heels. From the cupboard, they hauled out pots and pans and dented lids and Etha's flour sieve. Wooden spoons and tin ladles were handed around. Temple forced open the window facing Main Street.

The seven clustered around the sashes. The church bells came first, *dong-dong-dong*. Then car horns and whistles. The Odd Fellows burst through the doors of their banquet hall with loud whoops. Young folks at watch parties sang "Auld Lang Syne" along with Guy Lombardo.

The reverberations of the bells and horns and clanging pots washed across dusty rooftops and rolled headlong to the wind-whipped farmlands. The cacophony overtook a freight training swaying westward, its headlamp as incandescent as a harvest moon. And in response to the din, the train cast out two thick chords. Then a short blast. Then another. And for the moment, at least, all was well.

CHAPTER THIRTY-FIVE

TWENTY-FIVE. That was a laugh.

The window's cross-hatched grid of iron bars caged her sky into twenty-five squares. And that's how old she was too. Twenty-five. Funny, huh?

She'd counted those squares so many times in the past six months that the back of her brain continued reckoning—even when her thoughts carried her far away from the state penitentiary.

Today, for example, Thelma was at the other side of Oklahoma, in that boxcar where she and Lonnie had bunked. In some ways that had been their best time. A place of their own making. She'd set up the table and the chairs like she wanted. Cooked their meals. They both had work—he with the railroad, she at the hospital. They'd hitch a ride back from Vermillion each evening or, if the weather was fair, walk along the tracks hand in hand.

Then came that frigid night in November. Early dark. Couldn't get a lift to save themselves so they hoofed it in that sharp wind. As they tramped along, Lonnie told her he'd been canned. Hung his head as she'd hollered. As she'd shoved him hard with the heel of her hand. She was the one who decided they had to leave the boxcar. Find a place in Vermillion. Easier for him to find another job there, she reasoned. And she still had the hospital work.

They had to live separate for a bit. Cheapest setup they could find was her rooming with another girl and him bunking at the pool hall. If they hadn't been apart, maybe Lonnie wouldn't have gotten so nerved up. So nerved up that he did something stupid beyond belief. She'd worked a double shift that day. Was flopped on her bed in the rooming house when she got called back to the hospital. It was packed to the gills. Folks bleeding, burned. Limbs torn apart. The nurses and fancy Red Cross ladies and kitchen maids running around like chickens with their heads lopped off. She'd finally snuck outside for a cigarette around dawn.

Lonnie was lurking around the incinerator tower—looking like hell. Full of soot, eyes red and wild. His hands were shaking like he had the DTs. He hemmed and hawed and finally told her what he'd done—cocked the switch. She'd smacked him good. Saphead. Dope. Dumdum. He took it without a whimper. Said he was trying to get revenge on the fellow who'd fired him by derailing a freight that was due in. But the freight must have got held up and the passenger train and its occupants paid the price.

After a while, her fury spent, she'd considered what would happen next. No one had seen him cock the switch. But then he mentioned that a woman living close by might have spotted him right afterward when he tossed the lock and chain. She lived in the first house beyond the station. Thelma had wanted to walk away right then. Let him save himself. But he was so broken she knew he'd be in jail and on the way to the electric chair by nightfall. So she told Lonnie to go straight to his job with the highway. Then, after his shift, to get himself to the Idle Hour and, after it closed, join the all-night poker game in its back room.

As soon as the December dusk fell, she'd slinked along the tracks toward the house beyond the station. Squatted along a wire fence to study the yard. Unbuckled the thick leather belt of her coat. Tested its strength. Two hours passed. Then three. She'd expected that the woman would come outside with the dog as she had the night before. Folks were creatures of habit. But tonight was beginning to seem like a no-go. She'd have to try again tomorrow. Then the back door swung open and the woman stepped out. The dog sniffed around the grass. The woman came out the gate, turned to the left, her back to Thelma.

The wind howled. Thelma had inched up from behind, whipped the belt around the exposed throat, rammed a foot into the woman's spine, and pulled crossways—tight. The woman thrashed. Choking. Gurgling. Thelma kept pulling—*like a mule on a plow* is what her father used to say of her. *That little bit of a thing can pull the weight of a full-grown man.* He'd worked her like one.

Afterward, Thelma had dragged the body across the tracks and into the weeds to give herself time to beat it out of there if someone came along. The whole thing only took a couple of minutes. The stupid dog barking the whole time.

And in the end, she'd saved Lonnie. But then accidentally killed him. How do you like them apples? Har har. When her traveling thoughts encountered the wreck on Route 15, she turned and bolted back to her cell. To the bunk facing the window. To counting the squares.

The numbers kept unfurling, running under the current of her thoughts. She wouldn't live to see twenty-six. Everything was twenty-five.

During the trial, the prosecutor had doggedly reminded the jury of middle-aged men that she'd cohabited with Lonnie off and on for more than twelve years. Every time he brought that up, she watched the lips of the jowly farmers and tradesmen in the jury box contract in disapproval. In the end, she'd been found guilty of murder in the first degree and sentenced to the chair.

Every couple of weeks a letter from Mrs. Jennings arrived. One included an article the sheriff's wife had clipped from a newspaper. All about this twenty-one-year-old Virginia gal who'd murdered her father. After she was sentenced, some club ladies put together a defense fund. Made a stink that because women weren't permitted to serve on juries, the murderess had been denied a jury of her peers.

That got Thelma's hopes up. But when she'd asked her lawyer about it, he'd shot down the idea of making an appeal based on that argument. *Never see the light of day.*

So now she was just cooling her heels. She wouldn't see twenty-six, that was for certain. The chair would see to that. She pushed her thoughts back to the boxcar.

Acknowledgments

No matter how solitary and reserved the writer, no book comes into being without a host of guides, enthusiasts, and readers all along the way. The trail extends backward to grade-school teachers, librarians, and college professors, and forward to fellow writers, editors, and publishers.

I am indebted to the editors and early readers who worked hard with me to polish and streamline this book—which sometimes teetered too far afield.

Kaylie Jones has been teaching me the intricacies of writing fiction since 2007. She has championed my writing and published my books. I write for Kaylie, and if others read my work along the way, that is a bonus.

I am deeply grateful to the remarkable Johnny Temple, publisher of Akashic Books, who edited this novel, along with Johanna Ingalls, managing editor, and Aaron Petrovich, production manager. *Funeral Train* is infinitely better due to their sharp ears and eyes.

Additional thanks to these amazing folks at Kaylie Jones Books for making me look good on novels past and present: Kristin Ivey, Danie Watson-Goetz, Jake Cannington, Michelle Polizzi, and Renette Zimmerly. And to Akashic's Susannah Lawrence and Sobrab Habibion.